"Forgive me, Mr. Wallin, but I find your offer altogether unequal. What do you get out of the bargain?"

He frowned as if puzzled by the question. "Why, the chance to be helpful, ma'am."

"In my experience, people are not nearly so helpful."

"Then perhaps you know the wrong people, Mrs. Tyrrell."

She had no question on that score. Her experience with Frank had soured her on a lot of things.

She gazed down into Peter's dear face. His blue eyes, more gray than hers, gazed back, trusting. He offered her a smile as if to encourage her, and she couldn't help smiling back.

Didn't her son deserve something more than this narrow hotel room, the company of strangers? If what John Wallin was offering was even half-true, she could provide Peter a safe home and good food, perhaps even friends. Shouldn't she take the chance, for him?

"I believe your sister said Wallin Landing is about five miles from Seattle," she told John. "I'd be willing to move out, see if the area will suit Peter and me."

His smile was relieved. "Thank you, Mrs. Tyrrell. I promise you, you won't be disappointed."

She couldn't make herself believe that, either.

Regina Scott has always wanted to be a writer. Since her first book was published in 1998, her stories have traveled the globe, with translations in many languages. Fascinated by history, she learned to fence and sail a tall ship. She and her husband reside in Washington state with an overactive Irish terrier. You can find her online blogging at nineteenteen.com. Learn more about her at reginascott.com or connect with her on Facebook at Facebook.com/authorreginascott.

Books by Regina Scott

Love Inspired Historical

Frontier Bachelors

The Bride Ship
Would-Be Wilderness Wife
Frontier Engagement
Instant Frontier Family
A Convenient Christmas Wedding
Mail-Order Marriage Promise

Lone Star Cowboy League: Multiple Blessings

The Bride's Matchmaking Triplets

Lone Star Cowboy League: The Founding Years

A Rancher of Convenience

The Master Matchmakers

The Courting Campaign
The Wife Campaign
The Husband Campaign

Visit the Author Profile page at Harlequin.com.

REGINA SCOTT

*Mail-Order
Marriage
Promise*

HARLEQUIN® LOVE INSPIRED® HISTORICAL

Recycling programs for this product may not exist in your area.

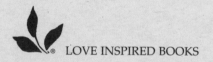

LOVE INSPIRED BOOKS

ISBN-13: 978-0-373-42538-9

Mail-Order Marriage Promise

Copyright © 2017 by Regina Lundgren

All rights reserved. Except for use in any review, the reproduction or utilization of this work in whole or in part in any form by any electronic, mechanical or other means, now known or hereinafter invented, including xerography, photocopying and recording, or in any information storage or retrieval system, is forbidden without the written permission of the editorial office, Love Inspired Books, 195 Broadway, New York, NY 10007 U.S.A.

This is a work of fiction. Names, characters, places and incidents are either the product of the author's imagination or are used fictitiously, and any resemblance to actual persons, living or dead, business establishments, events or locales is entirely coincidental.

This edition published by arrangement with Love Inspired Books.

® and TM are trademarks of Love Inspired Books, used under license. Trademarks indicated with ® are registered in the United States Patent and Trademark Office, the Canadian Intellectual Property Office and in other countries.

www.Harlequin.com

Printed in U.S.A.

Blessed are the peacemakers,
for they will be called children of God.
—*Matthew* 5:9,
New International Version

To everyday heroes, making our world safer and more peaceful, and to our Heavenly Father, for allowing even those of us who aren't heroes to contribute to His kingdom

Chapter One

Seattle, Washington Territory
April 1874

Dottie Tyrrell sat in the Pastry Emporium wondering what her groom looked like.

Not that she found looks all that indicative of character. Certainly Frank had been handsome, and he'd turned out to be a despicable rat. But it did seem odd to have traveled all the way from Cincinnati to Washington Territory and not have any picture in her mind of the man she had come to marry.

She settled her blue-and-purple-striped skirts around her on the wooden chair, then pushed a blond curl back from her face. Oh, but she was fussing, and why not? It wasn't every day you expected to see your husband come walking through the door.

His sister had tried to describe the fellow to Dottie in her letters, but Beth Wallin's reference points had meant little.

"John isn't as tall as Drew and Simon, our oldest

brothers," the young lady had written, "but he has a bit more muscle than Simon or James. His hair used to be red, but it's darkened over the years to look more like madrone tree bark, and his eyes are a darker green than Ma's were."

So Dottie had no idea of his height or weight. She'd never seen a madrone tree, but she could only assume John's hair was some shade of brown. Not particularly helpful!

She took a sip of the tea she had ordered earlier. The liquid trembled in the bone china cup. She was about to marry a stranger. Why, with everything she'd written to his sister, John Wallin knew more about Dottie than she knew about him!

Very likely he'd be able to pick her out the moment he walked in the door. The bakery was cozy, with a wide counter at the back next to a glass cabinet, where all manner of delicacies lay waiting for a hungry buyer. Six small wooden tables, all occupied, were clustered to one side so patrons could stop and enjoy their treats. The scents of cinnamon and vanilla hung in the air. With few women in the bakery, and all of them attended by a husband or children, the mail-order bride Mr. Wallin's sister had arranged for him would be glaringly apparent.

Dottie drew in a breath as she set down the teacup. A part of her, the part that remembered a mother and father deeply in love and that had gloried in stories of courtly romance, urged her to jump up and flee. Marriage was a sacred institution, meant to unite those committed to making a life together in love.

Funny how she still believed that even after Frank had made a mockery of their vows.

She pushed away the memory and her troubled emotions. She had given her word and accepted Mr. Wallin's money to travel to Seattle. She could sigh all she liked for what might have been, but she had to remember she had someone else depending on her now. For her son's sake, she would marry a man of stability and property, even if that meant tucking her heart away in a trunk with her wedding veil.

Another gentleman entered the restaurant, the fifth in the past quarter hour, and Dottie sat straighter, made herself smile in greeting. The telegram she'd received in San Francisco on her way to Seattle had said to meet John Wallin in this bakery, on this day, at this very hour. Was that her man?

He seemed more heavy than muscular in his plaid suit; she was certain the floorboards squeaked in protest as he marched to the counter. The tweed cap hid his hair, but his bushy beard was reddish brown. The same young lady with dark brown hair who had served Dottie tea nodded in welcome, and he snapped out an order for cinnamon rolls before turning to survey the crowd with narrowed eyes, fingers clasped self-importantly around his paunch.

Please, Lord, not him.

Dottie dropped her gaze to her gloved hands. That was unkind. She had no reason to expect anything special in her husband. She'd come all this way hoping to find a compassionate man who could provide for and protect her and little Peter. Perhaps someone who enjoyed literature as much as she did, though she wasn't even sure John Wallin could read or write, as his sister had corresponded for him.

Beth had explained that her brother was a very busy man and the lot of finding him a bride had fallen to her. Her writing had been so friendly and open that Dottie had dared to hope John Wallin would be equally so. If Dottie had been less than entirely open, it was only because she had learned the hard way to be more cautious. She'd said nothing to Beth about Peter and had arranged for him to stay back at the hotel with a lady they'd met on the boat. Time enough to introduce him once she'd had a chance to meet with John Wallin.

Now she made herself raise her head and return the gaze of the burly man at the counter. He lifted his brows, then grinned at her, and her stomach squirmed.

"Mrs. Tyrrell?"

Dottie blinked, then refocused on the young woman who had stepped up to her table. She had pale blond hair, fashionably done up like Dottie's to fall behind her, and wide, dark blue eyes. Her gown of sky blue crepe trimmed in ecru lace was right out of *Godey's Lady's Book*.

"Yes," Dottie said. "I'm Mrs. Tyrrell. Do I know you?"

The young lady's smile broadened on her round face and brightened the rainy day. "You most certainly do. I'm Beth Wallin."

Before Dottie could offer a greeting, John's younger sister pulled out the chair across from hers and took a seat. "I'm so glad to meet you in person at last! I've been waiting for this moment for so long, but then so have you. You're exactly as I pictured you. I just know John is going to love you."

The tea bubbled up inside Dottie, threatening to

choke her. She didn't believe John Wallin would love her. She certainly had no expectation of falling in love with him. She would be a good partner—working beside him on his farm, keeping his house. Beyond that, she was not willing to promise.

"Are we expecting your brother soon?" she asked, almost afraid to look toward the fellow at the counter again.

She nearly slid from her chair in relief when Beth glanced at the door instead. "Any moment. He had other business in town. He's very conscientious. And kind. And thoughtful. But I told you all that already."

She had. Dottie hated to admit even to herself how she'd clung to the words in Beth's effusive letters. "Kind" had been repeated many times. So had "sweet" and "good-natured." Even the initial ad that had opened their correspondence had seemed thoughtful, hopeful. Small wonder she'd chosen that one to answer.

She'd been in a bad way then, desperate enough to riffle through the local paper that reprinted ads for men seeking brides. The moment she'd sent off the letter in response to the ad from "a gentleman from Seattle," she'd regretted it. How could she, who had been lied to so cruelly, trust another man to tell her the truth? How could she take such a chance?

Because she needed to give Peter security, safety.

Beth Wallin's letters had calmed her spirit, made her feel welcomed, valued. But still doubts persisted. She had forced herself to take each step—giving up her one-room flat in Cincinnati, boarding the train to California, taking a ship north to Puget Sound. Now here she sat, waiting to meet the man who would be her new husband.

The young lady who had been behind the counter approached the table with a smile. Tall, slender and modestly dressed in a gray gown with a frilly white apron, she had brown eyes that seemed wiser than her years.

"Good to see you again, Beth," she said to John's sister. "What can I get for you today?"

Beth hopped to her feet and enfolded the girl in a hug. "Oh, Ciara, it's so good to see you! I was hoping you'd be working today." She released her, dimple popping into view beside her mouth, then turned to Dottie. "Mrs. Tyrrell, this is my good friend Ciara O'Rourke. Her older sister Maddie Haggerty owns this bakery."

Impressive. A shame Dottie didn't have any marketable skills, or she might have been able to raise Peter alone. But then again, what would she have done with him while she was working? That had been the problem in Cincinnati.

Dottie inclined her head in greeting, but Beth hurried on in the breathless way she had. "I see you brought Mrs. Tyrrell tea. I think we should have something to go with it. Did Maddie make lemon drops today?"

The girl shook her head. "I'm sorry. But I'm sure she would have if she'd known you'd be in. We do have iced shortbread."

Beth clapped her hands. "Perfect. We'll each take one."

With a nod, the girl hurried off.

Beth sat and turned to Dottie. "The lemon drops are wonderful. I'm sure we could get Maddie to bake some for your wedding reception. I was hoping you and John could be married out at Wallin Landing, but we haven't quite finished the church yet. It's on a beautiful spot overlooking the lake. I just know it's going to be a wonderful place for a wedding, but not yours. I guess we'll have to hold the ceremony in Seattle."

Dottie found herself gripping her teacup. "Perhaps we should discuss that with your brother."

Beth waved a hand. "He'll agree. He's very agreeable."

And kind and thoughtful, apparently. Dottie had wanted so much for this arrangement to work, but suddenly she found it difficult to believe this paragon of a gentleman existed. According to Beth's letters, John Wallin was twenty-eight, five years Dottie's senior, and had an established claim north of Seattle on Lake Union, in an area known as Wallin Landing, named after his family. He was supposed to be a pillar of the community, supporting civic and church functions alike. Yet he had no time to write letters, had delegated the task of finding a bride to his sister.

What sort of fellow was he?

The door opened again to admit another man. This one was tall and slender, with broad shoulders that showed to advantage in his navy wool coat. The golden light from the lamp hanging overhead sent red flames flickering through his short, wavy mahogany-colored hair. His features were firm, well formed, though his full lower lip hinted of a gentleness inside. She was certain she had never met him, yet there was something familiar about him. He glanced around until his gaze met hers, and something sizzled through her like the fizz from sassafras.

He came unerringly toward the table. Her mouth was dry as she pushed herself to her feet.

"Beth," he said in a warm voice, "you didn't tell me you were meeting a friend."

Beth hopped to her feet again to beam at him. "A very dear friend, to whom I've written any number of letters over the last eight months. John, this is Dorothy Tyrrell. I chose her to be your bride."

John Wallin's handsome face turned paler than the icing on the bakery's cinnamon rolls, and Dottie had a feeling that something was very wrong.

John felt as if every voice in Maddie Haggerty's busy bakery had suddenly shut off so that all he could hear was the rush of blood through his veins. Dorothy Tyrrell stared at him, her face paling, as if Beth's announcement shocked her as well.

He'd noticed the lovely blonde the moment he'd started into the room, and not just because she was sitting with his sister. No, it wasn't every day a fellow saw hair so golden and full, eyes such a purplish shade of blue that reminded him of the lavender Ma used to grow. The fitted blue bodice, with its tiny purple bows down the front, showed a supple figure, and her fingers in her proper gloves were long and shapely. He could imagine any number of men in Seattle rushing to pay her court.

But when it came to him marrying, his sister had to be joking.

"Beth, you shouldn't tease your friend," he said with a smile. "I promise you, Miss Tyrrell, I have no intention of proposing marriage."

Her pretty pink lips had been pursed in an O, most

likely in surprise. Now her mouth snapped shut, and she drew herself up. She was tall for a woman, and he was the shortest of his brothers at only six foot, so she could nearly look him in the eyes. That purple drew him in.

"A decided shame, Mr. Wallin," she said, voice tight, "because I came more than two thousand miles to marry you."

What was she talking about? He'd never met her before, certainly hadn't proposed marriage. He'd been busy of late, working on the church, looking for funding for the library he hoped to build next, but surely he'd recall courting such a beauty. He certainly remembered his last courtship, and how badly it had ended.

John glanced between the lady and Beth. "The joke's on me, then," he said. "Very funny, Beth. Did James put you up to this?"

His sister did not laugh. Indeed, her smile was rather stern.

"Sit down," she said, "both of you. We're making a scene."

She was right, of course. Already he could see patrons glancing their way. John took the chair beside his sister, and her friend suffered herself to sit as well. Still, those lavender eyes were dark enough to look like storm clouds.

Beth put one hand on John's shoulder and the other on her friend's fingers where they rested on the table, as if ensuring they each sat still long enough to listen to her.

"John," she said, "you know I worry about you, especially since last summer."

He caught himself squirming and pulled out of her grip. "This is not the time or place to discuss that, Beth."

"Yes, it is," she insisted. "You've retreated into a shell, won't listen to anything I have to say. You work yourself night and day for the betterment of the community, but you think nothing of caring for your own needs. You should have someone to help you, stand beside you, support you. So I took matters into my own hands and found you a bride."

He heard the lady suck in a breath. "Didn't you have your brother's permission to write to me? To propose marriage?"

"No," Beth admitted. "I'm sorry if I gave you that impression. But I can assure you that everything else in my letters about my brother and our family was true."

John felt ill. "Beth, you proposed to this woman for me? An agreement for a mail-order bride is a binding contract. She'll have spent money coming here in expectation."

Before his sister could respond, Ciara approached the table, a plate of iced shortbread in each hand. Her eyes were bright as she beamed at John. "Hello, John. Maddie's still singing your praises for helping her and Michael install the new ovens. Did I hear someone's getting married?"

"No," Beth's victim and John said in unison.

Ciara set down the plates on the table and backed away as if she thought John and the lady might come after her.

His sister, on the other hand, didn't look the least concerned as she drew one of the plates closer and picked up a cookie. "Yes, John, I invited Dottie to Seattle for a wedding, but I didn't ask her to pay her own way. I used the inheritance Ma left me to fund her passage." She took a bite of the shortbread.

She'd used her inheritance, money that was supposed to have gone toward building her future. It seemed his sister thought he needed it more. The very idea was lowering.

He would have to talk to Beth about what she'd done, find a way to pay back the money she'd spent. But at the moment, he was more concerned about the woman sitting beside him. How horrible this must be for her, how embarrassing. A woman had to be desperate to marry a stranger, from what he understood of the custom of mail-order brides. She had taken the ultimate chance in coming here, and now she had nothing to show for it.

He could not help feeling that it was partly his fault. If he had listened the many times Beth had tried to talk to him about taking a wife, he might have realized his sister's plans before they'd come to this. He had to find a way to make things right.

"Miss Tyrrell—" he began.

"Mrs. Tyrrell," she said.

She was a widow. Odd. She didn't look much older than Beth. How tragic to have already lost a husband. His guilt over how she'd been used ratcheted up higher.

"Mrs. Tyrrell," he acknowledged. "I can only commend you for your willingness to journey all the way to Seattle. My sister must have painted a very convincing picture."

"Thank you," Beth said, icing dripping off her chin.

John continued, undaunted. "But I am not prepared to marry."

"Yes, he is," Beth said, leaning forward, half-eaten cookie in one hand. "He has a nice house, a good farm and a steady nature. He just needs the right incentive."

"Beth." He had never been a man of temper. Indeed, his brothers were likely to tease him for being the peacemaker in the family. But his sister's actions were making him feel decidedly less than peaceful.

"You cannot think that a few letters I knew nothing about will encourage me to offer marriage," he told her. "I'm not interested in taking a wife."

Beth's lower lip and fingers trembled, sending a drop of icing to the table. "But, John, look at her. She's sweet and pretty. She loves books as much as you do. She'd be perfect for you."

He looked at Mrs. Tyrrell, whose eyes appeared suspiciously moist. Guilt wrapped itself around his heart.

Which was unfortunate, for his heart was entirely the problem. All his life, he'd tried to be the sort of man he'd read about in the adventure novels Pa had left them—bold, daring, determined, willing to brave great things for the woman he loved. His courtship last summer had made him painfully aware that he was no hero. That wasn't how God had made him.

Besides, Beth seemed to understand that his last attempt at courting had only wounded him. Why would she think he'd be willing to try again, and with a stranger?

"Mrs. Tyrrell is lovely," he said to Beth, though he kept his gaze on the woman who was supposed to be his bride. "I'm sure she'll make some gentleman a marvelous wife. But I will not be that man."

He could see Mrs. Tyrrell swallow even though she

had not taken a bite of the shortbread Ciara had left in front of her.

"I'm sorry you feel that way, Mr. Wallin," she said, her gaze holding his. "But I was promised a husband, and I won't leave without one."

Chapter Two

Oh, but she sounded so bold! What had happened to the girl her mother and father had once called sweet? Under other circumstances, Dottie would have apologized immediately, tried to appreciate John Wallin's position. Now all she could think about was Peter.

She could not return to Cincinnati and risk meeting Frank again. He'd been violent the last time she'd seen him, had warned her what would happen if she ever told anyone what she knew. The bruises on her arms where he'd grabbed her had taken weeks to fade.

Besides, she had no idea how he might react if he knew about Peter. He'd told her how much he wanted children. He might try to claim Peter. She'd used up the last of her money on the midwife to birth her son and most of John Wallin's—*Beth's*—money to reach Seattle, so she couldn't afford to leave. And without a place to stay and some reliable income, she couldn't make a new home here, either.

Across the table from her, Beth's round face was puckering. "This is not how I imagined your meeting to go."

Very likely not. Though she seemed about the same age as Dottie, Beth Wallin had clearly known little of the world. She still believed in love at first sight and happily-ever-after endings. Dottie had believed in all that, too, had dreamed of marrying the perfect man. She'd been a fool to accept Frank Reynolds's promises. Now she'd been lied to yet again.

"I could have told you a lady wouldn't fall in love with me after one meeting," John said to his sister, his voice kind. "Women don't react to me that way."

Well, at least he wasn't vain. Still, she could imagine another woman setting her cap at him. Forest green eyes and mahogany hair were a potent combination, especially with that warm voice and smile. It certainly seemed as if those broad shoulders could help carry a woman's burdens.

"And think of Mrs. Tyrrell," he continued as his sister sank in her chair, cookie falling to the plate. "You raised her hopes and put her in a difficult position."

Beth straightened with a show of defiance. "Not so difficult. Seattle is a much better place for her than where she was. I knew even if you could not be brought up to scratch, she could have her pick of husbands."

There was that. Ever since she'd arrived two days ago, she'd seen a predominance of gentlemen on the streets of the burgeoning town. But which of the miners, loggers, farmers and businessmen strolling past with approving looks were honest and hardworking? Which had left a wife behind when they'd journeyed west? She shuddered just remembering the day she'd discovered the truth about Frank.

She and Frank had been married a mere two months,

sharing a little apartment on Poplar, just north of the busy downtown area. Some days she didn't see him because he traveled for his work, but he was utterly devoted when he was home. That day, when she'd heard a knock on the door after Frank had left for work, she'd thought it must be one of the neighbor wives who liked to come over for a cup of tea. But her smile of welcome had faded when she found herself facing a finely dressed woman wringing her hands.

"I know he's here," the woman had said. "The detective agency gave me this address. Please, won't you let me see my husband?"

Even remembering, she felt the cold sickness sweep over her. She'd thought surely the so-called Mrs. Reynolds was mistaken. Frank would laugh off the story.

After he'd returned that evening, Frank had tried to keep up the pretense when Dottie told him what had happened.

"She's crazy, sweetheart," he'd said, taking Dottie in his arms. "You're the only girl for me."

But Mrs. Reynolds had returned the next day and the next, until Frank was forced to admit the truth. Unhappy in his marriage, he had found solace in another woman's arms.

In her arms. Dottie was the second Mrs. Reynolds, which meant she wasn't married at all. Small wonder she'd used her maiden name ever since.

"A good husband," she told Beth now, "is not so easy to come by. They generally don't wear labels like 'excellent provider' or 'kind to cats and children.'"

John Wallin smiled. Another man might have refused to have anything more to do with her after realizing his sister's scheme. But then again, he didn't know about Peter yet. Marrying a woman with a baby born out of wedlock might make even the kind, thoughtful Mr. Wallin turn tail.

"You might be better off seeking employment," he suggested. "My family knows many of the business owners in town."

And he believed she had the skills to succeed. That was refreshing. Too often men took one look at her lavender eyes and golden curls and assumed there was nothing behind them.

Beth straightened. "Of course! Maybe Maddie's hiring." She pushed back her chair. "I'll go ask."

Dottie raised her hand in protest, but Beth was already heading for the counter.

"She means well," John said. "Her heart just gets in the way of logic sometimes."

Dottie had been that way once, but she no longer had the luxury.

"I'm not sure about a position," she told him. "I never learned a trade. And I have some issues with my schedule." She took a breath and prepared to tell him about her son, but Beth bustled back to the table.

"They've just hired two more bakers," she reported. "So they don't need help at present."

Once more, the patrons were glancing their way. Perhaps this wasn't the best place to confess that she had a baby. Dottie rose, and John climbed to his feet as well.

"Thank you for asking about employment, Miss Wallin," Dottie said. "I think we should continue this discussion elsewhere."

Beth glanced around, cheeks turning pink as she

must have realized the amount of interest they were still generating. "Of course. Come with me."

Her brother stepped back to allow Dottie to go before him. She could feel him behind her, a steady presence, as she followed Beth out of the bakery.

The rain had stopped as they paused on the boardwalk of Second Avenue. Muddy puddles spanned the wide streets, and the signs plastered on the businesses on either side were shiny with moisture. The air hung with brine and wood smoke.

"Are you staying at Lowe's, as I suggested?" Beth asked.

Dottie nodded. The white-fronted hotel was neat and tidy, and she had felt safe staying there alone the last two nights.

"Allow us to escort you back," John said. He offered her his arm.

Dottie did not feel right taking it. Instead, she started forward, and he fell into step beside her, Beth trailing behind. That didn't stop her from continuing the conversation.

"Maybe Dottie could farm," she suggested. "She lived on a farm until she was twelve and her parents died. Then she went to live with her aunt and uncle in Cincinnati."

A reasonable thought, but not here, not now.

"I remember how to work on a farm," Dottie told Beth and her brother. "But I don't know if I could manage one alone, particularly starting from the wilderness."

John nodded in agreement. Beth, however, would not let the matter go.

"We could help," she insisted, voice bright. "Our

brother Drew logs. I'm sure he and his men could clear the fields for you and help you build a house. Simon has designed several, and John designed the church. I wrote you about my brothers."

Yes, she had. Dottie felt as if she knew all about the Wallin family. Both parents were gone, the father nearly two decades ago in a logging accident, the mother a couple years back from pleurisy. Beth had five brothers, three of whom had married and were raising families and one named Levi, who had headed north to seek his fortune in the Canadian gold fields. A shame Dottie knew the least about the man she had come to marry.

John walked beside her now, his smile pleasant. The people they passed—mostly dapper gentlemen in tall-crowned hats and rough workers in knit caps—nodded in greeting. Their looks to him were respectful; their looks to her speculative. John cast her a glance as if his green eyes could see inside her to her most cherished dreams. She could have told him she had only one dream that mattered—a safe, secure home for her and her son.

"Farming alone might be difficult," he agreed. "But we bear the responsibility for bringing you out to Seattle, Mrs. Tyrrell. I promise you I won't rest until you have a situation that suits you."

He sounded so sure of himself, so certain he could solve her problem. If only she could feel so sure, of Seattle and of him.

Mrs. Tyrrell did not look convinced by his statement, but John knew it for the truth. He still couldn't believe his sister's audacity in bringing him a bride. Did he truly seem so helpless?

Now Mrs. Tyrrell shook her head, her golden curls shining even under an overcast sky.

"I appreciate the thought, Mr. Wallin," she said, her voice soft yet firm, "but you know nothing about me. How could you possibly understand what would suit?"

"He may not know," Beth said, "but I do." She tugged on her brother's shoulder to get him to glance back at her. "I told you she enjoys reading, John. You should hire her for your library."

That Mrs. Tyrrell liked books was certainly a mark in her favor. Indeed, as John faced front once more, he saw a light spring to her eyes, making the lavender all the brighter.

"A library?" she asked, and he could hear hope in the word.

"John is building a free library at Wallin Landing," Beth said, "so everyone has a chance to improve."

"Admirable," Mrs. Tyrrell said, eyeing him as if he had surprised her.

Did she think everyone in Seattle illiterate? He'd seen articles from the newspapers back east that talked of the primitive conditions, the dangers from natives and animals, when they hadn't had a problem in years.

"Our family is committed to building a town at the northern end of Lake Union to honor our father's dream," John explained. "We have a school, a dispensary, a new store, a dock on the lake, decent roads and soon a church. We've even applied for a post office. A library seemed the next most important civic improvement."

"That's why John came into Seattle to ask the Literary Society to donate funds," Beth told Mrs. Tyrrell, and John nearly cringed at the proud tone. She tugged on his coat again, and he glanced back at her.

His sister's dark blue eyes sparkled with interest. "How did it go? Did they see the logic? Agree to support you?"

The six women of the Literary Society, which included his longtime friend Allegra Banks Howard, had seemed more interested in quizzing him about why a fine upstanding gentleman like himself hadn't married. He had been no more ready to confess his shortcomings to the most influential women in Seattle than he had been to the lovely lady beside him.

"Suffice it to say it will be some time before I have funds enough to build and staff the library," he told his sister. "I'll have to find some other occupation for Mrs. Tyrrell." He turned to Dottie. "Do you have enough money to see you through the next few days while I ask around?"

Her step quickened, as if she would distance herself from the very idea. "I can't take any of your money, Mr. Wallin. Now that I know we will not be married, it wouldn't be proper."

At least she wasn't a fortune hunter, not that he had all that much fortune to hunt. He leaned closer to her, catching a scent like fresh apricots over the salt from Puget Sound. "I wouldn't want to do anything to damage your reputation, ma'am. But my sister's promises that I would marry you are responsible for bringing you here. You must allow us to see to your needs."

She slowed her steps, body stiffening, until she reminded him of one of those golden-haired wax dolls on display at the Kellogg brothers' store. She had every right to be offended by this entire affair. She was likely questioning his character, and Beth's sanity.

At last she nodded. "Very well. I would appreciate it if you were to pay my room at the hotel for the next week, and I could use ten dollars for food and sundry."

It was a reasonable number, but he hadn't brought that much money with him to Seattle. "I'll return with the funds tomorrow, along with a report on my progress."

They were approaching the hotel, and she seemed loath to even allow them to enter the lobby with her. He supposed that was wise. Neither her future employer nor husband would approve of a rumor that she had received a gentleman caller in her room.

"Give your name at the front desk, and I'll come down to meet you," she told him. Then she dipped a curtsy. "Good day, Mr. Wallin, Miss Wallin." She straightened, then swept into the hotel.

Beth sighed as she and John turned for the livery stable, where their wagon and team were waiting. "I've made a mess of things, haven't I?"

"Yes," John agreed. "You meant well, Beth, but I wish you would have consulted me first."

"You would only have tried to dissuade me," she said, her chin coming up as they passed the mercantiles on Second Avenue. "You persist in seeing me as your little sister, John, for all I'm a grown woman."

She was wrong there. John and all his brothers knew she was grown. So did the gentlemen they were passing. Their smiles were appreciative as they tipped their hats in her direction. Beth paid them no heed whatsoever.

"Maybe you should think about your own wedding," John suggested with a smile, "instead of mine."

Beth's lips thinned. "My wedding is years off, if I even consent to marry. You, however, have been pining away. Oh, but I could shake Caroline Crawford!"

"She is entitled to marry a man she can love and respect," John said, finding his strides lengthening. "I am not that man."

"Then she is foolish and temperamental," Beth declared, scurrying to keep up.

Caroline hadn't seemed so to him. Indeed, when she and her parents had first moved out near Wallin Landing, John had thought he'd at last met the perfect wife for him. Petite, delicate, with great gray eyes, sleek raven tresses and a slender figure, Caroline Crawford had hung on every word of advice she requested from him after driving with him into Seattle for church services each Sunday for a month, her parents in a wagon just behind. Her attentiveness and bright smile had made him begin to hope for a future together.

But when he'd emboldened himself to propose, on bended knee in the moonlight no less, she'd refused.

"Oh, I could never marry a man like you, John," she'd said, as if surprised he'd think otherwise. "You have no gumption."

No gumption. No drive. No willingness to claw his way to ever greater achievements. He had built a farm from the wilderness, managed it well, assisted his brothers and Beth where he could, helped his neighbors, tithed to the church and supported the school, but apparently that was not enough.

Heroes did more.

Heroes put their own needs aside to raise their fatherless siblings, as Drew had done when Pa had died. Heroes protected ladies across wilderness areas as James had done for his bride, Rina. Heroes fought off dastardly relatives as Simon had done for his wife, Nora. Heroes braved the next frontier, like Levi.

A hero did not sit safely at home, reading adventure novels and the latest scientific and engineering theories while his cat purred in his lap before the hearth.

Yet that seemed to be his role in the family—the scholar, the peacemaker. When Pa had died, John had been all of ten, old enough to feel the loss, to recognize the pain in others. Drew had assumed leadership as Pa had directed him with his dying breath, but Simon and James hadn't sat well under it. Watching his brothers argue had just made John want to curl in on himself. And Ma had seemed so sad when her children didn't get along, as if it was somehow her fault she was raising them all alone.

Surrounded by sorrow and strife, John had done everything he could to make sure everyone got along. He encouraged the best in his brothers, helped them through the worst. He pointed out things that made Drew think about how James must be feeling, pushed James to see things from Simon's more logical perspective, reminded Simon that following Drew was what Pa wanted and tried to be an example to little Levi. Keeping things peaceable was how he contributed.

The trait was still with him. Now when John saw a problem, he was more likely to find a way to solve it quietly than to leap into the fray. He was the one who suggested compromises rather than demanding capitulation. A shame that habit kept him from living up to his image of a hero. Mrs. Tyrrell must have recognized that he lacked certain qualities, for she'd not held him to Beth's promise to wed. He had no need to drag his bruised heart out of hiding.

Still, he seemed to hear it whispering encouragement as he and Beth reached the livery stable. It would take more than a pretty mail-order bride to get him to listen.

Chapter Three

Dottie climbed the stairs to her second-floor hotel room, feeling heavy. How could she have let this happen? Why had she believed what Beth Wallin had written to her? Had she learned nothing from her terrible experience with Frank?

Of course, none of the letters Beth had sent her or the conversation with John had been anything like talking with Frank. A salesman for a manufacturing firm in Cincinnati, with clients all over the state, he'd had a way of making people feel important. She'd needed that fifteen months ago when she'd first met him.

Her uncle, who worked for the same firm, had brought Frank home for dinner to meet Dottie. Frank hadn't been the first fellow foisted upon her that way. Uncle Henry and Aunt Harriot lived in a manner her parents had found worrisome—drinking with friends most nights, holding their own riotous parties at least twice a month, saying vulgar words upon occasion and never attending church.

Though she tried not to complain, she could not bring

herself to act the way they did, causing her uncle to dub her "Dottie Do-Gooder." By word and action, they had made it very clear they wanted her out of the house as soon as possible. Only by doing all the cooking and cleaning had she convinced them to allow her to stay past her sixteenth birthday.

Every other man they had brought home to meet her had been just like them, favoring cheap cigars and alcohol. Frank had seemed different—polished, polite, friendly. Small wonder she'd begun to fancy she had found love. Frank had known just what to say, how to act, to get her to go along with his wishes and feel terribly happy about it as well.

Beth had also said all the right things, promising a kind, considerate husband well able to provide for Dottie's needs. That part hadn't been a lie. If anything, John Wallin was an even better man than his sister had described, if the way he had responded to Beth's interference was any indication. Yet what sort of man needed a sister to fetch him a bride?

John seemed neither stupid nor lazy. He was not crippled, and he appeared to be in good health. If he was intent on building a library, surely he wasn't the illiterate Dottie had feared. Most women would account him handsome. Even in Seattle, where there were far more men than women, he would likely be considered a catch.

So why did he lack a wife? Had he some flaw she hadn't noticed on first meeting?

She was still wondering as she let herself into the narrow hotel room with its single window looking down toward Puget Sound. Mrs. Gustafson rose from the chair as Dottie shut the door behind her. A heavy woman with button-brown eyes and a wide mouth, she exuded motherly warmth, even in the somewhat Spartan conditions of the hotel room.

"A little darling he was," she proclaimed in her thick German accent, looking fondly at the blanket spread on the floor. "Never once did he cry."

Dottie's son gurgled at her as she kneeled beside the blanket. He waved pudgy arms and begged to be picked up. She obliged, cuddling him close and feeling the soft tufts of his white-blond hair against her chin.

This was why she must stay strong. This was why she could not give up.

"Thank you for watching him," she told the older woman.

Mrs. Gustafson waved a beefy hand. "*Ach*, he is no trouble. And your young man, how did you like him?"

Dottie had confided her purpose in coming to Seattle, though she had let Mrs. Gustafson, like Beth, think she was a widow instead of a woman shamed. Now she considered how to answer. In truth, had she met John Wallin before she'd known Frank, she would likely have been willing to let him court her. Now she needed a man ready to take a chance on a woman and an illegitimate baby, a man willing to fight for family. John Wallin, for all his gentle ways, did not seem likely.

"He decided we will not suit," she told her friend.

The German lady recoiled. "*Vas?* Is he touched in the head? Such a lovely lady you are. And who could resist little Peter, eh?" She bent closer and stroked the baby's cheek. Peter watched her, wide-eyed.

"I'll simply have to find another way to support

Peter," Dottie said. "Surely someone here needs a worker and wouldn't mind having a baby along."

Mrs. Gustafson nodded as she straightened. "You could work on the railroad. I saw pictures all along the street here, asking everyone to come help on May Day."

Dottie had seen them as well, posters plastered to any bare spot on the wall along the streets of Seattle. *Come all ye adults of mankind. Nor let there be none left behind.* It seemed Seattle had lost its bid to be the terminus of the Northern Pacific Railway, which would be coming to Tacoma, to the south, instead. Now Seattle was determined to build its own railroad.

"I doubt they are planning to pay the workers much," she told her friend. "And I don't know how I'd be much help carrying Peter around. If you hear of anything else, though, please let me know."

"Oh, *yah*, of course," Mrs. Gustafson promised. "But I don't know of any places that will take a mother with child. And we leave tomorrow for the Duwamish. I would ask you to come, but it is my brother's place, and he only has room for me and my Dieter."

It was the same story every place Dottie tried that afternoon. Either the business did not want to take on a woman, or they needed her to work long hours away from Peter. The shops in Seattle, it seemed, were open by five in the morning and did not close until nearly ten at night. One of the owners even suggested that she give up her son, claiming many of the farmers in the area would be interested in adopting a baby that would grow into a strong young man. Clutching Peter close, she had hurried from the store. Peter was hers, not Frank's, not anyone else's. He was the one good thing to come from her bad marriage.

"You are a blessing," she told him as she carried him back to the hotel. A passing gentleman favored her with a gap-toothed grin as if he thought she was addressing him. Peter snuggled closer.

That night, after she'd settled her son to sleep beside her on the bed, she allowed herself a moment to pray, asking for help finding work, a safe place for her and Peter to live. But still she found no peace.

Her mother and father had always prayed before bed and at mealtimes. They'd attended church services as well, read to her from the Bible. All that had changed when they'd been killed in a train accident. Her uncle had taken her Bible away from her, told her it was just a book of nonsense. She hadn't seen the inside of a church in years. She shouldn't be surprised she no longer felt God's presence. She'd been the one to move away.

All Dottie could hope was that John Wallin had better connections in the frontier town than she ever would, and that he'd find something that would work for her and Peter.

John returned to Seattle the next day on horseback, leaving his mount at the livery stable while he canvassed the town. But it seemed Dottie had been unwilling to wait for his help, for most of the places he tried reported that she'd already been in.

"Lovely lady," the tallest Kellogg brother said when John asked at his store about a clerk position, "but we simply could not accommodate the hours she wanted."

He heard similar stories at other shops he tried. Dottie seemed determined to work as little as possible. He couldn't understand it. Had she been so tenderly raised that she had no idea what employers expected? Surely if she'd lived on a farm she knew that work went on from before sunrise to after sunset most days.

He wished he knew more about her. He'd asked Beth as they'd ridden back to Wallin Landing yesterday, but his sister had obviously recovered her usual buoyancy and determined that he was the villain in all this.

"Oh, no, John Wallin," she'd declared with a toss of her head. "You didn't wish to heed my advice and marry Dottie Tyrrell, so don't think you can get back into my good graces by appearing interested in her now. If you want to know more about her, I suggest you talk to her directly. I am quite finished playing matchmaker."

He didn't believe that for a minute. Beth had taken great delight in helping all their older brothers fall in love. She wouldn't stop until every last Wallin male was wed.

But John wasn't about to help her. He would find a better situation for Mrs. Tyrrell than marrying him.

Now he followed each lead to possible positions and talked to everyone with whom his family had built connections over the years. His quest eventually led him to the home of one of Seattle's founding families, the Maynards. Doc Maynard, who had first hired Drew's wife, Catherine, as a nurse years ago, had passed on last spring, leaving his wife as one of the area's most notable widows. An advocate for literacy, she had been one of the women to whom John had presented yesterday. Today she listened more intently and handed him her card to give to Dottie. Feeling as if a weight had been lifted from his shoulders, he hurried to the hotel.

He had to cool his heels awhile as Billy Prentice, the porter, went up to tell the lady she had a caller. John had stayed at Lowe's a time or two when he was needed in town, but looking around the plain white walls of the lobby, the hard-backed benches and brass spittoons, he wondered now whether it was the best place for a lady. As close as the hotel was to the businesses that catered to the workers at Yesler's mill, the noise at night could be considerable some days. If only Dottie would take the situation with Mrs. Maynard, all her problems would be solved.

Billy came back down the stairs. "Sorry, Mr. Wallin. Mrs. Tyrrell says she cannot see you at present. Perhaps tomorrow."

Tomorrow?

What was wrong with the woman? She came from a farming background. She had to know he had chores waiting for him, animals to feed, fields to till for spring planting. Wallin Landing was still several hours round trip from Seattle. He couldn't just make the jaunt when it suited her.

"Tell her I have urgent news," he insisted. "A position she'll want to hear about."

The porter raised a brow, but up the stairs he went again.

John tapped his hat against his thigh. She hadn't seemed so persnickety yesterday. Indeed, given the magnitude of his sister's mistake, Dottie Tyrrell had been remarkably calm. Besides, Beth surely would have noticed a high-handed manner in the letters they'd exchanged.

Any woman desperate enough to answer an ad for a mail-order bride couldn't afford to put on airs.

"I'm sorry," Billy said as he came down the stairs. "But Mrs. Tyrrell cannot see you now."

John drew in a deep breath. Here he was, known for his patience, and it was about to desert him. "Tell her that if I do not see her now, she will forfeit this opportunity, and I will bear no further responsibility for helping her."

Billy sighed. "If it wasn't you, Mr. Wallin, I wouldn't be going up the stairs again. But I never forgot how you helped me carry that luggage in out of the rain last winter. I'll try to get you a better answer from the lady." He turned and trudged up the stairs yet again. John was very glad when he returned with the news that Dottie would see him after all, even if it was in her room.

Odd, when she'd hesitated to be seen in the lobby with him yesterday. What had changed?

He climbed the stairs, then rapped on the door, hat in one hand. Though she had to know he was coming, Dottie took her time answering. When she did open the door, it was the merest crack, as if she expected him to come armed.

"Thank you for seeing me, Mrs. Tyrrell," he said, trying for a smile that he hoped would put her at ease. "I've brought the funds as promised and what I hope is good news. One of the greatest ladies of my acquaintance, Mrs. Maynard, is seeking a companion. She has a fine house right here in Seattle and is well respected by all. I'm sure she'd be thrilled for your company."

He had hoped for delight at the announcement, but if anything she looked sad, mouth dipping.

"I doubt a companion post will do, Mr. Wallin. I cannot be available the hours that would likely be expected."

That again. Once more, he felt the temper he hadn't known he had threatening. "Begging your pardon, ma'am, but most places expect a day's work for a day's pay."

"So I am coming to learn, but I'm afraid I must insist on it." Behind her came a coo, as if a dove had been let loose in the room.

John frowned, but she thrust out her hand. "If I could have the funds you promised?"

At least he could do that much for her. He dug into the pocket of his coat and offered her the money. "I wish you would reconsider," he told her. "I sincerely doubt you'll find another situation like this in Seattle. Folks who come here generally aren't afraid of hard work."

The coo had become a whine, accompanied by the sound of material rustling. Were there rats in the room? Perhaps he should find her somewhere else to stay.

"I'm not afraid of hard work, Mr. Wallin," she said, fingers tightening on the door. "I am simply unable to provide it at present. Thank you for your help, and good day." She started to shut the door, and a howl erupted behind her.

John's hand caught the door. "Wait. What was that? Are you all right?"

For a moment she hesitated, her gaze on his as if determining how easy it would be to refuse to answer him. Then she released the door and stepped back. "That, Mr. Wallin, is the reason I was willing to become a mail-order bride."

She turned and headed for the bed, and John stepped into the hotel room. Now he could see two chubby fists waving in the air above the bed. She bent down and swept up the baby.

"There now," she crooned. "It's all right. Mommy has her little man."

She had a child.

He drew in a breath. That explained so much—her reason for seeking a husband so urgently, her need for additional funds, her stringent requirements for a position. But it also meant his job of finding her a situation had just grown exponentially harder.

The baby calmed in her arms, blinking his eyes as he stuffed one fist into his mouth.

"What's his name?" John asked, venturing closer.

"Peter," she said, but so begrudgingly he wondered if she thought he'd argue over the matter.

The lad seemed about four months along. That was generally when they discovered their hands, if his nieces and nephews were any indication.

"I suppose Beth knows all about him," he said.

She blushed, the pink as deep as the sunrise. "Actually, I never wrote Beth about him. When I first answered the ad, I was rather sick, and I thought I might lose the baby. Why explain something that might never come to pass?"

She bounced the little fellow up and down on her hip, wiggling her nose at him and setting him to smiling. John fought a smile himself.

"And then when he was born," she continued, "I was afraid to tell her for fear you might not want to send for me. I thought, that is I hoped, you would want him, too."

And he hadn't given her the chance to find out. He could feel her yearning now, and something inside him rose to meet it. He shouldn't give in. She needed a better man than him.

"Is that why you didn't want me to come up?" he asked instead. "Because of Peter?"

She managed a smile. "I was more concerned that I didn't have a chaperone. I couldn't leave him alone to come downstairs."

John glanced back. "If we leave the door open, that ought to satisfy propriety. And you could have told Beth about Peter. She would probably have sent for you sooner. She loves babies."

"Do you?" She shot him a look equal parts challenge and concern.

He shrugged. "I'm an uncle eight times over. I'm used to babies."

Her frame relaxed, but she sighed. "What a very great shame you weren't the man who placed the ad I answered, then."

Perhaps it was a shame. But he didn't feel ready to be a husband, much less a father.

Peter reached out a hand, and John offered him a finger to squeeze. Such a strong grip for a little fellow. He seemed like a healthy lad, with round cheeks and sparkling eyes that might yet turn the purple of his mother's. His dressing gown of linen with its sweater over the top was clean and tidy, at least for the moment, but John knew exactly how many things a baby could do to clothing and anyone nearby. He'd been spit at, wet upon, and had a handful of hair yanked out at one

point or another. That fetching black-and-white check-
ered gown Dottie wore today didn't stand a chance.

"What did the ad say?" he asked, suddenly curious
as to what would have made this woman take a chance
on him. "What convinced you to answer it?"

She cocked her head, a smile hovering. "It said,
'Wanted—sweet-natured wife who will brave the wilderness and make a happy home filled with love.'"

Good thing no one else in his family knew he was
supposed to be the author, or he would never live it
down. "I'm sorry Beth raised your hopes."

Her smile faded, and the room seemed to darken.
"So am I. I truly have no idea what to do now. I know
no one in Seattle but you and Beth and two friends who
just left for the Duwamish. You can understand why
working could be difficult."

"You have no family?" John persisted.

Her mouth tightened. "None that will take in Peter.
They suggested I put him in an orphanage."

John cringed. Having been raised in a big, loving
family, he could not imagine giving away one of his
siblings. Even his youngest brother, Levi, at his worst
had been helped, not shunted aside.

"And his father's family?" he asked.

"Cannot be contacted," she said.

Why? Were they as heartless? Or had she and her
husband married against their wishes? Yet who would
refuse a grandchild, especially if their son was gone,
as must have been the case with her husband if she was
free to marry again?

As if the baby felt the hopelessness of their situation, his face sagged, and he began to whimper. She

drew him closer, rocked him from side to side. Her eyes closed as if she longed to block out their reality.

"I suppose," John heard himself say, "there's only one thing we can do. You better come out to Wallin Landing to live with me."

Chapter Four

Live with him? Dottie clutched Peter close. John Wallin had already told her he had no interest in marriage. How could she live with him?

She felt heat gathering in her cheeks. "I cannot like your assumption, Mr. Wallin. I don't know who gave you the impression that I'm the sort of woman who would put herself under a gentleman's protection, but I assure you that you are mistaken. I think you'd better leave."

His cheeks were as red as hers felt. "Please forgive me, Mrs. Tyrrell. I didn't mean… That is, it wasn't my intention…" He squared his shoulders and met her gaze straight on. His green eyes pleaded for understanding. "I have a good, solid farmhouse. You and Peter are welcome to live in it until you decide what to do next. My brother's logging crew has taken over my parents' cabin. I'm sure I can bunk with them in the meantime."

Nothing in that open face shouted of dishonesty. He was either the kindest man she'd ever met, or the wiliest.

Dottie cocked her head, watching him. "You'd give up your home, for me?"

He blew out a breath as if grateful he'd made his plan clear. "Yes, gladly. It's the least I can do for the trouble my family has put you through. I've several cows and chickens, so you can be assured of fresh milk and eggs. We still have vegetables and fruit canned from last harvest. My brothers and I hunt and fish during the week, so there's usually meat as well. All you'd have to do is take care of you and Peter while you consider your options."

It was too good to be true. "Forgive me, Mr. Wallin, but I find your offer altogether unequal. What do you get out of the bargain?"

He frowned as if puzzled by the question. "Why, the chance to be helpful, ma'am."

A laugh popped out of her, and she could hear the bitter ring to it. "In my experience, people are not nearly so helpful."

He shrugged, a hint of a smile on his lips. "Then perhaps you know the wrong people, Mrs. Tyrrell."

She had no question on that score. Her experience with Frank had soured her on a lot of things. Yet, was John Wallin the only man who had ever offered help to someone in need? She recalled her father allowing vagabonds to stay in the barn and feeding traveling families on their way to work on farms in the next county. He'd never asked for more recompense than a good night's sleep.

"What we do for others, we do for God," he'd said more than once.

She'd never fretted then. She'd been happy on the

farm, secure in the knowledge her parents loved her and would always be there for her. The latter had proved a lie.

Would John Wallin prove a liar?

She must have taken too long to answer, for he sighed, his gaze dropping to the hat in his hands. "If you prefer to stay in Seattle, I'll pay for the hotel as long as I can. I just thought Lowe's might not be the best place for a baby."

Or her. The more she moved about the hotel, going to seek work and returning, the more attention she attracted from the other residents. Several of the men had cast her interested glances, and not in a way she found admiring. And the clerk had told her a guest had complained about Peter's crying. What if the hotel manager asked her to leave? Where would she go then?

"If I agree to your offer," she began, setting John to beaming, "I would need assurances that Wallin Landing is a suitable place for a woman and child. Beth told me a great deal about it, but that was before I knew I would not be arriving as your wife."

He nodded, his hat gripped in his sturdy fingers. "Of course. My claim is the southernmost. It runs from Lake Union west over the top of the hill toward Puget Sound. My brother James and his wife, Rina, are adjacent, but our claims are narrow enough that you can cross them quickly. Just beyond live my oldest brother, Drew, and his wife, Catherine. She's a trained nurse and runs the dispensary. You'd have experienced medical help should Peter need it."

That was good to know. In Cincinnati and on the journey west, Peter had proved surprisingly resilient, with few of the fevers and ailments that seemed to trouble other babies. But she knew it was only a matter of time before something made him ill.

"There's also a school with fifteen students," he continued, stepping closer as if he sensed her resolve weakening. "Rina is the lead teacher. Beth helps sometimes, when she isn't working her claim, assisting my brother Simon's wife, Nora, or trying to boss our brothers or Drew's crew around. Nora watches the little ones while their mothers are working. The eight of them range from a sweet-natured toddler to a six-year-old who's convinced she's queen. I'm certain Nora wouldn't mind including Peter if you had work to do."

And she'd have a nanny of sorts, it seemed. Still, that voice inside her warned that it was all a trick. Hadn't she learned by now that anything good in life could be taken from her?

She gazed down into Peter's dear face. His blue eyes, more gray than hers, gazed back, trusting. He offered her a smile as if to encourage her, and she couldn't help smiling back.

Whatever happens, Lord, thank You for entrusting me with this precious boy.

And didn't her son deserve something more than this narrow hotel room, the company of strangers, here today and gone tomorrow? If what John Wallin was offering was even half true, she could provide Peter a safe home and good food, perhaps even friends. Shouldn't she take the chance, for him?

"I believe Beth said Wallin Landing is about five miles from Seattle," she told John, who was shifting from foot to foot as if he couldn't wait to hear her answer. "I'd be willing to move out, see if the area will suit Peter and me."

His smile showed his relief. "Thank you, Mrs. Tyrrell. I promise you, you won't be disappointed."

She couldn't make herself believe that.

She was coming with him. John wasn't sure why Dottie's decision raised his spirits so high, but he couldn't help whistling a tune as he went to the livery stable to see about hiring a wagon and stabling his horse overnight. She'd been reticent, but who could blame her? She'd already left everything behind to come to Seattle on a promise that had proved false. Why should she believe anything he said?

He'd simply have to show her he was a man who could be trusted.

He brought the wagon around to the hotel, carried her trunk down the stairs and heaved it into the bed. James still joked about the amount of baggage he had been required to move to bring Rina out to Wallin Landing to teach. Dottie's belongings seemed to amount to much less, especially when she was carrying clothing not only for herself, but also for a baby.

"Is there more?" he asked as she passed him by the front of the wagon.

She glanced back. She'd covered her gown with a navy wool cape that fell to her hips, and it twitched as she moved, drawing his attention to her slender figure.

"Just my valise with Peter's things." She held the case in one hand and cradled her son with the other.

An unencumbered female. That would be a novelty. Rina and Catherine had come to Seattle as part of the

Mercer Belles. The women had followed Asa Mercer to Washington Territory from the East Coast to work and marry, bringing fine silk and wool gowns with them. Nora had also been a Mercer Belle, but she'd brought fewer clothes. Still, she was a seamstress. Now she sewed herself something new on a fairly regular basis. And Beth had been known for her obsession with fashion, as depicted in *Godey's Lady's Book*, since she was ten.

He took the valise and stowed it behind the bench, where Dottie could reach it if needed, then turned to hand her up. Instead, she offered him the baby.

"If you'd hold Peter a moment?"

John accepted the soft weight. Peter regarded him solemnly, as if considering his character. Meeting the baby's gaze, John stood a little straighter. He felt the chuckle bubble up inside Peter's chest before the baby grinned. For some reason, John felt like celebrating.

"He likes you." Dottie sounded surprised. She had climbed up into the seat by herself and paused now to gaze down at her son. "He doesn't usually like strangers."

Neither did his mother, but John decided not to mention that.

"I'm used to babies," he said. "I guess they know that."

Dottie dropped her gaze, rearranging her skirts around her on the bench. Then she held open her arms. "I'll take him now."

Peter pouted as John gave him back to his mother. John felt the same way. There was something warm, something real, about holding a baby. The soft skin and sweet breath made him feel protective, strong. He'd felt the same way holding his nieces and nephews. Drew and Catherine had three children now, James and Rina three and Simon and Nora two.

Yet there was something different about Peter, with his too-solemn face. Perhaps he touched John's heart more than his nieces and nephews did because John knew they had two parents to love them. Dottie clearly cared about her son, but unless she remarried, the lad would grow up without a father. John remembered how it had felt to lose Pa, but Drew had stepped into the role. Who would step up to help raise Peter?

John came around, hopped up on the bench and took up the reins. "You won't regret this," he promised Dottie before calling to the horses to set off. Her tight smile showed she disagreed with him.

She cuddled the baby as they rolled through the streets, passing other wagons, men on horseback, ladies with baskets on their arms. Seattle had grown in the last few years. The fancy houses on Third Avenue that had once stood at the edge of town were eclipsed by the buildings on Fourth and Fifth. New streets with names like Cherry and Spring stretched east and west as well. They ran right up to the edge of the forest, which quickly wrapped around John and Dottie, narrowing the road and the world to the single rutted lane leading north.

Dottie glanced longingly back at the town that was disappearing behind them.

"More remote than you expected?" he asked.

She nodded, facing front again. "A bit. Do you have trouble with wild animals at Wallin Landing?"

"Not much," he admitted. "The more people move out our way, the more the animals flee. It's getting harder to find deer or rabbit near the claims. We may get a fox or weasel after the chickens once in a while, but I haven't seen a cougar up close in years."

"Well," she said, "I suppose that's good."

She didn't sound convinced.

"It's no Cincinnati," John acknowledged. "But you must have known that much when you agreed to come."

"Beth's letters were quite detailed, but I suppose it wouldn't have taken much for me to want to be elsewhere. I didn't like living in Cincinnati. I'm sure Wallin Landing will be fine."

He'd always thought so. "My brothers have done their best by the place. Ma and Pa brought us out before the Indian War here in '55. They each filed a claim, then each of us siblings, except my brother Levi, who went north, filed a claim when we reached our majority. Pa always wanted his own town."

John had grown up with the dream, but saying it aloud to Dottie felt odd. After living in a big city like Cincinnati, she could only see their goal of building a community as provincial. Why, Wallin Landing was small compared to Seattle!

She busied herself with her son, tucking the blanket around him, pulling a corner over his head and murmuring assurances. Not for the first time, he felt a stab of loss. Ma had been gone just two years, having met and loved each of her grandchildren, and he still missed her. He thought she'd like Mrs. Tyrrell. Ma had appreciated women who stood up for themselves.

The skies above the firs were heavy with rain, and John could hear it pattering down above them. Under the trees, however, it was drier. The cool air that brushed his cheeks carried the scent of Puget Sound. It might have been a pleasant ride, but he was all too concerned about the lady beside him. She'd come this far and the end of her journey wasn't in sight. Surely he could find some way to reassure her.

"It's nearly time to plant," he remarked. "We'll have corn and beans aplenty, and each claim has its own garden and orchard for fruit. Our neighbors are good about trading whatever's extra. You'll see the farms soon."

"How many people, all told?" she asked, sitting taller, as if she longed to spot any sign of civilization.

John frowned, considering. "With our claims and the neighbors to the north and south, perhaps sixty people."

"Sixty."

She said the word breathlessly, but he was fairly sure the number was far too small for her. He was just glad when they came out of the forest onto farmland, the fields dark as farmers turned the soil for new planting. He spotted neighbors out working as they passed. All raised a hand in greeting, and John waved back. Mrs. Tyrrell regarded him, brows tight over her nose, and he couldn't tell what was troubling her.

Peter had no such concerns. He closed his eyes and drowsed in her arms.

There had to be something that would please her. Through the trees ahead, he spotted a steeple rising. He pointed toward it. "That's our church."

"Beth said you designed it," Dottie replied, angling her head as if to try to glimpse more of the structure.

He couldn't quite prevent the pride from leaking into his voice. "I did. But Drew and his men felled the timber, James paid for it to be cut into board at Yesler's mill and my brothers and I all worked together to construct the building. It still needs paint, inside and out, and there are benches, steps and a pulpit to install."

"By summer, then," she said with a nod.

He grimaced. "Realistically, with planting coming, it might be a while before we finish. I'm hoping we'll start holding services there around harvest time, provided we can find a preacher willing to relocate out this way."

He spied an opening in the trees and turned the horses west, up the track that led to his house. The forest was thinner here. Drew and his crew had taken out most of the big firs years ago, but John had left a few vine maples and madrone to shield the house from the main road. His home and barn sat on a bench, with fields running down to the road and spreading out on either side, the forest rising at the back. The arrangement had proved both practical and pleasing.

Yet the closer they came, the more he tensed. Why? It was a good, solid house with a sturdy barn, just as he'd told her. He had no reason to feel as if its worth was tied to her approval.

He pulled the wagon up before the wide front porch he'd insisted on having when Simon had sketched out plans for the place.

"I want to be able to sit under the eaves and watch the sun come up," he'd told his brother.

Simon had frowned at him. "You get up before sunrise and head for work. When do you have time to sit?"

A literal man, his brother. But John had been firm. It was his house. He could do what he liked with it. Especially as it appeared he would never be sharing it with a wife.

"Here we are," he announced, setting the brake. He jumped down, tied the horses to the porch rail to make sure they didn't head for the barn and came around to help Dottie.

Her gaze was on the house. Did she wonder why a bachelor needed a second story or three chairs along the porch? Did she approve of the glass windows brought up from San Francisco? Or the blue paint he'd used to show off the door against the white of the house? Why did he care?

"It's lovely," she said, and he thought he might stand as tall as Drew for once.

He offered to help her down, but she merely handed him Peter. Now that the wagon had stopped moving, the baby cracked open his eyes. They widened as if Peter was surprised to see John holding him instead of his mother. John readied himself for the wail of protest. Instead, Peter's face brightened in a grin.

He kept the baby in his arms as he led Dottie into the house.

"Parlor's to the right," he explained, nodding through the open door. "Main bedroom's to the left. Kitchen runs across the back. Stairs lead up to a sleeping loft. Right now it's full of furs curing from the winter."

She wandered into the parlor, touched the bench Drew had carved for him, exclaimed over the woven rug his mother had made. John followed her, rocking Peter in his arms. The baby gazed about him, as if everything he saw was wonderful.

Not everyone was so entranced. A hiss told John he was in trouble. Glancing about, he sighted the ginger bullet on the windowsill a moment before it launched itself at him. John stepped back from the malevolent green glare.

"Oh," Dottie exclaimed, "you have a cat."

John managed a smile. "Mrs. Tyrrell, may I present Brian de Bois-Guilbert. He patrols for vermin."

That sounded a lot more manly than the cat's typical role—stalking John around the house with demands for attention.

Dottie's face brightened. "Brian de Bois-Guilbert, like in *Ivanhoe*?"

At the moment, the cat did indeed resemble the villain of the tale. His tail twitched as his eyes narrowed on Peter.

"No," John told him. "Down, boy."

Dottie looked at him in obvious amazement. "Does he obey you like a dog?"

He shrugged. "I thought it was worth a try."

She shook her head, then crouched on the rug and held out a hand to the cat. Brian refused to so much as glance in her direction. He busied himself licking his white mitten paws.

"Where did you get a cat out here?" she asked. "I'd think they'd get eaten by foxes."

"I found him in my barn," John told her, edging back from the cat in case Brian did have designs on Peter. "Pitiful thing, more bones than muscle. Some of our neighbors had cats, so Beth and I thought he might have escaped from a litter nearby. She named him after the knight in *Ivanhoe*, the one who couldn't decide whether he was a hero or a villain. I think she was hoping to keep him, but he seems to have attached himself to me."

As if to disprove it, Brian raised his head and let out another hiss, ears going back and eyes narrowing.

Dottie stood and glanced at Peter. The baby had started at the noise. Now he giggled. Dottie drew in a breath.

John wasn't nearly so pleased. The cat had been good company when he'd lived here alone, but Brian, like many of his kind, tended to do as he pleased. And he seemed to feel John was his personal companion. Would he attack Dottie or the baby? John wouldn't feel comfortable putting the cat out of the house on a permanent basis, but neither did he feel comfortable leaving Brian alone with Dottie and her son.

Dottie crouched again, ran her fingers along the rug. Brian watched each movement as if fascinated. Once more, John tensed.

"That might not be a good idea," he murmured.

Dottie didn't respond. Instead, she held out her hand again.

Brian eyed her a moment more, then his face and ears relaxed and his back came down. He wandered up to Dottie and ran his back under her fingers.

"Sweet kitty," she crooned. "Darling kitty."

As Brian turned for another pass, he glanced up at John as if to say *See? This is how it's done.*

Dottie gave the feline another pat before rising in a whisper of wool. "I think we'll get along just fine."

So it seemed. But, for the first time, John wondered just how many things would change in his life with Dottie and Peter at Wallin Landing.

Chapter Five

John Wallin had a cat.

Dottie wasn't sure why that surprised her so much. Perhaps it was because most of the men of her acquaintance preferred dogs, and then for hunting or protection. The majority of the felines she'd known had been barn cats at her parents' farm. They'd been wild, rangy things, used to hunting for their dinner. John claimed Brian de Bois-Guilbert served the same function here. She found that hard to believe. A lady at the apartment building in Cincinnati had had a cat she treated with the utmost courtesy. Brian had the same sleek, overfed, self-satisfied look.

Of course, for all Dottie knew, Beth had been the one doing the pampering. Dottie must not allow this whimsy to sway her opinion of John. Only time would tell if he was truly a gentleman worth trusting.

"It will just take me a minute to lead the horses to the barn, bring in your things and pack up mine," John told her now. He held out Peter to her.

That he seemed to be very good at cradling her son

was another mark in his favor. Some people had no idea how to treat an infant. She'd had to learn, first from her helpful neighbor Martha Duggin at the apartment building in Cincinnati, and then from Mrs. Gustafson on the boat. Now, as the baby passed between them, John's fingers brushed her arm, as soft as a caress. A tingle ran through her, and she stepped back lest he notice her reaction. She had to remember that a handsome face and a fine physique were no match for character. She was glad when he nodded respectfully and left the room. A moment more, and she heard the front door open as he must have gone out to the wagon.

Why did the room seem so empty without him?

She was used to emptiness, but she'd been a bit dismayed to find the land outside of Seattle so remote, the farms few and scattered. Beth's stories had made Wallin Landing sound so alive and vibrant. Dottie had needed to believe in a place like that. After Frank had left her, she'd felt so isolated. But now that she understood how far away the place was from Seattle, she could only wonder whether her isolation would be worse here.

Still, she could not deny that she felt welcome in John's house. The scrubbed wood floors gave off a patina that was reflected in the whitewashed walls and ceiling. The carved bench that served as the main seat for the parlor was draped with a quilt done in shades of brown and green, and the hearth was of rounded stones, browns and grays and whites, with splashes of gold almost the color of Brian's hair.

The cat strolled back and forth around her skirts, setting the wool to swinging. Peter reached out a hand as if he longed to touch the softness.

"He's a very handsome fellow, isn't he?" Dottie asked. Then she clamped her lips shut. She'd become accustomed to talking to Peter, even before he was born. After Frank had left her with the threat that she should keep quiet or else, she'd stayed in the apartment for days. Talking to her unborn baby had been the only way to stay sane. But if John Wallin had heard what she'd said right now, he might think she was talking about him!

Although she would have been speaking the truth. He was a handsome fellow.

Dottie raised her chin. "Come along, Peter. If we're going to live here, we might as well know where everything is."

She started in the kitchen at the back of the house, Brian strolling along beside her. The cast-iron stove along one wall stood between a cupboard and a wood box, both well filled. Copper pots and tin pans hung on the wall on either side. The wood table across from it could seat four, and she wondered who else might join him on occasion. The gingham curtains on the window overlooking the barn had been tied back with bows.

Beth must have done that.

"I'll be able to cook here," she told Peter, smiling down at his beaming face. "I can make you applesauce. Would you like that?"

Brian meowed as if he thought it sounded like a fine idea.

She returned down the corridor, heading for the bedroom across the entry from the parlor, and again the cat accompanied her. She felt a little odd peeking into John's room, but if the upstairs was full of curing furs, she would have no other choice than to sleep here. She was pleased to see the room contained a large bed made from hewn logs. The blue-and-green quilt in a block pattern looked thick and warm. Brian jumped up and dug his claws into it as if to prove as much. With a quick look out the window to make sure John had taken the wagon around to the barn and couldn't see her, she bounced on the mattress. Not too soft and not too hard. Good.

There was also a trunk at the foot of the bed, the beautifully carved top showing an owl sweeping out over a forest with the moon riding high above. She traced the bird's flight with one hand. "Look at this, Peter. Do you know what the owl says? Who-hoo."

Peter pursed his mouth as if he could make such a sound, but nothing came out.

Might as well say "what-what." What was she doing here so far from home? How could she make a way for her son with no husband, no employment?

From the back of the house, something clanked. Had John come in a back door instead of the front?

Brian's head snapped up, then he leaped off the bed and darted under it.

A shiver ran up Dottie's spine. She glanced out the window again but caught no sign of John. She swallowed nervously, then laid Peter on the center of the bed and pulled up one edge of the quilt to cover him. He'd just begun to roll over, but she didn't think he could manage it with the weight of the quilt.

"Here, kitty, kitty, kitty," she called, urging Brian out from hiding.

The cat poked his head out from under the bed, then

scampered across the floor like a streak of sunshine and flew out the door. Dottie followed.

She cocked her head and called toward the kitchen. "Hello, is someone there?"

In answer, the door swung open, and John moved into the corridor, her trunk balanced on his broad shoulders. It had taken two men to carry that from the cab to the train station in Cincinnati. She had a feeling it hadn't grown any lighter since then. Yet he walked as if it was no burden.

"Where would you like this?" he asked. And he wasn't even breathless!

She stepped aside to let him pass. "In the bedroom, please."

With a nod, he went to comply.

Oh, yes, quite a fine physique.

Blushing, Dottie followed John into the room. Peter was cooing from his bundle on the bed, hands reaching up toward a beam of sunlight that was coming through the window. John smiled as he straightened from positioning the trunk against the far wall. "He looks right at home."

Dottie felt it, too. But that was dangerous. This wasn't going to be home, not for more than a week or two at most. It was no more permanent than the hotel room in Seattle or the apartment she'd left behind in Cincinnati.

John was moving around the room. He opened his trunk and gathered some flannel shirts and wool trousers. She turned in case he meant to lift out his unmentionables. As she did so, she couldn't help noticing that even the windowsill was clean of dust.

Dottie frowned. Everything was clean. The floors had been swept, the gingham curtains on the bedroom window recently washed and ironed, and they also sported bows. Not one article of clothing had been strewn about the bedroom. No man she knew kept a house so clean, so lovingly decorated.

Anger flushed through her, and she rounded on John. "You lied to me! You have a wife. I demand that you return me to Seattle, immediately!"

John recoiled from Dottie's vehemence. Her face was red, her eyes flashing, and she marched to the bed and snatched up Peter as if to protect him from John.

He dropped his things into the trunk. "I'll take you back, if that's what you want, but I don't have a wife."

"Really." The single word held a world of suspicion. "And I suppose you'll tell me that you clean house for yourself."

He frowned. "I do. Ma insisted that all her sons know how to cook and clean and wash. Once in a while Beth comes by to help. I think she just likes having someone to look out for."

Her face puckered. "You really wash your own clothes?"

Was that so odd? As far as he knew, Drew, James and Simon helped on wash day in their houses. It was hot, heavy work, and someone had to make sure the children didn't go anywhere near the lye.

"Yes," he said, feeling as if she was questioning his manhood. "A bachelor needs clean clothes as much as anyone else. And I don't particularly like living in mud."

She put one hand on her hip. "And I suppose you like bows as well."

Bows? He glanced around the room, trying to see whether his sister might have left a hair bow lying around. "I'm not sure…" he began.

She stalked to the window and pointed at the fabric holding the curtains back. "Bows."

"The ties?" Now that he looked at them, they did resemble bows. He'd never noticed before. "Beth made them for all of us last Christmas."

Brian chose that moment to stroll back into the bedroom. He went immediately to John, wound himself around his ankles and glanced up with a pitiful meow. Normally John would have picked him up, stroked the ginger fur. But with Dottie looking at him as if he was some kind of oddity, he wasn't about to give her reason to doubt him further.

"I…see," she said. She drew in a breath. "I'm sorry, Mr. Wallin. I shouldn't have jumped to conclusions."

It was a strong reaction, but he supposed she had reason. He made himself shrug as Brian bumped his head against John's calf. "Strange location, strange people. Anyone might have done the same. But rest assured I have no wife or any intention of taking one."

She nodded, dropping her gaze. Brian reared up and dug his claws into John's trousers. John refused to so much as protest. The cat dropped back down and stalked out of the room in high dudgeon.

Very likely, Dottie would relax once he was out of the way. John gathered up his belongings again. "All the food is in the cupboard near the stove," he told her.

"The fire burns pretty evenly, but I've noticed you have to turn the biscuits to get a golden top all around."

She was staring at him again. Perhaps biscuits weren't the most manly thing to discuss, either.

"And there's a pump in the sink." That was better. Machinery, logging, buildings: those were things men discussed. "Sometimes it takes a few tries for the water to flow. Oh, and that window sticks when it rains, but you shouldn't need to open it this time of year."

She nodded. "I'm sure we can manage."

He straightened, arms laden. "Just don't let Brian outside for long. It's too easy for him to get eaten or end up in a trap."

She shuddered. "I'll be careful."

"Good. Right." John shuffled his feet. "Well, then, I suppose I better get going."

He started past her, and she caught his arm.

"Thank you," she murmured before standing on tip-toe and pressing a kiss to his cheek.

It ought to have been a neighborly kiss, a sisterly kiss, but the floor seemed to be rippling like a wave on the Sound. He had to stop himself from turning his head and meeting her lips with his own.

"Ho! John!"

His brother's voice seemed to come from somewhere far beyond the little bubble that enclosed him and Dottie. She dropped to her soles, lavender eyes wide. Peter giggled.

James strolled past the door of the bedroom. "John? Are you here? I saw a wagon out back."

"Excuse me," John murmured, passing Dottie to the hallway.

James turned at the sound of his movement. "Ah, there you are. What, is it wash day already? What a tidy fellow you are. Ma would be so proud."

John had a sudden urge to push his brother out the door. "Can I help you with something?" he asked instead.

James smiled. His next closest brother in outlook, James had a few inches on John, though he remained whip-thin. He'd also inherited Pa's light brown hair and dark blue eyes. "Rina's tooth is bothering her," he explained. "Catherine's given her a powder, but she'd prefer to take the day off tomorrow. She wondered if you'd step in."

John and Beth had both substituted for James's wife, who taught in the one-room school at Wallin Landing. Beth must have something else to do tomorrow that James would come for John.

"Of course," John assured him. "Just have her write down what they're studying in the various subjects. Last time Danny tried to convince me he couldn't do more than add so he could get out of working on his multiplication. And perhaps Simon can return the wagon and horses to Seattle and bring back my horse."

James opened his mouth, most likely to make some quip, as he was wont to do, but his gaze swept past John and no words came out.

John turned to find Dottie in the doorway to the bedroom. She smiled shyly at his brother before focusing on John.

"Forgive me. I just realized. You said you had cows and chickens. Do you need me to feed them? Milk the cows? Gather eggs?"

"I'll tend to the cows and milk morning and evening,"

John promised. "If you'd like to gather the eggs, that would be appreciated. You'll see the coop at the side of the barn."

James cleared his throat.

John kept his smile tight. "Mrs. Tyrrell, this is my brother James Wallin. He has the claim next to mine, as I mentioned. James, Mrs. Tyrrell and her son will be staying in my house until she decides where to settle in the area."

James swept her a bow. "Dear lady, welcome to Wallin Landing. I'm John's most charming brother and father to three adorable children. May I see yours?"

Dottie widened her grasp so he could peer down at Peter. The baby's lower lip trembled, and he buried his face in his mother's arms.

Funny. Peter hadn't been particularly shy with John. He wasn't sure why that made him feel as if he'd finally gotten the better of his witty brother.

"Probably ready for a nap," James acknowledged. "A shame John doesn't have a cradle." He tsked as if John had been entirely shortsighted.

"I haven't needed one before," John reminded him.

James beamed at Dottie. "I have it! My beloved wife and I have a cradle, and none of our darlings is sleeping in it at present. We'd be delighted to see it go to good use. Why don't you come with me, John, and fetch it back for the lady?"

Why not? It would keep John from saying more ridiculous things that would only give Dottie Tyrrell a further disgust of him. And the way his brother's brows were wiggling, he had something to say to John in private.

"I'll be right back," John told her. He nodded to James, who bowed again to Dottie and then headed out the front door.

John fell into step beside him, arms still laden with clothing.

"Who is she?" James demanded. "Where did you meet her? Why does she have a baby?"

John started for the trees that marked the dividing line between his claim and James's. "She's a widow from back east. She and Beth have been corresponding for months, and Beth convinced her to relocate to Seattle."

James whistled. "So that's the mail-order bride. I didn't realize she'd arrived."

John jerked to a stop on the well-worn path. "You knew?"

James shrugged. "Beth had to confide in someone."

"And you didn't think to warn me?"

"She swore me to silence." James shook his head. "Besides, it wasn't as if I expected the woman to agree to come. This isn't exactly an admirable situation— far from civilization and the things a lady generally prefers."

John glanced back at the house, barely visible through the trees. "You think she can't be happy here?"

"Who knows?" James clapped him on the shoulder. "That's what courtship is about, learning what the other person can tolerate."

John started forward once more. "We aren't courting. She's just staying here until she can determine her next steps."

"Ah, I see."

Somehow his brother made it sound as if he saw more than John intended.

"I mean it, James," John warned. "Mrs. Tyrrell and I are not courting. I have no interest in marrying."

James matched his stride. "Can't say I blame you. There are already too many blondes at Wallin Landing, though none, mind you, with quite that glorious shade of gold. And a trim figure, while all the rage in Beth's precious magazine, probably indicates she hasn't the strength to muck stalls and haul timber."

"I'd hardly expect a wife to muck stalls or haul timber," John protested.

"No? How progressive of you. But it probably doesn't matter. Very likely Mrs. Tyrrell is too educated for you."

John frowned at him. "You think so?"

James barked a laugh. "No, scholar that you are. From what Beth tells me, you and Mrs. Tyrrell are evenly matched. I say propose and get it over with."

"No." John could hear the obstinacy in his tone. "You and Beth may know all about her, but I don't. And I'm not sure I want to. A woman like that is looking for a hero. I'm no hero."

James chuckled, but he didn't argue the point. "It's not me you need to convince."

"Mrs. Tyrrell and I understand each other," John assured him.

"Oh, very likely," James agreed. "But you both may be outvoted. Do you really think you can resist the combined forces of the female population of Wallin Landing?"

John felt as if the shadows of the trees crept closer. "You don't think…"

"I do. Once Beth, Rina, Catherine and Nora learn that Mrs. Tyrrell and her baby have arrived, you might as well go buy the ring, my lad, for you'll be as good as married."

Chapter Six

By the time John and his brother returned with the cradle, Dottie had taken herself in hand. She knew why she'd assumed John had a wife, but her reaction troubled her all the same. Everything she'd read in Beth's letters, everything she'd seen so far, told her that John and his family were kind, helpful people. She didn't want to judge them, or anyone else she met, by Frank's behavior. Yet how could she trust her own judgment? She'd been wrong before, with disastrous results.

"That should do it," John said now, stepping back as if to admire the placement of the cradle next to the bed. The cradle was beautiful, the wood carved with doves and lambs and polished to a warm glow. Already Peter snuggled in the soft blankets, eyes drifting shut.

"Is everything to your liking, Mrs. Tyrrell?" John asked.

"Yes, Mr. Wallin," she replied. "You've been most kind."

He smiled, but his brother made a face. "'Mrs. Tyrrell, Mr. Wallin.' We're not nearly so formal here at

Wallin Landing." He bowed extravagantly to Dottie. "I shall be James, this paltry fellow, John. And what shall we call you, fair lady?"

"James," John said in warning.

His brother shook his head. "No, no, we can't call her James. It would be entirely too confusing."

Dottie smiled. It should be permissible to go by first names. She was living in John's house, after all. "My name is Dorothy, but everyone calls me Dottie."

James seized her hand. "A pleasure to meet you, my dear Dottie. And now I must go, but I leave you in good hands." He transferred her hand to John's arm, wiggled his light brown brows and backed from the room.

John shook his head, shifting so that Dottie's hand fell to her side. "Forgive him. He tends to be a bit theatrical."

"Was he in the theater?" Dottie asked, bending to check on Peter. Her son was dozing in the cradle as if it had always been his bed.

"Never," John told her. "Unless you count the school productions over the years. Rina used to have to enlist all of us in the plays—she didn't have enough students at first." He took a step closer. "You're sure you'll be all right?"

She glanced up and felt herself slipping into the green of his gaze. Odd how the color looked warm on him. She forced herself to step away. "We'll be fine. Thank you."

"If you need anything, look for a break in the trees to the north. That path will take you past James's house and down to the main house. Someone's always available there. Now, rest easy." His boots clumped as he headed for the door.

Rest easy. If only she could. It seemed forever since she'd had a good night's sleep. Before Peter had been born, she'd lie awake each night, thinking about the future. When she'd ordered Frank from her life, he'd left her some money. For her trouble and her silence, he'd said, as if the funds could in any way compensate for his broken promise, her shattered dreams. She'd been tempted to donate the money to charity, but she'd soon realized she'd need it for Peter. She'd taken pains to economize so that the money would go as far as it could.

Once Peter had been born, his needs had woken her several times a night at first. Rocking him in the darkness, she kept wondering what would happen if Frank discovered he had a son. He had been a terrible husband to both his wives, betraying them in the worst way, but the law was on the father's side. If Frank had reconciled with his first wife, and he learned about Peter, he could easily take Dottie's son from her, claiming her as a fallen woman, a seductress who had attempted to steal Frank from his wife.

Those concerns had driven her from Cincinnati, made her accept a stranger's offer to be his bride, brought her to the far side of the country. Surely that distance would be enough to protect Peter. Surely she could finally rest, as John suggested.

But as the day faded and evening approached, she couldn't seem to relax. Sounds she had forgotten when she'd lived in the city came back to her now. An owl hooted from the nearby forest; something rustled against the roof. And the smells—the tang of fir, the dark scent of fields freshly turned. With no streetlamps, no lights from businesses, it was so very black outside. Danger could be lurking ten feet from the house, and she'd never know.

Peter must have sensed her agitation, for he was unusually fussy, even as she nursed. Now she held him as she stood in the doorway, looking out over the porch, watching the darkness and listening.

But even as the night made her shiver, she began to notice pinpricks of light. The closest to the north was likely the home of James and Rina. The largest might be the house where John was staying. Was he asleep yet? Did he fret over the responsibility he'd agreed to take on?

Then, on the breeze, she caught the strains of a violin, plaintive, calling. And it seemed good and right that John moved out of the shadows to approach the porch.

He'd put a thick coat over his shirt, but he'd left his hat behind. The breeze fingered through his hair, which looked almost black in the night. He gave her a nod but made no move to enter the house.

"Still up, I see," he said from the foot of the porch. "I just thought I'd check on the house and the barn. Everything all right?"

Everything felt more than all right with him here. Even her breath seemed to come easier.

"We're fine," she assured him. "Who's that playing?"

He cocked his head as if to listen. "Simon. He often plays for his family at night." He hummed a snatch of the tune.

"I don't know the song," she said.

"Pa taught it to us when we were children.

"I would not die in summer
When music's on the breeze,
And soft, delicious murmurs
Float ever through the trees,
And fairy birds are singing
From morn till close of day
No: with its transient glories
I would not pass away."

His warm baritone wrapped around her, the words reminding her of better times, a place of hope, where everything felt good. In her arms, Peter sighed and closed his eyes, a smile playing on his lips.

Could it be she'd finally found a place she could feel at home?

John wasn't sure why he'd sung to Dottie and Peter. He remembered Pa playing and Ma singing when he was a boy. Certainly he'd sung to a fussy baby before. But never to a lady whose smile made him feel the most talented of all men.

"I'd best put Peter to bed," she murmured now. "Good night, John."

"Good night, Dottie." He watched her until she closed the door. The night felt colder, and he tugged his coat closer.

He checked the barn and then walked back to the main house with a smile. It wasn't just the sound of his brother's playing, which always encouraged him. No, it was Dottie's company that warmed him. He knew she wasn't his to keep, but nothing said he couldn't enjoy being around her for now.

Still, it was odd settling to sleep on the pallet in the loft of the main house at Wallin Landing. Growing up, he'd shared the space with Drew, Simon, James and Levi, while Beth had slept on the other side of the hearth in a bed near their parents. There had been a simple arch between the two spaces so Ma and Pa could call over to settle squabbles among his brothers or hurry to deal with a sick child.

Now the rooms were completely separate, and Harry Yeager, one of Drew's men, slept in Ma and Pa's room. Beth lived in Simon's old cabin, since Simon and Nora had relocated to a larger house up on the ridge and Beth had yet to decide on the house she wanted to build on her claim. Instead of his brothers sleeping around him, the other two loggers of Drew's crew were bundled under blankets. The sharp snore belonged to Thomas Convers. Dickie Morgan muttered something in his sleep, and the pallet rustled as he rolled closer to the wall.

John pulled the covers up over his ears, tried to focus on something besides the unfamiliar noises. Perhaps he'd lived alone for too long. He'd filed his claim when he was twenty-one. With his brothers' help, he'd built the house and barn and moved in before he was twenty-two. Many times in the last six years one or more of the family members had stayed with him for one reason or another, but they'd used the loft, leaving him to his bedroom.

The bedroom Dottie was now sharing with Peter.

He could imagine her lying there, golden curls spread across the goose-feather pillow. Would she use the lamp to read one of his books? Would she fall asleep with a smile on those perfect pink lips?

The lips that had felt soft and sweet against his cheek.

He rolled over, gave the pillow a good punch. There was no future in dreaming about Dottie Tyrrell, or any other woman for that matter. He was the one women chose as a friend, a confidante, not a husband. He knew that. He was rather proud of the fact that he could be of assistance to any who needed it.

But somehow, the role had never seemed less satisfying.

John must have fallen asleep at last, for he woke to the smell of bacon frying and the sound of a baby crying. Funny. He'd thought all his nieces and nephews were too old now to make that distressed mewling. And who was cooking in his kitchen?

Then he remembered where he was. One of the loggers or Beth, who sometimes helped, must be cooking. But how could there be a baby in the house?

Only if Dottie had come with Peter.

He scrambled out of bed, yanked on his trousers and grabbed his flannel shirt, shoving his arms into the sleeves as he went. As he started down the open stairs that ran along one wall of the main room of the house, he spotted a head of golden curls near the table, surrounded by men with broad shoulders. Beth stood in the doorway to the kitchen, wiping her hands on her apron and beaming at the group clustered around Dottie.

Drew was standing at the bottom of the stairs, arms crossed over his chest.

"I understand I have you to thank for this," he said,

jerking his head toward his men. "They were supposed to report to work an hour ago. First time I ever had to come looking for them."

That was saying a lot. From the moment his brother had assumed leadership of the family on their father's death, no one had disobeyed his orders very often. And why would they? Drew was the tallest of them, the strongest. His hair was the most blond, his eyes the darkest blue. Drew was a rock of safety, a mighty cedar sheltering any who came near. Even his work crew knew that.

"I'll get them back to work," John said, pulling his suspenders up over his shoulders. He waded into the crowd.

Dottie was in the middle, rocking Peter and making soft shushing noises. Today she wore a dress the color of spring leaves, with ruffles running up from her waist all the way to form a collar against her neck. Peter wore a long blue shirt that covered his toes, and his bubbling sobs were evident, his face puckered and red.

"Mr. Wallin taught me how to whittle," Dickie said to Dottie. "I could carve little Peter a rattle. That might make him feel better."

Dickie was young enough that he ought to be playing with toys himself, in John's opinion. With blond hair that reminded John of the hay in his barn and bright blue eyes, Dickie's round face held more than one pimple.

"No, what he needs is a wagon so you don't have to hold him all the time," Tom argued, squaring his shoulders so that the plaid flannel stretched taut. The most experienced on Drew's crew, the dark-haired fellow was forever putting forth opinions on one subject or another.

"I'll make you one," Harry offered. "I can get Mr. Yesler to give me some of the lumber."

That was Harry, always sure of himself. He had wavy brown hair, sharp brown eyes and a chiseled chin. Harry had been quick to push himself into a place of leadership among the loggers, until he was considered second to Drew himself.

"Mr. Yesler is only going to give you timber if you actually cut down the trees," John pointed out. He made a show of glancing out the window at the brightening day. "Which you should have been doing an hour ago."

Harry elbowed him good-naturedly. "You gave her your house. Can't blame us for giving her our time."

Dickie heaved a sigh. "Especially since Miss Beth won't hardly look at us."

John couldn't see his sister over Harry, but he heard her righteous huff.

Drew cleared his throat with a deep rumble. "The trees are waiting. If this takes much longer, they'll grow too big to be used for spars."

With joking protests, his men begged Dottie's pardon and followed their boss toward the door. Dottie watched them go. John knew, because he was watching Dottie.

Then he noticed that Peter was watching him. The red faded from his face, and he offered John a watery smile. John smiled back.

"They didn't even eat their breakfast," Beth complained, coming to the table. "You two better sit, because this food has to go somewhere."

With a laugh, Dottie went to sit at the table. John joined her.

"Your friends are very kind," she murmured, gaze on

Peter, who had grasped one of her fingers and seemed to be examining it in amazement.

John nodded, though he could only be annoyed with the men's behavior. He couldn't remember a time he'd simply "forgotten" to go to work. Cows had to be milked, fields tended, wood chopped. A pretty face had never stopped him from doing his duty.

Then again, there weren't many faces as pretty as Dottie's.

"Drew has a great crew," Beth assured her, bringing a plate of bacon and another of pancakes to the table. "And Harry and Tom have filed their claims, so they'll have homes of their own soon."

"And none of them are married?" Dottie asked, serving herself a pancake. She asked the question so casually, as if the answer was of no importance. John's shoulders tightened.

"None," Beth told her, taking a seat across from her. "Go on and eat, John. You never eat enough. Sometimes I wonder that you don't blow away."

Dottie eyed his shoulders, and he found himself sitting taller. He was fully aware his physique was as powerful as Harry's, and he was taller than either Dickie or Tom.

And what difference did that make? It wasn't as if he was in competition with them. He piled the pancakes onto his plate and pushed the bacon alongside them.

"They're fine men," Beth continued, slathering her stack of pancakes with butter. "Considerate, clever even. Any one of them would make a good husband."

A piece of bacon in his mouth, John nearly choked. "Husband?"

Beth pointed the butter knife at him. "I warned you, John. Dottie is bound to attract the attention of another man. Just because you refuse to wed doesn't mean everyone else feels the same way."

"But didn't Mr. Morgan say you refused to wed any of your brother's crew?" Dottie asked Beth.

Simon would have approved of her logic. So did John. He swallowed his bacon, settling in his seat.

Beth blushed, but she reached for the jar of blackberry preserves and dumped them onto her pancakes. "I'm not attracted to Harry, Dickie or Tom. And we are talking about you, Dottie. I feel responsible for bringing you all this way. I won't rest until I see you well settled."

John snorted. "You don't have to play matchmaker this time, Beth. I'd think Dottie would know what she prefers in a husband."

Beside him, Dottie shifted, her gaze dropping to Peter in her arms. He was eyeing the pancakes as if wondering how they might taste.

Beth raised her chin. "Very likely. But I know the local gentlemen and which are suitable."

Suitable. Sometimes he didn't think his sister knew the meaning of the word. Look how many fellows had tried to court her. Look how many had come away as no more than friends.

"You can't choose a husband like you choose a dress out of *Godey's*," he told her.

Beth cut into her stack of pancakes. "I don't see why not. I take particular care in choosing my gowns. I'd think choosing to court would take just the same amount of consideration."

"Dottie doesn't need to marry any old Tom, Dick or Harry," John blurted out.

Beth stared at him a moment, then her laughter peeled. "Why, John, James would be so proud of you for that quip."

Dottie seemed to be fighting a smile, though her cheeks were turning that delicate shade of pink again.

"I just thought it might be a little soon to be planning a wedding," he told his sister. "Dottie just met them."

"Sometimes it only takes one look to know you've found the right fellow," Beth informed him.

She'd read their father's adventure novels, too. A shame real life didn't usually follow that pattern.

"And sometimes it takes months of courting to know," John insisted.

"You're right." Dottie spoke softly, gaze still on her son, who was examining his own fingers now. "But I can't stay in your house for months, John. I must find employment or a husband."

"Employment," John told her. Just saying the word eased the tension in his shoulders. "There has to be someone out here who needs help cooking or sewing."

"Or teaching," Beth suggested. "Rina has enough students that I wonder whether we could convince the board to hire her an assistant."

Rina. The school.

John shot to his feet. "I promised Rina I'd teach school this morning!"

Beth glanced out the window. "By the looks of things, the students have found other methods of education."

John could see them now, too, running around the school door. Worse, he could hear them. From across the clearing came whoops and hollering, and the shrill shriek of a girl annoyed.

It seemed no matter what he did, he showed himself to disadvantage in front of Dottie. Perhaps Beth was right. Dottie needed to find the right man for her, and it clearly wasn't him.

Chapter Seven

Dottie could see exactly what had concerned John. A half-dozen children ran about the clearing in front of the main house. Others hung off the split-rail fence, calling to the horses in the pasture or holding out clumps of grass to lure the animals closer. One enterprising lad tugged on the rope for the school bell, setting it to pealing.

"Excuse me," John said, starting for the door.

"John!" Beth cried. "Where are your boots?"

He glanced down at his feet, which Dottie noticed for the first time were clad only in brown wool stockings. Then he rolled his head skyward as if begging the good Lord for help and plunged out the door anyway. Peter began to whimper once more.

Dottie met Beth's gaze as she rocked her son. "Will John be all right?"

Beth shrugged.

Dottie glanced out the window again. He had made it to the schoolroom door and was calling the children to him. Most came willingly enough, but a few dragged their feet. The boy who had rung the bell went so far as to hide around the corner of the schoolhouse.

"Poor John," Beth said as if she'd seen the same problem. "Even Rina struggles to get them to calm down long enough to learn some days. I help her on occasion, but I'm too busy today." She swung a leg under her lavender skirts, setting them to swinging.

"What are you doing today?" Dottie asked, eyeing her pretty dress. Those purple bows and the scalloped trim did not seem conducive to hard work. Was Beth heading back into Seattle? Should Dottie hitch a ride?

Beth rose and came around the table to her, holding out her arms. "Why, I'm watching Peter so you can settle in, of course."

Of course. Dottie didn't remember agreeing to any such plan, and she seemed to recall James remarking, before anyone else had known that Dottie had arrived in Wallin Landing, that Beth had been too busy to teach today. She ought to protest the imposition on Beth, but she had to own that a few moments to herself would be most welcome. As John had suggested last night, she had followed the path down to the main house this morning to see if she could locate Beth and ask about employment opportunities in the area. Perhaps she could go to the trading post along the lake she'd seen when she'd walked to the main house and ask if the owner needed any help.

If Peter would be amenable.

He regarded Beth solemnly, a slight frown on his face. Beth wrinkled her nose at him, and his frown deepened.

"Oh, we'll get along fine," she said, taking him from Dottie's arms. "You just wait and see."

Peter didn't smile, but then, he didn't cry, either.

"Well, if you're sure," Dottie said.

Beth beamed at her. "Absolutely sure. We'll be right here when you want us."

Dottie lifted the bag she had tucked under the table earlier. "There are diapers in here. I nursed him before I came, so he should be fine for a while. If he fusses too much, try singing to him. He seems to like that." Well, he liked it when John sang to him. Dottie could only hope he would like the sound of Beth's voice as well.

"I've diapered and cared for all my nieces and nephews," Beth assured her, rocking Peter in her arms. "I'll just take him around to meet the others. If Peter needs you, I'll be sure to send someone to find you." She glanced up. "Though you might take John his boots before you go. Let's go find them, shall we, little man?" She whisked Peter up the stairs before Dottie could protest.

Alone in the main cabin, she glanced around. The log walls, plank table by the window and stone fireplace gave the place a sturdy look, while the quilts thrown over the wooden chairs, settee and bentwood rocker made it feel more homey. She could imagine John and his brothers running down the stairs for breakfast in the morning.

She accepted the worn leather boots Beth brought down, pressed a kiss against Peter's head and started for the door, but something made her turn. "You mustn't let him go to anyone else, even if they claim kinship."

Beth brightened. "Oh, do you have family in Seattle after all?"

It was on the tip of her tongue to tell Beth the truth. She had been nothing but kind, her falsehood about her brother's interest in marrying notwithstanding. But Dottie couldn't admit how foolish she'd been, couldn't watch Beth's smile turn to disdain.

"No, not that I know of," Dottie told her. "But stranger things have happened." She hurried out the door before Beth could question her further.

She'd gotten a good look at the clearing when she'd walked over from John's house earlier. The main house, barn and schoolhouse were clustered inside a ring of trees, the lake at the front and a hill rising at the back. Even now, mist clung to the treetops, making the peaceful clearing seem sheltered out of time and place.

The schoolhouse, however, was far from peaceful. John was out on the porch, peering one way and another while faces crowded at the window. She spotted the last of his students still lurking around the corner of the school, clinging to the log wall.

Dottie caught John's gaze and raised the boots with one hand. He beckoned her closer.

"Beth thought you might need these," she said, trying not to look down at the stockinged feet sticking out below his rough trousers. There was something vulnerable about those wiggling toes.

He sat on the porch and pulled on the boots. "Thanks. Hard enough to teach in stockings. Even harder to go searching for a lost lamb."

"I know something about lambs." Dottie pointed silently to the side of the building. John didn't look that way. He merely inclined his head in thanks, stood and strolled in that direction. A moment more, and he pounced on the lad.

Dottie thought he might reprimand the boy or set him to some labor as punishment. That was what most of the schoolmasters she'd known would have done. John merely threw the boy over his shoulder and carried him back to the school.

The child's voice echoed across the clearing. "Oh, please, Mr. Wallin. Can't I play one day?"

John's answer was hidden by the closing of the schoolroom door behind him.

The sounds from his students were not nearly so quiet. Squeals and laughter rang out, followed by thuds and bangs. What was he doing in there?

Dottie glanced about the clearing. She could see no one else. Drew had left with his men. Beth was busy in the main house. Likely Simon and his wife were up in their home on the ridge, with Drew's wife at the dispensary. No one would notice if she took a peek.

Dottie gathered her skirts and climbed up onto the porch. The schoolhouse had grown silent, and she pictured children bent over their desks, slaving away as John tapped a ruler against his palm. She had not taken him for a strict disciplinarian, but she had mistaken a man's character before.

She carefully tilted her head to see through the window.

John sat at the front of the class on the teacher's chair, the children gathered around him on the floor. Their postures were still, their gazes rapt.

"'But no sooner were my eyes open,'" he said, voice

rich, "'but I saw my Poll sitting on top of the hedge; and immediately knew that it was he that spoke to me; for just in such bemoaning language had I used to talk to him, and teach him.'"

Was that *Robinson Crusoe*? Surely it wasn't part of the curriculum. She had to admit he had calmed them enough to sit still and listen, and with evident interest stamped on each young face. She found herself listening just as intently as he read a few more passages of the story.

He glanced up, and their gazes met. He winked at her.

Dottie jerked back. What must he think to find her spying on him? She drew in a breath and climbed off the porch. Really, she should just accept the fact that he was the kind, considerate fellow his sister had extolled in her letters.

But everyone had thought Frank the perfect gentleman, too. Her uncle had had no idea of his other life on the far side of town. Cincinnati was big enough that a man could have had several wives stashed away in different corners.

So what secrets was John Wallin hiding?

She glanced at the main house and considered going to question Beth, but John's sister had already written so much about the man. And would a man confide his darkest secrets to his sister in any event? No, it was more likely his brothers who knew him best. That was where she should start.

Not that she had any designs on John, she assured herself as she picked up her skirts and headed for the store on the shores of Lake Union. It was only because she was staying in his house, beholden to him and his family, that she wanted to know more about him. She was merely being cautious.

The store, which was more of a trading post, was a square block of shaved logs with a plank door painted a welcoming blue. Hitching rails stood on either side, and she could see a dock running out from the back into deeper water. Smoke curled from the chimney, so she knew someone was inside. She hesitated a moment, wondering whether she should knock. In the end, she merely grasped the latch and opened the door.

Inside, the walls were lined with wide shelves crammed with such an assortment of items she wasn't sure where to look first. Kegs of nails stood next to bolts of calico, tins of tobacco beside jars of honey. At the counter near the front sat John's brother James, chin propped on his hand.

He straightened at the sight of Dottie. "Well, my dear, welcome to my treasure cave. What can I get for you? Pearls from the Orient? Silk from China?"

Dottie wandered closer, skirts brushing a woven trap she guessed was for fishing and a bundle of beaver pelts. "Do you really sell pearls and silk?"

"No," James said with a grin. "But they sounded better than saltpeter and molasses."

Dottie couldn't help smiling. "You're the owner of this fine establishment?"

He puffed out his chest. "Owner, founder, builder." He slumped. "And clerk. Humbling, isn't it?"

"I think it a noble calling," she assured him. "Why, everyone for miles around must come here at some point for something they need."

"That was the idea," James told her. "What can I get you today? John has plenty of food, so I doubt the tin of ham would amuse. Needles for sewing a young man's shirt?"

For a moment, she thought he meant John, then she realized he was likely talking about Peter. "I'm all set on needles, actually. It's employment I need."

"Ah." He pulled a rag out from under the counter and set about buffing the wood, which already gave back a dim reflection of his light brown hair. "I wish I could help you. But this store is just beginning to show a profit, and not enough to allow me to hire another worker."

"Of course." Dottie tried not to show her disappointment. "Do you know anyone else in the area who needs help?"

He paused in his buffing. He was a handsome man, like his brother, but his features were sharper, his build more slender. "You might ask Nora, Simon's wife. She's a seamstress of some talent. She always seems behind in her commissions." He grinned. "Or maybe it's just my commissions she finds difficult to complete. I can be quite exacting in my standards." He put his nose in the air.

Dottie laughed. "I'm sure you'd be very kind to your sister-in-law."

"All of them," he assured her, lowering his nose with a grin. "Even the ones who aren't quite there yet."

Oh, but he was going to put her to the blush. "I can be just as exacting in my standards, sir."

He nodded. "As you should be. But you won't find anyone better than John."

Dottie cocked her head. "Really. I've only met you and Drew so far, but the Wallin men seem to be tall of stature and fine of character. What makes John better than the rest of you?"

He gave an exaggerated sigh. "Oh, will you make me praise someone other than myself? I don't know if I have it in me."

"I have faith in your abilities," Dottie said.

He laughed. "That's one of us. But very well. Drew has ever been the leader—brunt, determined, focused. He built this family, and his logging business. Simon is the thinker—he sees every angle and lets you know the flaw in your argument. He makes sure we're all fed and housed appropriately. Levi is the adventurer, never satisfied with staying put. He'll do great things one day, you mark my words. And I'm the charming one, as I believe I mentioned."

Dottie inclined her head with a smile.

"And then there's John," James continued, tossing his rag into the air and catching it. "John is the one you turn to when everything is going wrong. He'll listen, commiserate and stand beside you, whatever you determine to be the right course."

He'd certainly done that with her. "And what is his dream?" Dottie asked. "What mark will John leave on the world?"

James frowned. "I don't know." He chuckled. "I'm afraid John is also the one most likely to be overlooked."

How sad. If he really was the shoulder on which all his brothers leaned in times of trouble, he should not be ignored when times were good. On the other hand, had he so little faith in his future that he had never told his brothers about his dream of a library in the wilderness?

She chatted with James a while longer, then thanked him for his trouble and left the store. James's position gave him insight into the farmers and other residents all around. If he didn't know of any work besides helping his seamstress sister-in-law, Dottie wasn't sanguine about her ability to find it.

But as she reached the main clearing again, she spotted two women bearing down on her. One had pale blond hair smoothed back from her face and an elegant figure; the other was shorter and more sturdily built, with flyaway black hair. Both seemed entirely too well dressed for the wilderness. The shorter woman's fashionable puce gown quite put Dottie's dress to shame.

What was more concerning was the wolf that appeared to be trotting along at the dark-haired woman's side.

Dottie took a step back. The creature seemed to see that as an attempt to escape, which she supposed it was, and bounded toward her. She forced herself to stand still as it circled her, pink tongue lolling.

"Don't be afraid," the dark-haired woman said with a smile directed equally at Dottie and the animal. "My dog Fleet just wants to become better acquainted."

A dog? Dottie glanced down to where Fleet had sat at the woman's side. She had only read stories of wolves, had never seen one in person, but perhaps they didn't have that black fur around their head and back. The markings made Fleet appear as if he was wearing a cape. Those bright eyes were entirely too canny, as if he could see inside her. Whatever he saw, however, appeared to make him smile.

"There now," his mistress told him. "You've met our new friend. Go have some fun."

He bolted off as if intent on finding more interesting company in the woods.

"We'd like to make friends as well," the lighter-haired woman said. "Welcome to Wallin Landing. I'm Catherine, and this is Nora. We're married to John's brothers."

Catherine—she was the nurse married to Drew, if Dottie remembered correctly. And Nora was Simon's wife and the seamstress James had mentioned. Small wonder her gown was so beautifully done.

"Very pleased to meet you," Dottie said. "Beth probably told you that I'm Dottie Tyrrell."

Nora nodded, and Catherine smiled. "We won't detain you for long. As it is, we had to enlist Simon's aid to watch the little ones so Nora and I could come meet you. Rina, James's wife, would have joined us, but she's nursing a sore tooth."

"So I heard," Dottie told Catherine.

Nora beamed. "Oh, good. You're already threaded onto the spool."

Dottie blinked.

"Beth," Catherine explained. "She hears all, sees all. If you have any questions, ask her."

Dottie nodded. "Thank you. I certainly will."

"When are you and John marrying?" Nora asked.

"Nora!" Catherine scolded before Dottie could answer.

Nora spread her hands. "I must know when the gown is needed."

"John and I have no intention of marrying," Dottie told her.

Nora frowned. "Why not? I always thought he was the nicest of the brothers, for all Simon was the one for me."

Catherine was frowning as well. "I cannot conceive he would do anything to offend you, Mrs. Tyrrell. John is unrelentingly kind and considerate."

"And determined to remain a bachelor," Dottie said.

Catherine and Nora exchanged glances.

"Oh," Nora said. "If *that's* the only difficulty…"

Catherine nodded. "It won't be a difficulty for long. His brothers all had reasons for refusing to wed, yet here they are, happily married."

"It just took the right woman," Nora agreed, her face turning dreamy for a moment. Then she cocked her head. "I wonder why John decided not to wed."

So did Dottie.

"It doesn't matter," Catherine insisted. "With our help, John will shortly see that you are the right woman for him. Trust us, Mrs. Tyrrell. We only want what's best for John, and from what Beth's told us, you are the best. We won't rest until you and John are married."

Later that afternoon, John settled Rina's chair back under her desk at the schoolhouse. The room had changed since he and his brothers had built it eight years ago. Then, the best they had been able to do was put in benches. Now each student had a desk and chair. Then, everyone wrote on slates. Now, besides the slates, they had paper, inkwells and quill pens. And how he would have loved growing up with a schoolteacher like

Rina. Ma had done her best to instruct her children in reading, writing and ciphering, but most of what he knew he'd learned from his brothers or from the precious books he'd been able to buy or borrow.

"Will you come back tomorrow and read to us, Mr. Wallin?" Isaiah Blaycock, a local fisherman's son, asked as he set the broom he'd been using back in its spot by the hearth. "I want to see how Mr. Crusoe makes it off the island."

"It depends on how Mrs. Wallin is feeling," John told him, joining him by the door. "But you could read the book yourself."

The boy hung his head. "Pa doesn't hold much with storybooks. He says money needs to go for clothes and food and such."

"The Bible says man cannot live on bread alone," John told him. "I'll see if I can find a copy for you to borrow."

Isaiah beamed at him. "That would be great, Mr. Wallin. Thanks." Whistling, he hopped off the porch and scampered toward the south, where his father had taken over the old Rankin claim by the lake.

John shut the door behind him. That was why Wallin Landing needed a library. Most people in the area were just getting by. Any extra money went toward improving their claims. They didn't have funds for art or music or books. Some had never had access to such things. And he couldn't help feeling that their lives had been the poorer because of it.

He couldn't do anything about the art or music, but when it came to books, he could share.

He met Nora and Catherine coming back across the

clearing. Before he could even utter a greeting, Nora rushed up to him and wrapped her arms about his waist. He was used to his sister-in-law's mercurial ways, but this seemed a bit much even for Nora.

"Thirty, maybe thirty-two," she muttered, pulling back. "Probably fifty-two at the shoulders."

"Nora?" John asked with a frown.

"How did school go today?" Catherine asked brightly, drawing his attention to her. "Did Danny and Ben behave for you?"

He wouldn't have told tales on the local boys even if they had misbehaved. "Good as gold. Have you seen Rina? Can she return to duty tomorrow?"

"I'm on my way there now," Catherine assured him. "I'll send Harry back with the verdict when he gets off work. I'm sure he'd like an excuse to spend more time with Mrs. Tyrrell."

"Wouldn't you?" Nora asked.

They were both watching him.

John offered them a smile. "No need for matchmaking, ladies. I'm just helping Dottie while she gets settled."

"Very kind of you," Catherine said.

"Just what we would expect," Nora agreed.

They were up to something. He could feel it. "We have no intention of marrying."

Nora slapped her skirts. "That's what she said!"

At least he could count on Dottie for support.

Catherine nodded. "Until we talked to her, of course. We told her the splendid sort of fellow you are."

John's heart sank. "The sort of fellow?"

"Yes," Nora said. "You know. Kind, considerate."

"Someone a lady can depend upon," Catherine added.

"A friend," Nora said.

John cringed.

"That's exactly the sort of man women don't want," he told them. "If Dottie Tyrrell had any interest in having me court her, I guarantee she's running for the hills right now."

Chapter Eight

John's family was certainly persistent. Dottie could not help but admire how they championed what they felt to be the best course of action for him. Catherine and Nora had sung his praises, as had James and Beth before them. But Dottie could not make herself believe he was so very perfect. Everyone had a flaw. What was his?

She had taken a moment to ask Nora about helping her sew. The seamstress had brightened. "Oh, do you like sewing?"

Not particularly, but it was something she could do while tending Peter. "I am competent," Dottie had assured her. "You probably shouldn't trust me with your most complicated commissions, but I can hem, sew on a button or add trim."

Nora had promised to look at her work and bring Dottie something the next day.

It was a start, Dottie told herself as she retrieved Peter from Beth and returned to John's house.

She thought he might come to his claim later that afternoon to check on the animals. She had gathered eggs that morning, with a wide-eyed Peter in her arms. Every time a chicken squawked, he had reared back in amazement.

That was one of the things she loved about her son. Everything in the world fascinated him, from his own fingers to a grass blowing in the breeze. She wished she could return to such an open acceptance. She remembered naming the lambs after flowers, climbing out her bedroom window to read in the branches of the oak that grew next to the farmhouse. Every character, every story, seemed to carve itself on her heart. After her betrayal by Frank, sometimes she feared her heart was forever hardened.

Still, she knew what was most important now— finding a permanent, safe, secure home for her and Peter. Living here in John's house was only temporary.

When she heard a knock on the door as evening approached, she hastened to answer it, thinking it must be John. Instead, Harry Yeager stood on the porch. She pushed back the disappointment that threatened. She should make an attempt to get to know all the suitable bachelors in the area. If she couldn't find work, she might well have to marry, however unappealing that sounded now that she'd escaped Cincinnati.

Mr. Yeager had seemed the most commanding of the men she'd met that morning, certainly the one most sure of himself. His thick brown hair was tousled from his day logging, and his flannel shirt gave testimony to how hard he'd worked. Still, that square-jawed face broke into a grin at the sight of her in the doorway, with Peter in her arms. He propped a booted foot up on the porch and gave them a nod.

"Mrs. Wallin wanted me to tell John the other Mrs. Wallin won't be needing his services at the school tomorrow," he said. "Is he about?"

For some reason, she didn't like the idea of admitting she was alone. "He said he'd come by this afternoon. He may be in the barn." Mindful of the cat not far behind her, she moved out onto the porch and shut the door.

Harry nodded again, but he took a step up onto the porch. "How are you settling in? Is there anything I can do to help?"

My, but they were the friendliest people at Wallin Landing. Peter didn't seem to agree, for he hunched closer to her at the sound of Mr. Yeager's voice so near.

"We're fine," she assured the logger, jiggling Peter up and down to cheer him.

Harry hooked his thumbs in the suspenders over his broad chest. "Cute little fellow." He bent closer to smile at her son. "How are you doing, little man?"

Peter's lower lip quivered, a sure sign a squall was coming.

Dottie lifted him in her arms so he looked over her shoulder at the house instead of at the logger. "Have you had much experience with children, Mr. Yeager? Brothers and sisters perhaps?"

He shook his head as he straightened, towering over her. "I was an only child. My parents died when I was a youth, and I struck out on my own."

She knew a little about that. "What brought you to Wallin Landing?"

He chuckled. "I like to knock things down. It got me in trouble once or twice, but Mr. Wallin showed me how to make a good living from the habit."

Knock things down? She had an image of Frank falling over after a strike from Harry's meaty fists. But as much as the violence might feel warranted, she didn't want to be the cause.

"And will you be content to continue knocking things down, Mr. Yeager?" she asked.

He shrugged, like a mountain under an earthquake. "I could be persuaded to try something else, for a good reason."

He eyed her as if waiting for her to proclaim she could be that reason. She knew other young ladies might have flirted that way, batting their eyes and flattering his consequence. She had never felt comfortable doing that, and she couldn't find the words now.

What was wrong with her? She'd wanted someone who could protect her and Peter. One look from this man would likely send Frank running. Yet everything in her recoiled from encouraging Harry.

"Hey, ho."

The call and the familiar voice raised her head. John was strolling toward them across the field, some sort of chair hooked over one arm.

"Afternoon, Harry," he said, stepping up onto the porch. "Work done so soon?"

Harry shrugged again. He had to outweigh John by nearly forty pounds of pure muscle, but their heads were on a level and something brighter seemed to shine from John's green eyes.

"We finished the order of spars earlier than we expected," Harry told him. "Mrs. Wallin asked me to come back and let you know that you won't be needed at the schoolhouse tomorrow. I thought I'd check on Mrs.

Tyrrell and little Peter while I was here." He reached out and put a hand on Peter's head.

Peter jerked back and wailed.

As Dottie rocked him to calm him, Harry stepped away. "I didn't mean to hurt him." His face was white, his eyes wide in alarm.

John didn't seem to be troubled by the sudden noise. "Babies can be tricky," he commiserated, setting down the chair on the porch. "Some want to be cuddled close, others like the freedom to explore. May I?"

He held out his arms to Dottie. He wanted to hold Peter when her son was fussy? That sounded like a bad idea.

"Perhaps I better keep him," she said. "He has a hard time with people he doesn't know well."

John's arms did not fall. "Trust me."

Well, that was entirely the problem, wasn't it?

Harry's look darted between them as Peter's wails grew sharper. Next thing she knew, the logger would be offering to help, too. Perhaps both of them should see just how challenging a baby could be.

Dottie held out her son. "Very well, Mr. Wallin, but don't say I didn't warn you."

With a smile, John took Peter from her.

Peter twisted in his grip, trying to keep his gaze on Dottie, and she shoved out her arms, ready to grab him if he fell. But John didn't drop the squirming bundle. Carefully repositioning his hands, he held the baby close to his chest, face out. John's fingers rubbed Peter's shoulder.

"There now," he said, voice soft. "I'm thinking you just wanted to see more of the world."

Peter gazed about him, sobs quieting. His hands and feet twitched as they often did when he was absorbed in something. His blue-gray gaze met Dottie's, and he gurgled a happy greeting.

Harry shook his head. "I don't know how you do it, John. No wonder all the ladies want you to tend their young'uns."

Color tinged John's cheeks, but his smile didn't waver. "Nice to be considered trustworthy."

Now Harry's cheeks reddened. "I should see if Miss Beth needs any help with supper." He inclined his head to Dottie. "Evening, Mrs. Tyrrell. If you need anyone to chop wood or move furniture, I'm your man. I may not know much about children, but I can still help around the house. And no one ever claimed my head was in the clouds."

John's look narrowed, but Harry strode back down the path toward the other claims.

Head in the clouds? Dottie glanced at John, who stood there so patiently while Peter looked his fill at the porch and lands beyond. Was that the flaw in this good man? Did he have trouble seeing the darker side of the world, keeping himself grounded in reality?

Would he be able to protect her if Frank came calling?

Peter wiggled in John's arms, and he shifted the baby to look toward Harry's retreating back. He shouldn't have tried to show up the logger by proving how well he could get along with Dottie's son, but finding Harry chatting so freely with Dottie made him feel as if someone had prodded his back with a flaming branch. And hearing him voice the complaint John's family had leveled at him over the years hadn't helped. *Head in the clouds*. Eyes on a book more likely. At least he thought about something more than when the cows had to be milked or which tree to chop down next.

Still, he shouldn't have nettled Harry. Dottie was looking for a husband. Harry was strong enough and clever enough to make some woman happy. But surely Dottie could do better.

He nodded toward the chair he'd brought with him. "Rina asked me to deliver that to you. It's a special chair, for a baby to sit in."

She bent her head to look more closely at it, running a hand over the smooth wood. "Please thank her for me. It will be just the thing as Peter starts eating solid food." She drew back her hand, straightening. "Forgive me. We don't intend to encroach on you that long."

"You're not encroaching," he told her. "Or did things go particularly well today? Any leads on employment?"

She smiled. It was a polite upturn of her lips, as if she thought the other person expected it. There was little warmth behind it.

"I spoke to your brother James and sister-in-law Nora. He doesn't need any help at the store, but she might have work for me."

John brightened. "Well, that's good news."

She nodded. "I suppose it is. I should have realized it might be even harder to find work here than in Seattle. You all made a way in the wilderness. You're used to being very self-sufficient. I don't know how I can contribute."

"I've felt the same way," he admitted, shifting to change Peter's view. A moth fluttered by, and the baby raised a chubby fist toward it, missing by inches. "Drew has his logging, Simon the main farm and James the store. Sometimes I think our youngest brother, Levi, left because he didn't see a place for him."

"And where do you see your place, John?" she asked.

At your side.

The words almost tumbled out, but he managed to cough instead. Peter glanced up at him with a concerned frown. What was John thinking? Dottie had come here to find a future, and that future wasn't with him.

"I have my claim," he told her, hearing the words come out more than a little defensive. "The crops I grow help feed the others. The eggs and milk can be sold in James's store. When I'm needed, I help with the school or with Catherine at the dispensary. I'm Drew's fifth man when he has a big contract. I keep busy."

"Commendable." She took a step closer, lavender eyes gazing up at him. "You help all your family. But what about you? What do you want?"

Those lips were pink and soft-looking, and all he could think about was how they'd feel against his. He swallowed.

"If I can build the library I want, I'll be content."

It was a true statement, or at least it had been true before he'd met her. And suddenly, it was the most important thing in the world that she understand.

"Come on," he said. "Let me show you." Keeping Peter in one arm, he grabbed the chair with the other and took them both into the house.

Dottie followed him, but then, what choice did she have? He was holding her son.

Brian had been pacing in the entry as if waiting for

Dottie and Peter to return. Now he paused and eyed John as if disappointed to find him in attendance. Even his cat preferred other company, it seemed. Pushing aside the dismal thought, he set the chair aside and led Dottie up the stairs to the loft. Peter giggled as they climbed, as if he liked the movement.

It was darker in the loft, the only light coming from a window at either end and through the door at the top of the stairs. This space had been intended to house John's children, like the loft at his parents' house had housed him, his brothers and Beth. Now the pelts of the animals he'd trapped this winter were stretched on frames against the rafters, and casks and baskets held the last of fall's harvest. Dottie came in beside him and gazed around as wide-eyed as her son.

John kept up a steady bob for Peter as he nodded toward the stacks of books along the far wall. "Those are what I've been able to gather so far. I figure there's enough so every person within an easy walk of Wallin Landing can borrow a book a month."

She wandered over, tilted her head to read the titles on the leather spines, golden curls spilling down one side of her face. "Science, philosophy, literature, the arts, scripture." She straightened and glanced back at him. "You've thought of everything."

He felt as if someone had inflated a hot-air balloon in his chest, lifting his countenance, his head and his spirit. "That's just the beginning. I want everyone to be able to read about whatever interests them. Books can take you places you'd never go otherwise, to faraway lands or long-ago times. They teach you things you would spend a lifetime learning otherwise."

"The wisdom of the ages," she murmured.

He nodded, turning to keep Peter from grasping one of the furs. "They can help shape your opinions, your character. A place truly isn't civilized until it has a library."

Peter gurgled in his arms as if he quite agreed.

John shifted on his feet. "Sorry. I didn't mean to prattle on that way."

"You never prattle," Dottie assured him, turning for the stairs. "I find your vision inspiring. I only wish I could help."

John followed her down. "As I told Beth, I can't afford to hire myself as librarian, much less anyone else."

"I know." She came out on the level and paused to let him catch up. "But I brought a few books with me. You're welcome to add them to the collection."

John stared at her. "Are you sure? I wouldn't want to deprive you and Peter of them. I know how precious books can be out here."

This time her smile set her face to glowing. He felt the answering glow inside him.

"If Peter and I settle here at Wallin Landing, we can borrow those books from the library. But this way, others can enjoy them, too."

His heart swelled, and he balanced Peter in one arm as he seized her hand in the other to shake it. "Thank you, Dottie. This means so much to me, to the whole community."

That smile and those lips were only a few inches from his own. Another step closer, and he could kiss her. She smelled like the apricots of summer, but he thought she'd taste even sweeter.

And he had no business thinking about her lips at all.

Brian seemed to agree, for he darted between them and disappeared into the bedroom.

John dropped Dottie's hand and stepped back, lowering his gaze to check on Peter. The baby looked up at him as if he was just as aghast at John's thoughts.

John had told Dottie he had no intention of marrying. There were men who had no trouble charming a lady and stealing a kiss, with no thought of the consequences. He wasn't one of those men. A kiss was a promise, a commitment. He couldn't have one without the other.

Harry would have kissed her.

The thought came unbidden, but he knew it for the truth. Even James had kissed a girl or two before he married Rina. He'd been more than happy to let his brothers know about it. But John wasn't Harry or James. He didn't have their easy way. He was the one ladies depended on for help, not romance. He should focus on Dottie's needs rather than his own.

"I'm glad to hear you're going to help Nora," he said. "She always seems to have a project or two waiting."

She licked her lips, drawing his gaze there once more. "I think she may have taken up a new one today," she admitted.

John bobbed Peter to keep him entertained. "There you are, then."

Dottie grimaced. "I doubt she'll ask my help with it. She intends to make me a wedding gown."

Something twisted inside him. Well, of course Dottie would need a wedding gown if she found the right groom. "That's kind of her," he said.

"You may not think so when you hear the other part of the project," Dottie told him. "She also intends to make you a wedding suit."

So that was why Nora had been muttering numbers!

"I'll explain things to her," he promised. "Again. I'm sorry, Dottie, if her assumptions troubled you. My family is well-meaning."

"They are very kind to want to help," she agreed. "I couldn't talk her out of creating the gown, but I suppose it might be needed at some point."

The air in the room seemed to have soured. "It seems you like Harry."

She actually shuddered, and he almost danced. Instead, he turned Peter in a circle, earning him a giggle from the lad.

"Mr. Yeager seems like a fine fellow," Dottie said, watching him, "but only time will tell if he's ready to support a wife and child."

"Perhaps," John said, feeling a bit like a traitor to poor Harry. Peter wiggled as if he wanted to spin again, and John turned him in his arms to look into his face. "What do you think, little fellow? Do you want Harry Yeager to be your papa?"

Peter babbled something that sounded like a negative and reached for John instead.

"I better take him now," Dottie said, intercepting the baby's fingers before they could close on John's face. "He'll get tired soon. Thank you for all your help. Good evening, John."

The entire speech had been said so quickly it sounded more like her son's babble. She moved just as swiftly to the door and held it open for John. He could only nod farewell as he left. His last sight was of Peter pouting, as if he was sorry to see John go.

It was clear her baby liked him, but it was also clear Dottie had taken his measure. He wasn't what she wanted in a husband.

But he was beginning to think no man could measure up to the fellow John thought she deserved.

Chapter Nine

Dottie shut the door behind John and leaned against it a moment. From her arms, Peter stared at her accusingly.

"Why him?" she asked her son. "He doesn't even want a wife."

Peter gabbled quite the lecture, face serious and determined. He even waved his fist for emphasis. Dottie shook her head with a laugh as she pushed off the door and headed for the kitchen. Brian slunk out from the bedroom and followed her.

She had a hard time putting dinner together that evening. Meeting so many new people and having her hopes for employment raised even the slightest were enough to fill her mind with ideas, her heart with hope. Then there was the way Peter reacted to John. Her son liked him more than any other man to whom Dottie had introduced him, but she could not convince herself that that was any indication of character. Peter didn't know enough about the world to be discerning.

Still, there was something fine about John. She couldn't help remembering how his eyes had glowed, his face brightened, when he'd described the wonders of the library he hoped to build. What a splendid calling, and one she firmly believed in. If only she could believe in him as much.

She had risen the next morning and gathered the eggs when she received callers. Once again, she dared to hope it was John tapping at the back door, but instead Tom Convers and Beth stood waiting. He held up a brace of trout, still wiggling on the string.

"Breakfast," he announced, beaming.

"I'm here for propriety's sake," Beth explained to Dottie with a smile, twitching aside her rose-colored skirts to enter. "I enlisted John's help to cook for the others."

Of course. And of course, John would agree. Likely he was trying to help his sister, but Beth was just as clearly bent on matchmaking.

Mr. Convers followed Beth in. Like Harry, the logger had dark hair, but his was slicked down on his head, making his face look long. In fact, he was long all through, from his tall, slender frame to his big hands and feet. She thought he would head for the sink and clean the fish, but he tossed the trout on the sideboard and went to take a seat at the table, looking expectantly at the two women.

Beth glared back at him. "Tom?" She nodded toward the sink.

He frowned as if he had no idea what she wanted, then his brow cleared. He rose and went to wash his hands, leaving the fish flapping on the sideboard.

Peter started to cry.

"You better see to him," Mr. Convers said, returning to his chair. "Nothing like a crying baby to spoil a meal."

Dottie knew her brows must be as high as her hairline.

Beth marched over, grabbed the logger by the ear and tugged him to his feet.

"Ow!" He jerked away. "What did I do now?"

"You brought a lady smelly fish and left them on the sideboard," Beth informed him. "You clean those fish right now, and, if you're quick about it, we might think about cooking them for you."

Well, that was one way of dealing with a fellow. How would Frank have reacted if Dottie had been so bold? Of course, Frank had never done anything to disturb her in their few short months of courtship and marriage. That was, until he'd broken her heart.

Now Mr. Convers, muttering under his breath and rubbing his ear, went to retrieve the trout as Dottie put the eggs she'd gathered earlier into a bowl by the stove.

"It's just because he's been on his own too long," Beth confided to Dottie, keeping an eye on the logger. "He has a good heart."

"Let me do the cooking," Dottie suggested. "You watch Peter. And we'll both watch Mr. Convers."

Beth nodded with a grin.

Dottie thought her gentleman caller might protest her busyness. His appearance at the door was obviously his attempt to start courting, and courting meant getting to know the other person, after all. But the logger didn't seem disposed to talk. After he'd cleaned and filleted the fish, he brought them to Dottie and returned to the table. Leaning back, he eyed Peter in the chair John had brought yesterday, then patted the pocket of his flannel shirt where something bulged. Beth glared at him as if daring him to draw it out. Chewing tobacco, perhaps? Dottie fought a grimace.

A while later, they gathered around the table before buttermilk biscuits, fried trout and scrambled eggs. Dottie was rather pleased with the spread she'd put together so quickly in a strange kitchen. After cooking for her aunt and uncle, she liked to think she had some proficiency. Mr. Convers took one bite of the trout, reached for the salt cellar and dumped it on the food.

Beth hopped to her feet. "That's it. Out. Now. And don't expect to be invited back anytime soon."

Frowning, he picked up his plate and fork and marched out the door.

"Entirely too full of himself," Beth proclaimed, throwing herself back in her seat as he slammed the door behind him. "Doesn't help around the house, doesn't appreciate good cooking." She forked up a mouthful of the trout and sighed as she swallowed.

"Delicious," she assured Dottie. "And I'm certain everything else is, too. You can do better than him."

She hoped so. How nice to be truly appreciated for what she did, who she was. And, truth be told, a second pair of hands would be welcome, at least until her son was old enough to take on chores. Of course, Frank had never helped around the house, but she'd believed his story about being tired from his work and travels. She hadn't known he'd had another house he was likely expected to support.

"Harry appears to be interested," Beth told her. "And

then there's Dickie. I'll send him to the house later so you can see whether you like him. He's terribly sweet."

He was also a bit young for her and very shy. He stopped by the house that afternoon, stammering a greeting with his gaze on his feet, and asked what he could do for her. His blond hair, sticking out in all directions, only added to the picture of pathos. She was afraid she'd crush his heart if she told him she was fine, so she asked him to fix the window John said stuck. Mr. Morgan came inside, took one look into the bedchamber and backed toward the parlor.

"Oh, I couldn't," he said. "That's where you sleep, ma'am. It wouldn't be seemly. Why don't I just go chop you some wood?"

Harry had made the same offer. It seemed when courting, that was a logger's preferred way to show a lady he cared.

"So the fireboxes by the stove and the hearth are overflowing," she reported to Beth, when the young lady came over that evening with a commission from Nora. "And I have an entire woodpile, neatly stacked, outside the kitchen door. But I still know nothing about Dickie's dreams or his character."

Beth stuck out her lower lip in commiseration. "It might take some time with that one. But cheer up. John went into town and brought back the mail, and there's a letter for you."

For her? Dottie's fingers trembled as she reached out to take the letter. Beth must have noticed, for she frowned.

"Dottie? Is something wrong? Were you expecting bad news?"

She hadn't been expecting news at all. The only person she'd told where she was going, and then in only the most general of terms, was Martha Duggin. Dear Martha had been a rock on which Dottie could lean during those dark days, but Dottie hadn't wanted to leave any evidence behind that might tell Frank where to find her if he ever came looking.

"I don't know who would write to me," she told Beth, turning the envelope in her hands. She didn't recognize the handwriting, but then she'd never seen Martha write anything, and she'd only seen Frank make his signature on the wedding certificate.

A certificate that had proved utterly worthless.

"Well, it's a lovely surprise, then," Beth said. "Go on, open it. Unless you'd rather I left."

She felt as if a snake lurked inside that paper. She refused to open it while Beth was there to see her distress. She set the letter on the bench beside her. "That's all right. I'll read it later."

Beth smiled, but Dottie felt her disappointment. Unfortunately, this was one thread that Dottie could not allow to go on Beth's spool.

Even after her friend left, however, Dottie could not make herself open the letter. She cooked dinner, then prowled around the parlor, swishing a rag she'd found in the kitchen over the mantel, the backs of the bench and the wood chairs that flanked it. Peter, seated on the floor in front of the bench, kept craning his neck as if to look at the letter on the seat above him. Even Brian jumped up and sniffed at the envelope.

Dottie threw up her hands. "Oh, all right. I'll open it."

She sat on the bench, lifted Peter onto her lap, took

up the letter and slid her finger under the flap. Her gaze darted to the signature at the bottom. Relief surged through her when she saw Martha's name.

But her relief quickly faded as she read the note aloud.

"'Dear Dottie,
I hope this finds you and little Peter happy and settled. You had told me you were going to Washington Territory, so I'm sending this to the postmaster in Seattle in hopes it will reach you. We are all in fine health here, and a nice widow lady with a cat has settled into your old apartment.'"

She cast a glance at Brian, who was looking over her arm as if reading the note along with her.

"'But I wanted you to know that that dastardly Frank Reynolds has left Cincinnati. His wife came by looking for you, begging to know if you'd run away with him. Supposedly he's headed west. I guess you could come home now if you wanted. Let me know, and I will see if I can find a place for you and Peter. I miss our talks.
Your friend always,
Martha.'"

Dottie's fingers were shaking once more, and Brian pounced on the paper, knocking it from her hand. She didn't retrieve it as he pushed it across the bench to Peter's delight. She cuddled her son close instead.

Frank was headed west. That was a lot of territory,

she knew from her travels. He might settle in some state between here and Ohio. He might go all the way to San Francisco.

But please, please, Lord, don't let him come to Seattle.

What if he did? Beth had said new settlers arrived every day. And Seattle was just the sort of place Frank might like, full of opportunities, strangers easily taken in by his charm.

Perhaps she should leave now. But where would she go? Martha advised her to come home, yet Cincinnati was no longer home. She didn't want to go back there, even if Frank never returned. She wanted someplace new, someplace clean, someplace all her own. She had a chance for all of that here at Wallin Landing. She couldn't let a list of maybes and might-haves scare her away.

Apparently disgusted with her lack of movement, Brian jumped down from the bench. He started across the floor, then paused, gaze going to the back of the house. His whole body stiffened.

Had he heard something? Was she in danger? Had Frank found her?

John carried the pail of milk toward the back door. The night was clear for once, with stars sparkling above the trees. He followed the path from the barn to the house from long practice. But he couldn't help that his feet dragged.

Beth had told him in excruciating detail all the ways Drew's crew was trying to impress Dottie. Fresh trout for breakfast, wood for the fire. He should have thought of those things.

But then again, he had said he wasn't courting her.

So why did he hesitate now to see how happy she was with their attentions? She deserved all that, and more.

He opened the door and backed through it, only to hear a cry behind him. He dropped the pail and whirled. "Dottie?"

She stood in the doorway, hand gripping the handle of a cast-iron skillet she held up and at the ready like a club. "Oh, John." Her voice was breathless. For all her brave stance, the pan shook in her grip.

He held up his hands. "It's all right, Dottie. It's just me. I'm sorry if I startled you."

With a sharp intake of breath, she set the pan back on the stove with a clatter. "Sorry. I heard a noise."

And had been scared out of her wits by it. He'd never seen a woman so pale. With a step, he moved forward and put his hand on her arm.

"I didn't see anything moving outside," he assured her. He glanced around the kitchen and spotted the ginger tail twitching under the sideboard. "But perhaps your noise came from inside." He went to bend over and peer under the furniture. "Here now, Brian. What do you mean by scaring Dottie and Peter?"

The cat's green eyes flickered in the shadows. John straightened. "Just Brian. Maybe he was actually doing his job for once."

"Perhaps he heard a mouse." She rubbed a hand along her arm as if she wanted to feel the security of the pan in her grip once more.

John tried for a smile. "There's nothing to fear here, Dottie."

Her smile said she didn't believe him.

"Where's Peter?" he asked, going to retrieve the pail. The tall can in the corner and the cool night temperatures would keep the milk until morning.

"I put him in his cradle before coming to check on the noise," she said.

"I imagine he's sleeping like a baby," he joked.

Ah, there was the smile he prized. "Perhaps. But he doesn't know any better."

And she was sure she did.

"I can't deny that the wilderness holds dangers," he told her, pouring the milk into the steel can. "But my family has worked hard for nearly twenty years to tame the wilderness. If you look closer, you may find things to love about the area." He set the pail on the floor. "Here, let me show you."

He held out his hand. She looked at it as if the gesture was foreign to her. Then a shudder went through her. He refused to back down. He couldn't see her going to sleep this worried.

He almost shouted a hallelujah when she slipped her fingers into his grip.

He led her through the house, pausing in the bedroom doorway to check on Peter, who had indeed fallen asleep, then out onto the porch. The velvet black of the night wrapped around them. He pointed up at the semicircle of stars. "See there?"

He could barely make her out in the darkness, but he saw her shadow move as she must have looked up. "The stars?" she asked.

"Exactly." He leaned closer, caught that sweet apricot

scent. "See that long dip down and across? That's Ursa Major, the great bear."

He heard the smile in her voice. "Peter would like that."

"You might like this one better. See that *M* shape? That's Cassiopeia, the queen."

She must have turned her head to look at him, for he felt her breath brush his ear. "Where did you learn that?"

"I read about it in a book." He felt a little self-conscious admitting it. Men were supposed to go out and discover things, not sit at home and read about them. "Catherine's friend Allegra Banks Howard loaned it to me. It had the latest scientific theories about stars and galaxies. Do you know Earth is only one planet among a group of planets, and that group is only one of perhaps millions out there in space?"

"My word." She sounded as awed as he'd felt when he'd read the book.

"Those stars look like tiny pricks of light to us, but they're as big, or bigger, than the sun. We're the ones who are tiny, in the scheme of things."

"I feel that way sometimes," she murmured, and he thought she was looking up again.

"But they're so far away," John told her. "There's nothing there to harm us. Now, listen."

She stilled beside him.

"Do you hear that *shush-shush* sound? That's the waves on Lake Union."

She nodded, and a curl caressed his cheek. "I didn't know a lake could have waves."

"I understand larger ones do. Lake Union isn't that

large, but the breeze from the Sound encourages the water to move. Now, take a deep breath."

She inhaled.

"What do you smell?" he asked.

"Something dry and flowery, and just a touch of brine."

"The pungent flowery scent is the cedar not far from the house. It's a massive thing, probably been growing more than a hundred years. I didn't have the heart to cut it down. I'll show it to you and Peter. And the touch of brine is Puget Sound, beyond the hill behind us. To me, this is the smell of home."

She drew in another breath as if she wanted to sense it, too.

He put his hands on her shoulders, turned her to look down toward the main clearing. "Now, see those lights? That's Drew and Catherine, James and Rina, Beth, Harry, Tom and Dickie. You shout loud enough, and every one of them will come running to help you." He turned her back to face him. "And so will I."

"Will you?" Her voice begged him for the truth.

"Always," John promised. "You're safe here at Wallin Landing, Dottie."

He felt her trembling in his grip. He only wanted to assure her that nothing could hurt her, that he wouldn't let anything hurt her. It seemed only right to lower his head and kiss her.

As he'd expected, her lips were soft and sweet, and something rose inside him, demanding that he protect her, cherish her, take the risk that she could be the one for him.

He'd meant to comfort her, lessen her fears. Why was he the one who was suddenly afraid?

Chapter Ten

John Wallin was kissing her.

It was a lovely kiss, warm, sweet. Something inside her rose to meet it, begging her not to let it stop. Why couldn't she feel loved, protected?

Why did the moment have to end?

He drew back, and she was glad for the dark, for she felt the air turning the tears on her cheeks cold.

"Do you want me to stay with you tonight?" he asked. "I could sleep in the loft."

How nice to know help would be only over her head. But she couldn't accept the offer. It wasn't proper. "No. Thank you. You've helped me so much already, John. Peter and I will be fine. As you said, I only have to shout if I need help."

"Remember that." His fingers brushed her cheek, and she heard him suck in a breath. "You're crying. I'm sorry. I didn't mean..."

Dottie caught his hand. "Don't apologize. I know you meant that kiss for a kindness. I won't refine on it."

"That makes one of us."

Had he meant the kiss as more than she'd thought? A tingle ran through her, but she shook it off. "Good night, John."

He stepped back from her. "Good night, Dottie. Sweet dreams."

She rather hoped she didn't dream at all.

As it was, sleep was a long time coming. Inside the house, she couldn't see the stars or smell the cedar, but she fancied she could still hear the waves over the sound of Peter's breathing. More, she felt John's kiss against her lips, so tender. Was he coming to care for her after all? She'd said she wouldn't refine on his kiss, but she couldn't seem to stop herself.

Still, her concerns persisted. Would he be man enough to stop Frank if Peter's father moved to Seattle? Or was it selfish of her to even think of inflicting her problems on this idyllic place? John had built a nice, safe life for himself. It didn't seem right to burden him with her troubles.

Not for the first time, she wished she still had her Bible. What comfort to read over the familiar words. A shame she hadn't been able to spend the funds to purchase a new one.

She sat up in bed, glanced at the ceiling. Why pine for the scriptures when at least two copies lay just overhead? She'd spotted them the other day when John had shown her the beginnings of his library. She'd noticed them again when she'd gone up to add the three novels she'd purchased before she'd discovered Frank's secret. She lit the lamp and went to fetch one of the Bibles. Brian, who had been sleeping near the foot of the bed, raised his head and followed her.

The loft smelled musty, but she thought it was more because of the furs than the books. It took her only a moment to find a Bible, this one with a crimson cover. Tucking it under one arm, she shooed Brian away from a fur he was sniffing and returned to the warmth of the bed.

But as she leaned against the headboard, covers pulled close, the cat came and curled against her side, staring at the book as if just as eager to read it as she was. She gave him a stroke before opening the cover. Her gaze fell on the name written there.

Hannah Elisabeth Wallin.

Dottie frowned. She knew the names of all the Wallin ladies. Had this belonged to John's mother? Was John willing to share it beyond the family?

She flipped to the pages at the back, where her father and mother had noted family information. Sure enough, there was the Wallin family in summary. Lars and Hannah, along with their birthdays and wedding anniversary, were followed by Andrew, Simon, James, John and Levi. Then a Mary with a death noted only a few days after her birth, and finally Beth.

Dottie couldn't help glancing at Peter, sleeping so sweetly. His little lips puckered as if he offered her a kiss. How horrid to lose a child. How could she bear it if Frank took Peter away from her?

She forced herself to focus on the Bible. The date of Lars Wallin's death was smudged, as if a tear had fallen on the ink. It seemed John's mother had been a widow for more than fifteen years, raising her youngest children alone. No, not alone. Drew, Simon and James had been old enough to help at first. And though John had been only ten at the time of his father's death, she could imagine him being a comfort to his mother.

She turned the book in her hands, and it fell open to psalms. She spent a little while reading. It was surprising how often the writer cried out to God, pleading for help with some problem. But surely they had been godly men, not someone like her, who'd made so many mistakes, even in allowing circumstances to distance her from her faith.

But she had taken her life in her hands at last. She could read the Bible as often and as long as she liked. It was quite some time before she set it down.

When Dottie awoke the next morning, she smiled at the well-worn cover as she pinned up her hair. Brian strolled past, then backed up as if inviting her to run her hand over his soft fur. Peter watched her from the cradle, singing a song in which all the words involved "ooh" and "aah." Over his piping, however, she heard the thud of boots on the porch. Oh, no, she was not going to allow herself to become excited. That sounded like more than one man, so it could not be John.

Or, thankfully, Frank.

She set the last pin in place and picked up Peter, then went to see who had come calling now. As if he didn't think he'd like her visitors, Brian darted off into the depths of the house.

All three of the loggers stood on the porch, shuffling their feet and casting narrow-eyed glances at each other. Unlike when they had visited her before, they were dressed in dark suits, hair plastered down, faces freshly shaved and scrubbed. Harry was the first to step forward, earning him a glare from Tom and Dickie.

YOUR PARTICIPATION IS REQUESTED!

Dear Reader,

Since you are a lover of our books – we would like to get to know you!

Inside you will find a short Reader's Survey. Sharing your answers with us will help our editorial staff understand who you are and what activities you enjoy.

To thank you for your participation, we would like to send you up to 4 books and 2 gifts – **ABSOLUTELY FREE!**

Enjoy your gifts with our appreciation,

Pam Powers

**SEE INSIDE
FOR READER'S
SURVEY**

Get up to 4 Free Books!

Romance ⟩⟨ Historical

We'll send you 2 Free Books from each series you choose plus 2 Free Gifts!

Try **Love Inspired® Romance Larger-Print** books featuring Christian characters facing modern-day challenges.

Try **Love Inspired® Historical** novels featuring Christian characters confronting challenges in vivid historical periods.

Or **TRY BOTH!**

YOUR READER'S SURVEY
"THANK YOU" FREE GIFTS INCLUDE:

▶ 2 lovely surprise gifts   ▶ Up to 4 FREE books

PLEASE FILL IN THE CIRCLES COMPLETELY TO RESPOND

1) What type of fiction books do you enjoy reading? (Check all that apply)
   ○ Suspense/Thrillers ○ Action/Adventure ○ Modern-day Romances
   ○ Historical Romance ○ Humor   ○ Paranormal Romance

2) What attracted you most to the last fiction book you purchased on impulse?
   ○ The Title   ○ The Cover   ○ The Author   ○ The Story

3) What is usually the greatest influencer when you <u>plan</u> to buy a book?
   ○ Advertising   ○ Referral   ○ Book Review

4) How often do you access the internet?
   ○ Daily ○ Weekly ○ Monthly ○ Rarely or never

YES! I have completed the Reader's Survey. Please send me 2 FREE books and 2 FREE gifts (gifts are worth about $10 retail) from each series selected below. I understand that I am under no obligation to purchase any books, as explained on the back of this card.

Select the series you prefer (check one or both):

❑ **Love Inspired® Romance Larger-Print** (122/322 IDL GMRL)

❑ **Love Inspired® Historical** (102/302 IDL GMRL)

❑ **Try Both** (122/322/102/302 IDL GLYY)

FIRST NAME   LAST NAME

ADDRESS

APT.#   CITY

STATE/PROV.   ZIP/POSTAL CODE

HLI-817-SCT17

▶ DETACH AND MAIL CARD TODAY! ▶

READER SERVICE—Here's how it works:

"I'm here to escort you to church services, Mrs. Tyr-rell," he announced.

Tom elbowed him aside. "*We're* here to escort you to services."

"You—you do want to go, don't you, ma'am?" Dickie asked.

Her spirit rose inside her like a bird set free from a cage. Her aunt and uncle and even Frank had made light of the role of faith in her life, and she'd had no opportunity to attend church since leaving Cincinnati. Now the thought of joining others in worship made her heart beat faster.

"I'd be delighted, gentlemen. Give me a moment to change into a more appropriate gown. Perhaps one of you could watch Peter for me?"

Dickie blanched, Tom took a step back and Harry made a face. Peter clung to her as if he had grave misgivings about the whole matter.

"You know I'm not that good with babies," Harry told Dottie. Then he straightened. "But here comes the perfect fellow."

Dottie followed his gaze and saw that John was just coming out of the trees. Like the loggers, he was dressed in a suit, his the color of the firs that grew so abundantly here. She had a feeling Nora had sewn it for him, for it was tailored to his muscular form. The misty morning seemed to brighten as he came up to the porch.

"Tom, Dickie, Harry," he greeted them. "I'm surprised to see you up so early on your day off."

Tom shrugged, Dickie looked down at his feet and Harry laughed.

"I might say the same about you," he told John. "I came—"

"We came," Tom reminded him.

"We came to take Mrs. Tyrrell to church. She needs help with the baby."

John glanced around at them all. "So why isn't one of you helping?"

"He's such a little feller," Dickie said, his Adam's apple bobbing with his nervousness.

"He might puke on my shirt," Tom explained with a wrinkle of his long nose.

"Holding babies is a woman's job," Harry argued.

Dottie knew her brows were up again. Why, these big, strong men made it sound as if her little son was a danger to them!

John must have found their excuses just as ridiculous, for he shook his head before turning to her. "What do you need, Dottie?"

At the use of her first name, the others stilled. Dickie glanced between Dottie and John and heaved a sigh as if resigned to his lonely fate. Tom and Harry stepped closer to Dottie as if prepared to assert their claims.

Which was just as ridiculous as their posturing, because none of them had a claim on her.

"I just need someone to hold Peter while I change into my church clothes," Dottie said. To be fair, she glanced around at all the men.

Harry stepped forward. "Oh, all right. I'll hold him."

She hesitated. He'd just called the act woman's work, and she thought he saw taking on the task as a noble sacrifice. Besides, he had claimed he wasn't good with babies. He'd certainly had trouble with Peter the last time he'd called. Or was she being too cautious?

She glanced at John, who gave her an encouraging smile. She knew he wouldn't let anything happen to Peter.

"Very well," she said, and she offered Peter to Harry.

Harry took him so carefully her son might have been made of fine crystal. "You're safe, little fellow," he murmured, meeting Peter's inquisitive look.

Peter frowned at him, but he didn't raise a fuss.

"Go on," John urged her. "I'll come for you if he needs you."

She nodded, excused herself from the others and hurried into the house. She knew John would be as good as his word. He'd come for her if Peter needed her.

But what concerned her was how much she was coming to need John.

John stood on the porch, watching Harry hold Peter in his arms. He was such a solemn baby, studying those around him. What was he looking for? What did he see?

"He's too quiet," Tom said, eyeing the baby. "Is he sickening?"

Harry frowned and peered closer. Peter stared back.

"He looks fine to me," the big logger declared.

John told himself to be patient. They didn't have eight nieces and nephews. Harry and Tom didn't even have little brothers and sisters to go by. Dickie, the oldest of seven siblings, at least had an idea of how to deal with babies.

He, however, looked the least comfortable. As Peter

uttered a belch that made Harry's brows go up, Dickie took a step back.

"Babies get sick all the time," he said. "Then they make you sick. That's how I got the measles last winter."

An idea beckoned, but John couldn't quite make himself follow where it led. It would be all too easy to scare off these would-be suitors by claiming Peter had some dreaded disease. But that wasn't fair to Tom, Dickie or Harry.

Of course, John wasn't feeling all that charitable at the moment. He'd come over to the house with the express purpose of escorting Dottie to worship, hoping to further the connection they'd been building, especially after last night. That kiss had been impossible to forget. But then he'd found Drew's men clustered around her. He couldn't convince himself any of them was the right man for her.

"Never had much interest in babies," Tom said. "But I guess I better get used to it if me and Mrs. Tyrrell reach an understanding."

He sounded as if having Peter around was a bother rather than a blessing. That tore it. John peered down into the baby's face as well, earning him a smile from Peter.

"Is that a spot?" he asked, lacing his voice with concern.

"Where?" Harry demanded.

At the logger's troubled tone, Peter's lower lip began trembling.

"There," Dickie insisted, shoving a finger toward the baby's cheek. "I see it, too. Could be cow pox or chicken pox or one of those other splotchy things."

Peter reached up and grabbed Dickie's finger. Dickie yanked away as if he had been attacked.

"Nah," Harry scoffed. "He's fine, I tell you."

Dickie moved back. "I'll just meet you at the house." He turned, jumped off the porch and hurried across the field.

Tom shook his head. "Coward. Getting sick now and again would be a small price to pay for a wife as pretty as Mrs. Tyrrell."

As if he disagreed, Peter scrunched up his face and turned red.

"What's wrong with him?" Harry demanded. "What do I do?"

John was fairly certain he knew. "He's fine. Give him a moment."

With a sigh, Peter relaxed.

Thomas wrinkled his nose as if it itched. "Smell that? Funny scent, like sour milk."

Harry stared down at Peter, horrified. "I think it's him." He thrust the baby at Tom. "Here, you take him."

Tom scuttled back out of reach. "Not me. Call Mrs. Tyrrell. It's her baby."

John intercepted Peter, afraid that Harry might drop the lad the way the logger was shaking. "I'll take him. Maybe you two should wait at the main house with Dickie."

Neither Tom nor Harry argued with him. They were across the yard and into the trees before John could promise he'd bring Dottie along as well.

Peter wiggled in his grip, clearly uncomfortable.

"It's all right, little man," John told him, heading for the house. "I have some experience in these matters."

He met Dottie coming out the door. She'd put on the blue-and-purple dress she'd worn when he'd first met her, and he was honored to think she'd chosen her church clothes that day.

"What's wrong?" she asked, seeing him with Peter. "Where are the others?"

"They went ahead," John said. "And there's nothing wrong a clean diaper won't fix."

She reached for her son. "I'll take him."

John eyed the pretty dress with the purple bows running down the front. "Why don't I change him this time? You can supervise to make sure I do it to your liking."

She raised a brow but led him into the house and bedchamber.

He'd been sleeping in that room for years, and she hadn't changed anything other than to add her trunk and the cradle, yet somehow it felt warmer, more welcoming than he remembered. Even Brian seemed to think so, for he was curled up in the center of the quilt and only opened an eye long enough to confirm it was someone he knew coming to disturb his sleep.

"Sorry, old fellow," John told him before shooing him off the bed to make room for Peter.

Nose in the air, Brian stalked off to the nether parts of the house.

Dottie brought John a clean diaper, and, in short order, he removed the soiled one, cleaned Peter with a cloth Dottie provided and put the baby in a fresh diaper. The whole time, Peter gurgled happily, reaching for his toes as often as he could as if finding them fascinating.

John finished pinning the diaper in place and stepped aside to let Dottie pick up Peter.

"Well?" he asked. "Do I pass muster, General Tyrrell?"

"You're a very handy fellow to have around, John Wallin," she replied as she tugged on Peter's shirt to cover his toes. The baby frowned as if wondering where his feet had gone.

But John couldn't help noticing that something sparkled on Dottie's cheeks. Had he made her cry again? Now what had he done wrong?

"Please don't cry, Dottie," he said. "I wasn't trying to interfere."

Her son in one arm, she put her other hand on his. "You didn't interfere. I know it may sound silly to you, but sometimes I cry when I'm happy."

It didn't sound silly, but it did sound odd to him. "You're happy with me?"

"Very," she assured him. "It's wonderful to have help."

Help. A friend. Well, he was that if nothing else. He turned to go rinse his hands in water from the washbasin in the corner. "I'll try to stop by more often. I forget—my brother's wives all have my brothers for help. It's just you and Peter."

She started walking toward the door, faster than he expected. Did she think they were late for services? While his family had a general time they started worship, he knew they'd wait until he and Dottie joined them. That could change once the church was finished. Their minister might have a more stringent idea of when things happened on the Lord's Day.

They set off across the field, and John purposefully

slowed his steps. Not Dottie. She kept moving, her gaze darting to the trees as if she expected something huge to come thundering out of them.

"Did one of them tell you he saw a bear on the way over?" John asked.

Dottie clutched Peter closer. "No. Did you see a bear?"

"No," John told her. "Or a cougar, or even a cranky cow. So it might be safe to walk at a normal pace."

She drew in a breath and slowed her steps. "Sorry. Perhaps I'm just eager for services."

Perhaps. Or perhaps he hadn't made it clear last night that she was safe. For all he knew, she'd been scared of what else might happen since the day she'd become a widow.

"When did Peter's father die?" he asked.

When she didn't answer, he glanced her way. She was rocking the baby as she walked, head down and shoulders tight.

John put a hand to her elbow. "Is Peter all right? Tom and Dickie thought he might be getting sick, but it seemed to me they were just afraid of babies in general."

"He's fine," she assured him, relaxing her hold enough that he could see Peter's face gazing up at him. The boy bubbled a greeting as if he hadn't seen John in days instead of a few minutes.

John touched Peter's head, feeling the downy hair against his palm. "Good. For a moment there, I thought I might have hurt him."

"You couldn't," she murmured. "You've been very good to us, John. I feel as if you and I have been friends for years."

She had no idea she was heaping coals on his head. "I hear that a lot," he said, dropping his hand.

She frowned. "And you sound saddened by the fact. Why? I think it admirable that you are a friend to all."

Admirable? Perhaps. He turned his gaze to the path ahead as it pointed toward James's claim, trees crowding on either side. "Well, I've been told there is a category of gentleman a lady considers a friend and a category of gentleman she considers courting. I seem to be confined to the friend category."

She picked up her skirts with one hand to step over a root in the path. "Is that such a terrible thing? Friends can be valued."

He grimaced. "Nothing wrong with being a friend, unless you were hoping for more."

"Ah." She cast him a quick glance, then focused once again on the path. "I suppose every woman has an inner image of the perfect husband. I imagine some prefer shoulders as broad as Harry Yeager's or a fortune as deep as I hear the Denny family has amassed. I think it more important that a man be steady, supportive, reliable. And that he provide for and protect his family."

His family would attest to his steady, reliable nature. His farm was sufficient to provide for a family of six or more. And he certainly had the desire to protect her and little Peter from whatever life brought them. But he couldn't believe it was so simple. Surely Catherine, Rina and Nora had wanted more from a husband. They'd chosen his brothers.

"What of ambition?" John persisted. "Drive? The passion to succeed?"

"Those can be commendable," she acknowledged,

shifting Peter in her arms as they started down the hill past James's cabin. "But they can also be a hindrance to a loving family. I know men more interested in their businesses than their wives and children, husbands who put their needs first at all times."

There was a tremor in her voice. Had her husband been that way? Had he worked himself to an early grave? Small wonder ambition meant so little to her.

"So, is that what you seek in a husband?" he asked, leading her into the main clearing. "Someone steady, someone willing to give all for family?"

She paused as they left the trees, as if just as loath to share their time with others. "Yes, John, I think I could be very happy with a husband like that, whatever else his situation." She tugged Peter's shirt down as if to avoid John's gaze. Very likely she was a little concerned about what she'd just confessed.

It was a simple criterion, but one that would not be easy to meet, he guessed. Indeed, he found it hard to picture the brash Harry, the self-centered Tom or the shy Dickie rising to the occasion.

The question was, could he?

Chapter Eleven

Dottie wasn't sure what to expect of a worship service at Wallin Landing, especially when a pastor had yet to join the community. The church building wasn't even finished. Beth had told her that John and James had been taking turns painting the interior and setting in the steps to the front door in the last week. Besides, church services had been solemn occasions back home, a time to dress in your best and contemplate the sermon the pastor would give. Though the loggers and John were certainly dressed finer than they usually were, she had a hard time seeing them sitting piously in a pew.

But John didn't lead her to the church. Instead, he headed unerringly for the cabin in which he and the loggers were living.

"Until the church is finished," he explained as they neared the door, "we hold service here for our family and the crew." He paused with his hand on the latch. "Be warned—we're a lively bunch, but everyone settles down once service starts."

He opened the door to chaos.

The chairs and benches from the table had been arranged in the middle of the room facing the stone hearth, but no one was sitting in them. Dottie glanced from one group to another, identifying people she'd met. Catherine was kneeling near the hearth, talking with a girl of about six who kept shifting on her feet, her pink skirts swinging, as she watched three boys about four or five years of age chase each other around the room, with Beth in hot pursuit.

Nora had corralled another set of three children, one of whom was just beginning to walk, if his unsteady steps were any indication, and was attempting to settle them on the rug in front of the chairs. A tall, lean man, who looked a bit like James, stood in the opening of the chairs as if to keep the children from straying.

A regal woman with hair a shade lighter than Dottie's was standing next to the window with James, a girl of about five who was nearly as elegant at their side. By the look in James's eyes, he wanted to run with the boys Beth was chasing.

Tom, Dickie and Harry were pressed up against the stairs at the far side of the room as if determined to fend off barbarians. As she entered, Harry nodded in Dottie's direction, Tom crossed his arms over his chest and Dickie bowed his head and scurried to the kitchen.

John's brother Drew waded into the center of the room and put two fingers to his lips. The shrill whistle made the elegant little girl clap her hands over her ears and the three boys pause in their game.

"Seats," he said, eyeing the boys. "Now."

They glanced at each other, then ambled over to find a spot on the rug. Beth, smiling gratefully at her oldest brother, followed them and took a chair. The boys were still wiggling when John led Dottie to a spot near the side. He nodded to the archway in the wall to her right.

"Use the kitchen for Peter if you need to."

He thought of everything. "Thank you."

Tom plunked himself down next to Dottie and leveled his gaze on Peter and then on John. "He looks fine."

John shrugged. "What can I say? Babies are resilient."

"Was something wrong with Peter?" Dottie asked, glancing between the two men, then down at her son, who was gazing around, seemingly fascinated by all the movement.

"Apparently not," Tom said. "But I'm beginning to think there's something wrong with this whole situation."

Before she could question him, the tall man who had been helping Nora stepped up to the hearth. He raised a violin and set it under his chin. This must be John's brother Simon, the one she'd heard playing the other night. Dottie leaned forward, eager for the music. Around her, the others took their seats. John drew up a chair on the other side of her.

Simon played two hymns, the tunes familiar. Dottie remembered the words from her childhood and sang along with the others, sopranos blending with tenors and underscored by Drew's bass. When Simon lowered his instrument with a tender smile that transformed the stern lines of his face, James moved up to take his place and led them in a surprisingly sweet prayer of thanks. Dottie waited to see who would bring the sermon, guessing it would be Drew. He was the acknowledged leader, after all.

Instead, John rose from her side and went to the hearth.

"We are reading in the book of John today," he said. The girl who had been standing with Catherine giggled, then covered her mouth with her hands.

"It's a very important book," he assured the children, who were clustered in the middle of the semi-circle of chairs.

"Did you write it, Uncle John?" one of the boys asked.

"No, silly," the elegant girl scolded. "Jesus wrote it."

"Well, not quite," John said with a smile. "It was written by a man named John. He was Jesus's good friend, so he knew a lot about Jesus. Let me read some of what he wrote."

He pulled a Bible from the mantel. The black leather cover was scratched and torn in places, the gilt nearly gone from the edges of the pages. Since the Bible Dottie had found at John's house had been his mother's, this must have been his father's. Beside her, Tom leaned back to listen, and Peter turned his face to John.

"'So Jesus came again into Cana of Galilee,'" John read, "'where he had turned water into wine. And there was a certain nobleman, whose son was sick at Capernaum.'"

Just like the school children earlier in the week, John's nieces and nephews quieted to listen to him. There was something about his voice, a conviction, a strength. Even Tom stilled as if he was paying attention, and Dickie peered out of the kitchen.

"'When he heard that Jesus was come out of Judea into Galilee,'" John continued, "'he went unto him, and besought him that he would come down, and heal his son: for he was at the point of death. Then Jesus said unto him, "Except ye see signs and wonders, ye will not believe." The nobleman saith unto him, "Sir, come down ere my child die."'"

Dottie shivered. How desperate the nobleman must have been to go to a man of another faith for help. She knew something of that feeling of helplessness. She glanced down at Peter, but the baby's gaze was all for John.

"'Jesus saith unto him, "Go thy way; thy son liveth." And the man believed the word that Jesus had spoken unto him, and he went his way. And as he was now going down, his servants met him and told him, saying, "Thy son liveth."'"

"Huzzah!" one of the boys cheered, and the other children nodded agreement while their parents exchanged glances and smiled.

John smiled at his nieces and nephews, too. "Good news indeed. And do you know that the boy began to heal the exact hour that Jesus spoke to the father?"

All of the children regarded him with wide eyes.

"The Bible calls that a miracle," John told them, raising his head to look at his family and friends, even as he closed the book. "But sometimes it seems as if the only miracles are in the Bible. We look around us and just see everyday life, nothing special. But you know what I see when I look around?"

The children shook their heads, and even Dottie found herself waiting for his answer.

"I notice the wonders of God's creation," he told

them. "Have you ever seen anything taller than Mount Rainier?"

Again they shook their heads.

"Ever hear anything louder than thunder rolling down the lake?"

One of the boys rubbed his ears as if hearing the rumble even now.

"Ever smell anything sweeter than the honeysuckle Catherine grows along the fence?"

"Mama's apple pie," one of them offered.

John smiled. "It smells pretty good, too, I'll give you that. But I think those are all special, and so are the people God puts in our lives—our family, our friends."

His gaze met Dottie's, and warmth spread through her. He had a unique way of looking at the world. She felt as if she'd been groping in the dark for so long, feeling alone. Perhaps the light, and God, had been there all along. Perhaps He had been working on her behalf, bringing her someplace she could make a future.

Perhaps all she had to do was start looking.

John stepped aside and returned to his seat to let Drew lead them in the concluding prayer. He liked the pattern of their services. Each of the adults took turns at explaining the reading for that week. He'd been part of the rotation since he'd turned eighteen. He remembered how nervous he'd felt the first time, sure he'd stutter or mumble.

Today had been the best he'd ever read.

Though he was used to comments from the children, he'd never been so aware of the members of his audience as he was with Dottie. He noticed when her golden brows drew together. He heard the sigh escape her near the end. Her smile was almost as rewarding as sharing his thoughts on the Word.

Of course, he should probably have skipped ahead rather than read that section about a deathly sick child. He'd seen her clutch Peter close for a moment. And likely every mother and father in the room had felt the same way.

So did he. He'd spelled Drew when little Mary had had pneumonia, walking back and forth across the wooden planks with the feverish girl in his arms, keeping her upright to ease her breathing. He'd ridden hard to Seattle to fetch the medicine Catherine had said would save James's son Seth from whooping cough. Nothing tore at the heart more than a child in danger.

He glanced at Peter now, where the baby dozed in Dottie's arms. He seemed a sturdy little fellow, with chubby pink cheeks and bright blue eyes. He grasped a finger with strength. But what would Dottie do if he sickened one night, and there was no one there to help her?

Drew concluded the prayer, and his family and friends rose, began gathering up belongings, children, spouses. James and Simon returned the chairs and benches to their usual places. Tom seemed in no hurry to leave, although Dickie remained hiding in the kitchen. Harry glanced their way.

Beth hurried over. "Stay and visit awhile, Dottie. I know Catherine and Rina would love a chance to hold Peter." She glanced at John. "I'm sure you could find something else to do while you wait to escort her home."

Very likely he could. Already James was nodding in

his direction as if looking for a private word, and Drew glanced his way, arms full of children, as if hoping John might be amenable to helping.

Dottie drew herself up. "Your brother was very kind to escort Peter and me to church, Beth. I wouldn't want to keep him from his other plans for the day."

John couldn't help his smile. He never minded helping, but it was rather gratifying to have someone consider his plans for once.

Beth had no such thoughts. She waved a hand. "Oh, John won't mind. Besides, it's Sunday. Our family only does what's absolutely necessary on Sunday. It's supposed to be a day of reflection, of family gatherings."

"Then I shouldn't intrude," Dottie said with a look to John.

"No intrusion," he assured her. "I'm sure the ladies would love to talk with you."

Dottie smiled at him. "And you'll join us, of course."

With that look in her eye, he refused to be anywhere else.

Beth shook her head, but she suffered him to come over to where his sisters-in-law were gathering at the table. John didn't realize Harry had followed them until he attempted to slide onto the bench next to Dottie.

Beth held up a finger. "Oh, no, Mr. Yeager. This gathering is for women only."

"Except John, of course," Dottie added with a smile John's way.

Harry laughed, straightening. "I think Miss Beth had the right of it. Enjoy your little get-together, *ladies*."

John willed himself not to respond.

Catherine slid in next to Dottie, so John went around

to the other side, back to the window, where he could see Dottie. Rina seated herself next to him. Beth sat in Drew's old chair at the head of the table, and Nora took Ma's spot at the foot.

Catherine peered over Dottie's arm at the sleeping Peter.

"Dottie," Beth began, "have you had encouraging interest from any of the local gentlemen since a certain fellow could not be brought up to snuff?"

John refused to rise to the bait. His sister was being difficult. She had seemed more annoyed than pleased when he'd returned the money she'd given Dottie earlier. Besides, Dottie had entirely too much interest, if the looks being directed her way from across the room were any indication. Tom was still glowering, Harry was watching the table openly and even Dickie had ventured outside the safety of the kitchen to cast a longing glance in Dottie's direction.

Her back to the men, Dottie merely rocked Peter in her arms. "I've had the opportunity to converse with Mr. Yeager, Mr. Convers and Mr. Morgan. They seem honest and conscientious."

He supposed they were. Across the way, Tom said something to Harry, and Dickie gave him a shove, earning them both a glare from Drew, who was busy shepherding his children out the door.

Rina's lips thinned, as if she'd seen the display as well. "They have good hearts, but they seem too young to me to settle down as husbands and fathers. Or perhaps I am getting old."

"Certainly not," Catherine said. "We've simply been married long enough, and know what a marriage takes, that we can spot the characteristics in others. And I quite agree. Drew's workers, while admirable fellows, are not what you need, Dottie."

"A shame Scout isn't here," Rina said. "He knew how to be a gentleman."

Their old family friend Scout had grown from a scrawny youth into a fine man, with none of his late father's unsavory habits.

"A shame he and Levi felt it necessary to seek their fortunes elsewhere," Catherine agreed.

Nora sighed. "I do miss them."

"Be that as it may," Beth said, "we must find a husband for Dottie."

Dottie kept her gaze on her son. "Or perhaps permanent employment."

Beth shook her head. "A husband who could provide would be better. Surely we know someone suitable." She speared John with a look.

He shifted on the bench, finding the seat unaccountably hard. He certainly wasn't going to suggest a fellow. Neither were his brothers. James, Drew and Simon were already out the door. Across the room, Tom, Dickie and Harry were studying the floor and the ceiling as if wondering what other trouble they could get into on a Sunday.

"What about the younger Mr. Kellogg?" Nora suggested. "He's ever so kind."

Beth made a face. "And far too self-righteous."

"Rolland Denny," Rina suggested. "His family is very well connected."

"But he has a reputation for not wanting to settle down," Catherine argued.

Beth brightened. "Rupert Hollingsworth. He's so handsome."

"Engaged," Rina reported. "To Caroline Crawford."

John stiffened. It seemed Caroline had found her man with gumption. Hollingsworth certainly qualified. A recent immigrant from back east, he had immediately ingratiated himself with the Dennys and Borens, earning him a place in county government. His claim to the north, however, languished from lack of care. His family might, as well. Still, knowing Caroline had settled on another man ought to leave him devastated, depressed.

Instead, he felt relieved.

"I know the perfect man," Nora proclaimed. "Deputy McCormick. He's—"

"No," Beth said, face reddening. "Not him."

Odd. Beth had always been partial to the deputy, who was ten years her senior. Catherine must have been surprised by Beth's refusal, too, for she peered at her.

"But, Beth, I was under the impression you thought Mr. McCormick the epitome of a gentleman."

"The best and brightest of mankind, I believe you called him," Rina added.

"And you sigh every time he rides into the clearing," Nora reminded her.

Beth sat straighter. "Just trust me on this. I have reason to know that Hart McCormick is not the man we thought him. He will not do for Dottie at all."

"I appreciate your concern," Dottie said, glancing around. "But I must keep my own counsel when it comes to marrying. For now, I'm grateful for Nora's patronage to begin earning my keep."

Nora beamed at her.

Beth tapped her chin. "I wonder. An advertisement brought you out here. What if we were to put an advertisement in the Seattle paper? 'Lovely lady with darling infant son seeks proper husband.' I'd think we'd get quite a few responses."

Dottie paled. "Oh, I couldn't."

"And you shouldn't," John told her. "Beth is right—you'd get more than your share of responses, but most of them would be from men you wouldn't want as a husband." He glanced at his sisters-in-law. "Don't you remember what it was like when Mercer brought you to Seattle?"

Catherine, Rina and Nora turned varying shades of pink.

"Mercer?" Dottie asked.

"Asa Mercer, to be exact," Beth explained. "He realized there were widows and orphans left after the War Between the States, but an even larger number of bachelors on the frontier searching for brides, so he went back east to fetch them some."

Catherine raised her chin. "He told us that Seattle needed nurses…"

"And teachers," Rina interjected.

"And seamstresses," Nora added.

Catherine nodded. "He never mentioned that he'd taken money from lonely bachelors to bring them wives."

"We were deluged," Nora confided. "Surrounded the moment we hit the dock." She sighed as if she remembered that time fondly.

Rina shivered instead. "It was dreadful. I'm simply grateful the bachelors were persuaded to act like gentlemen."

"For the most part," Catherine agreed. "So John is quite right that you wouldn't want to start a fervor like that, Dottie."

Beth deflated.

"There must be other ways to meet eligible gentlemen," Nora mused.

"There is!" Beth hopped to her feet. "The May Day picnic! Everyone in town will be there to help build the railway."

Dottie frowned. "Work on the railway? I'm not sure I'd be suited."

John snorted. "No one is suited. It's a ridiculous idea born of vanity."

"I heard that." Harry wandered closer once more. If he had been listening to the conversation, he couldn't like Rina's assessment of his maturity.

"Mrs. Tyrrell should come to the picnic," he said now, gaze on Dottie. "It's a grand civic gesture, and she's sure to meet people who could help her."

"A gesture is a good description," John insisted, turning his look to Dottie. "Seattle was hoping to be the terminus of the Northern Pacific Railway, but Tacoma to the south was selected instead. Our leaders were so angry they decided to build their own railway from Seattle over the Cascade Mountains to the wheat fields in Eastern Washington."

"To Walla Walla," Harry confirmed. "All those mining riches, all that produce, pouring into Seattle while Tacoma cries on the tide flats. I call that a worthy cause."

"Does that mean you'll be volunteering on May Day, Mr. Yeager?" Dottie asked.

He puffed out his chest. "Yes, ma'am. Me and every other able-bodied man in Seattle. The ladies will cook for us to keep us strong for the work. You can learn a lot about a man by how hard he works." He cast John a glance.

Once more, John refused to acknowledge the comment. "We'd be better served to put the labor into the church and library."

Harry waved a hand. "The church and library will still need building. When do you get a chance to be part of history?"

"It does sound like an amazing feat," Dottie said. She glanced at John. "I'd be willing to help the ladies cook. Will you be working that day, John?"

They were all watching him. His family knew where he stood on the issue. He'd just made it clear to Harry. Building a railroad to spite Tacoma was a fool's quest.

But those lavender eyes were compelling.

"Certainly, Dottie," he said. "If you'll be there, I'll be there, rain or shine."

Chapter Twelve

The strangest feeling came over Dottie as she sat at the table talking about things with John and the Wallin women. It took her a moment to recognize the feeling as joy. After all, she still had no real lead on employment other than helping Nora. She wasn't any too sure about Harry's, Tom's and Dickie's potential as husbands, and the Wallin ladies had ruled out every other eligible man of their acquaintance. But for the first time in a long time, she felt like part of a family.

She didn't know what they would all do next. They had said the day was for contemplation, so she was surprised when James ushered in an older man with salt-and-pepper hair and a grizzled chin. At the sight of the ladies, he yanked off his tweed cap.

"You're needed, John," James announced. "And better you than me."

John cast Dottie a smile before sliding off the bench. "Mr. Blaycock, how can I help?"

The man turned his cap in his hands as if well aware he was imposing. "My anchor's snarled on the dock again. I told your brother that wasn't the best place to build the dock. Too many water lilies." He scowled at James.

James held up a hand. "I can't stop them from growing. Believe me, I've tried."

"It's just a matter of pulling them up from the roots," John told them. "If you cut off the stalks, they just grow faster."

Had he read that in a book? Peter, who had gone willingly to Rina a few moments ago, nodded as if he quite agreed with John's assessment.

"Well, something's snagged the anchor chain," Mr. Blaycock complained. "I can't mind the boat and fix the anchor at the same time, and my boy's still too young to help." He looked around the room as if seeking someone to take his son's place, and Harry, Tom and Dickie quickly made themselves scarce.

"I'll help you," John said. "It shouldn't take long. Just give me a moment."

She thought surely he'd go up the stairs and change out of his suit, but he returned to her side instead. "Will you be all right, Dottie?"

His family and neighbors relied on him, and yet he thought of her first. She didn't remember anyone treating her that way.

She smiled at him. "I'll be fine, John. Go where you're needed."

His face tightened, as if her words had somehow hurt him, but he nodded and headed for the stairs at last.

Beth slapped her hands down on the table, gaining her everyone's attention. "Dinner in two hours. I have the venison simmering for stew."

Nora rose as well. "I still have carrots and turnips."

"I made an apple cobbler for dessert," Catherine said.

The need to contribute was strong, yet what could she give? Everything she had John had given her.

"Dottie makes lovely biscuits," Beth said as if she knew Dottie's thoughts. "Almost as good as Levi's."

The other women sighed, as if that was high praise indeed.

"I'll be happy to make some," Dottie told them.

The plan agreed, Rina returned Peter to Dottie, and the women separated for their own homes. Only Beth remained behind, keeping up a steady conversation as she set the main house to rights. Dottie took the opportunity slip away to the rocker and nurse Peter, responding to Beth's comments on the weather, the Wallins' plans for the growing community and Beth's apparent indecision about how best to use her claim. Then the two adjourned to the kitchen to bake the biscuits.

One look at the massive cast-iron stove across the back wall, and Dottie sighed with envy. Even Peter stared at it.

Beth ran a hand along the silver appointments on the upper warming drawers. "Isn't she a beauty? Drew and John installed her when we opened the house to Drew's crew. Six burners, two ovens and double warming drawers. I call her Mrs. Heatsworth." She picked up a spoon and lifted the lid on the large pot on one of the back burners. A tangy scent rose with the steam.

"Of course, we had a little trouble getting the firebox to draw properly," Beth said, giving the pot a stir. "But John fixed it. He's very handy, you know. Catherine told me she hopes to get him to fix the pump at the dispensary—it keeps hanging up. And Simon wants him to help level the road after the winter rains and frost. And we should really widen the road north so Drew can move timber through there easier."

"There is the matter of John's library," Dottie reminded her. How would the poor fellow ever move forward on it if everyone kept commandeering his time?

As it was, he didn't return until the others were arriving for dinner, and then his wet shirt and trousers clung to him as he headed for the stairs, dripping mud across the floor.

Once more, it was a rowdy bunch, with children, parents and loggers crammed together around the table. Dottie found herself and Peter wedged between Harry and James, with John, now dressed in fresh clothes, down the table. While she and Beth had cooked, she'd taken the opportunity to quiz John's sister about him but hadn't learned anything new. As James had mentioned, it seemed the entire Wallin family found John easy to overlook.

Harry stayed close to her side that afternoon, even going so far as to tickle Peter's toes where they stuck out from under his shirt. Her son drew up his feet, little face scowling as if he was highly offended by the familiarity. John seemed to be the only one who had noticed, for she caught him fighting a smile. Though Harry showed every inclination of walking her home, Dottie made sure to latch on to John's arm instead.

He walked beside her now, gaze moving about the forest. Sunlight slanted past the broad trunks, and the air sparkled, full of a dry, clean scent. Birds flitted through the branches, and squirrels scampered up the bark. Seeing Peter watching him, John wrinkled his nose and stuck his tongue out between his teeth.

Peter giggled so hard he wiggled.

Dottie beamed at her son. "I love how he laughs with his whole body."

John relaxed his face and straightened. "So do I. Must be nice to feel so free."

She cast him a glance as they came out of the trees onto the field before his house. "Don't you feel free, John? I'd say you have the best of all worlds—loving family, good farm and home, a dream to achieve."

His steps seemed to lengthen, as if he could outrun the image. "A dream that isn't going anywhere without some more funding. It isn't practical to house the books in the loft, piled up like that. They need to be in a building accessible to all, organized on shelves so people can find the right book when they need it. And we should keep adding to the collection. All that takes money."

"And time," she pointed out as they approached the porch. "I believe that may be the larger impediment, with everyone coming to you for help."

She knew she should go inside, leave him to his reflections on this sacred day, but she was loath to lose his company. She sat on one of the chairs on the porch and settled Peter on her skirts. He waved his fists at John as if beckoning him closer.

John came to sit on another chair. "Those are no impositions, Dottie. I like helping people."

"And you are tremendously good at it," Dottie assured him. Peter babbled something that sounded like agreement. "But perhaps we've all grown too accustomed to your help. It's easy to ask you, not even considering what else you might be planning that day. That's what can happen with those we care about. We become so used to their presence in our lives that we take them for granted. Then one day, they're gone, and the world seems harder and colder."

He put a hand on her arm, his face sad. "I'm sorry for your loss, Dottie."

She stroked Peter's soft hair with her free hand. "My parents have been gone for more than ten years now. I've accustomed myself to their absence."

He frowned, and too late she remembered that she was supposed to be a grieving widow. Once more, the words pressed against her lips, even as her heart begged her to tell him the truth. How sweet to unburden herself, to cry against those broad shoulders, to feel his arms come around her as his warm voice told her she was safe and valued.

How horrid to see those kind eyes darken with disgust.

She rose, lifting Peter up in her arms once more. "I should practice what I preach and allow you to do whatever you had planned for the rest of your day."

John nodded, rising as well. "I had hoped to spend the evening with you and Peter."

And wouldn't that be nice? She could imagine them going through the books together, sharing memories of reading the stories. She could picture the three of them around the table in the kitchen, talking. But that was for a married couple, a family. Much as she had enjoyed today, she had to remember she didn't really belong to the Wallin family. She had to find a place for her and Peter.

"Nonsense," she said, making herself smile. "Look at the lovely sky. Surely you'll want to be out in the nature you love so much. Peter and I will just take a nap, I think."

He darted in front of her to open the door of the house. Always the servant, always the helper.

Dottie passed him, then paused in the doorway. "You are the strangest man I've ever met, John Wallin."

Hand still on the door, he raised his brows. "Ma'am?"

Dottie held out Peter, and John immediately lowered his hands, catching the door with his shoulder as he took her son. He held him gently as if he knew more about holding babies than she did. Given the number of nieces and nephews he had, he might very well know more about babies than she did. Certainly Peter was comfortable in his hands. He gazed up at John and began telling him a long story, face turning from solemn to happy.

"See?" she challenged. "Most men I know would have hesitated. You saw Mr. Yeager, Mr. Convers and Mr. Morgan this morning. I heard their excuses. Babies are an inconvenience. Babies make messes or get sick. Big, strong men don't hold babies. You are a big, strong man, and you hold him as if you were born to the role."

His cheeks were pinking again. "That's me. Nanny, cook, shoulder to cry on."

"That's you," Dottie agreed. "Kind, considerate, putting other's needs before your own. You would make some woman a marvelous husband."

There, she'd said what had been building in her heart. She didn't know what made John Wallin refuse to wed. Certainly he wasn't afraid of Peter. He was clearly capable of courting if the way he treated her so respectfully was any indication. And that kiss!

Better not think about that kiss. Already her gaze was moving toward his lips. She made herself focus on his eyes instead.

He was staring at her as if she'd grown a second nose.

"Are you saying you'd be willing to marry me?" he asked.

Now she was the one who wanted to run. She could say yes. Simply forget everything that had happened to her and fall into life with the Wallin family. She and John and Peter could make a family of their own. But was that fair to him when she wasn't sure where Frank was or whether he'd show up to claim Peter? When she couldn't even bring herself to tell John the truth?

"I don't know," she told him.

He shifted Peter into one arm and laid a hand on her cheek. She thought he would kiss her again, and her body leaned toward him even as her pulse sped.

But he swallowed, and she knew he was going to say something she wouldn't like. He'd say it kindly, of course. He would never be cruel.

"Dottie," he said, gaze holding hers as gently as his hand cupped her cheek. "You deserve a husband who will love and cherish you. You don't have to settle for me."

Tears were starting. She sniffed them back. "Then you don't want to marry me. Still."

He looked troubled, brows drawing down and mouth dipping. "I don't want you to regret marrying me. I've probably read too many adventure novels, but I think marriage should be between two people who love each other deeply. I sincerely doubt you love me."

Perhaps not yet, but she was beginning to believe it possible. "Cannot love grow over time?" she asked, hating the begging tone that had crept into her voice.

"Certainly," he acknowledged. "Under the right circumstances. I can easily see a man falling in love with you."

The tears were coming faster. John took a step closer and held out Peter, whose little face was crumpling as if he felt her pain.

"Don't cry, Dottie," John said as she took her son. "I know there's a husband for you. We'll look at the May Day picnic. And we'll keep looking if needed. I won't rest until you have the life you deserve."

He turned, jumped off the porch and strode off toward the woods before she could tell him she was very much afraid the only husband she'd ever want was him, and that he wouldn't want her as his wife if he knew about Frank.

John tore through the woods, feeling as if someone had branded his chest with an iron rod. The look on Dottie's beautiful face, the tremor in her words, touched something deep inside him. He could see them making a marriage, working beside each other on the farm, partnering in raising Peter. But she wouldn't be happy. He wasn't the sort of man women came to love.

And she had every right to marry a man she could love and respect, a man who would love and honor her all the days of her life. He knew giving her that chance was the right thing to do, the unselfish thing.

But, for once in his life, he wanted to be selfish.

He passed James's cabin, making for the main house. The air stung his cheeks, and he realized he was crying. Crying! What was wrong with him? A man didn't cry. He was tough, like Drew; stoic, like Simon. Even James passed off hurt with a quip. Why was John so different?

"Hey, ho!" James bounded out of his barn, which leaned ever so slightly to the north. "I've been watching for you, brother. I could use a hand." He skidded to a stop beside John and peered at him. "Is it raining?" He glanced up at the cloudless sky.

John swiped the tear from his cheek. "Must have walked through a spiderweb. You know how they can hold the dew. How can I help you?"

James lowered his gaze and clapped John on the shoulder. "That's more like it. Come this way, and I'll show you."

John drew in a breath, pasted on a smile and followed his brother up the slope behind the cabin.

They had logged the area some years ago. Simon and James had extended the farm from the portion Nora had brought to her marriage onto the upper half of James's claim. Now the fields stretched along the ridge, black and rich and ready for planting. The blue waters of the lake glistened below. He could see Simon's house in the distance, a long, low affair with rooms for a half-dozen children.

At least his brother had gumption.

James led him to the edge of the field, where trees anchored the slope in place. Drew was seated on some tree roots, while Simon paced back and forth in front of him, boots making a dent in the moss of the path.

"What's happened that you need all four of us?" John asked as he and James joined them.

Drew had a blade of grass between his teeth. Now he pulled it out. "Catherine seems concerned about Mrs. Tyrrell."

Simon paused to stare at John accusingly. "So does Nora."

As John glanced at James, his brother shrugged. "Rina feels equally concerned, but I told her you would work it out."

"So?" Simon demanded. "Are you working it out?"

Never had a smile felt more difficult. "Certainly," John said. "I am helping Dottie find the right man for her."

"Good," James said with a nod. "Now go and marry her."

John pulled back. "I'm not the right man."

"Why not?" Simon stepped closer, eyes narrowing. That was Simon, facing every problem head-on, like a charging bull. "You've settled your claim, you're respected in the community."

"Thank you for that," John told him. "But she should marry a man she loves. She doesn't love me."

"Oh, ho," James declared, hands on his hips. "I beg to differ. The lady positively hangs on your arm."

"Because she doesn't know anyone else," John protested.

"She knows Nora," Simon countered. "She knows Beth. She shows a decided preference for your company."

"I'm good with Peter," John said. "What she feels for me is ease and convenience. Not love."

Drew glanced up. "Do you love her?"

John swallowed. It would be easy to claim he didn't. But a part of him informed him that was a lie. How could he fail to appreciate her bravery, her beauty? It would take little to fall in love with her.

And that way led heartache.

"It doesn't matter," he told Drew. "Everyone knows I'm not the sort of man to inspire a woman's heart."

Simon stiffened. "Who said that? Point him out to me, and I'll be glad to show him his error."

"I don't need you to fight my battles, Simon," John informed him.

Drew rose, towering over John and James. "No one can fight this battle but you, John. If you don't believe you're the man for Dottie Tyrrell, nothing we can say will convince you."

Finally, the voice of reason. "Thank you," John said.

"But I think you should ask yourself why you aren't that man," Drew continued. "Because from where I'm standing, you are the best of our brothers."

John blinked, stunned.

"Well, I like that," James teased.

Simon was nodding. "Drew's right. You understand logic."

"You have a sense of humor," James said.

Drew nodded, too. "You are the one we all count on for help. There isn't a person at Wallin Landing who isn't indebted to you in one way or another. At times, I've wished I had half of your ability to see the good in the world. Life might have been easier."

"And more peaceful," James added.

John looked from one face to another. Drew's smile

was kind, Simon's determined and James's commiserating. All stood ready to help in any way.

"Funny," John said. "I've always compared myself to you, Drew."

"Who hasn't?" James complained with an exaggerated sigh.

Drew shuffled on his feet as if uncomfortable with the idea. "Pa told me to raise you the way he would have. But you each had to find the best path for you. That's just what you've done, John. Pa would be proud of the man you've become. I just want you to be proud of yourself as well."

"I am," John assured him. When they all narrowed their eyes again, he laughed. "All right, I am sometimes. Then I look at the three of you and I ask myself where I went wrong. I'm not as strong as you, Drew. I'll never be as clever as Simon or as charming as James."

James sighed again. "So few are."

Simon cuffed him on the shoulder.

"We each have our talents," Drew said. "There's a passage in the Bible that talks about a hand not wishing to be a foot, an eye being content to be an eye. You're the hands of Wallin Landing, John."

Was he? So many times he'd wondered why he was so different from his brothers. Had God needed someone like him to help the family?

Did Dottie need someone like him?

"I appreciate the compliment," he told his brother, "but you have to admit that there are other men who could make Dottie a better husband."

"I'll admit nothing of the kind," Simon said. "She couldn't do better than a Wallin."

"And since Drew, Simon and I are taken," James reminded him, "and Levi's off to parts unknown, she's pretty much stuck with you."

Drew sent him a look, then turned to John. "You and Mrs. Tyrrell could make a strong marriage, John, if that's what you want."

They were all watching him, waiting to see if their words had taken effect. He wanted to believe his brothers. Who knew him better than they did? But, in the end, it didn't matter what they thought. It mattered what Dottie thought.

"I'm not sure what I want," he told them, "except that I want Dottie and Peter to be happy."

"That's it, then," James declared. "We better finish that church, because I see a wedding in your future."

Now if he could just make himself see that.

Chapter Thirteen

The next week gave Dottie much to think about. She had plenty of work from Nora, enough so that she began to wonder if she could make a way for her and Peter by helping the seamstress. Of course, she'd have to find her own house, and it wouldn't come stocked with milk, eggs and canned goods. It might not even be out at Wallin Landing, unless she staked her own claim in the area. But how would she build a house, furnish it and manage it all alone?

She certainly wasn't alone very often in John's house. The Wallin ladies stopped by to chat, snuggle Peter and offer extra food or bedding. While Tom and Dickie seemed to have given up the field, Harry continued his efforts to charm her. She had been ready to dismiss the fellow as a suitor, but he was so very constant. He left firewood for her every morning and came by after work to see what else she might need. As for John, he came by morning and evening to milk the cows, and, more often than not, he stopped by at least once during the day to check on her. Often he, too, brought something with him.

One day it was a set of little wheels. She couldn't imagine what they were for until he sat on the kitchen floor and began affixing them to the legs of Peter's chair. Her son bounced up and down in her arms as if he knew the purpose.

"And which brother should I thank for borrowing these?" Dottie asked.

John's gaze remained on his work. "None. I bought the wheels from Kelloggs'. This way, you can push Peter's chair around to wherever you're working."

He thought of everything. Her eyes felt hot. Oh, why did she keep crying around him? "You are far too kind to us," she murmured, unable to look at his face or her son's.

"I hope that's happiness again," he'd said, his voice hinting of a smile.

Dottie had nodded, laughing through her tears.

She supposed she should have realized that Harry and John would bump into each other at some point. It wasn't as if she was trying to hide her friendship from either man. They'd known each other far longer than she'd known either. But the inevitable meeting did not go well.

John was bringing in the milk one evening just as Harry came into the kitchen. Brian, who had been cuddled in the warmth from the stove, hissed and darted away at the sight of the logger.

"Fixed that stuck window," Harry told Dottie with an eye to John as if to accuse him of not trying hard enough to fix it himself. "You need other help, Dottie, you just let me know."

He'd taken to using her first name, and she hadn't protested. As frequently as he visited, it had seemed only a courtesy.

"Thank you, Harry," she said, seeing him to the door.

From his chair, Peter burbled a farewell. Funny how he always seemed more pleased to see Harry leave than arrive.

John stepped aside to let Harry and Dottie pass, but his face was still, his eyes shadowed. Had she hurt him by befriending Harry? No, not her unselfish Mr. Wallin.

Harry turned on the back stoop. "I may not be here tomorrow afternoon, Dottie. Weather's supposed to be fine, so I'm going to start work on my cabin."

Beth had said the man had filed a claim in the area. Dottie knew that keeping the claim required Harry to prove it up, building a residence and clearing the land within five years.

"Good for you," she told him. "You might talk with John. I understand he knows something about designing."

Harry snorted. "Well, he may know something about drawing and such, but I know more about building." He flexed his arms as if to show off the already evident muscles under his flannel shirt.

"And fixing things," Dottie acknowledged with a smile. "I'm sure your house will be lovely."

"Lovely," he scoffed. "My house will suit my needs. Front room large enough to welcome friends, hearth big enough to roast a deer and plenty of bedrooms for a wife and children."

"Sounds like you know exactly what you want," Dottie told him.

"I do." He reared up on the step and planted a kiss on her cheek. Before she could protest, he sauntered off toward the forest.

Dottie turned to find John watching her.

"Sounds like you know exactly what you want as well," he said.

Dottie came in and shut the door behind her. Peter banged on the high chair with the wooden spoon she'd given him. She went over and touched his silky hair. "I do. A safe home for Peter and me."

"You have that here," John said, going to pour the milk into the container. Brian ventured out from under the sideboard and went to circle the can, head up as if hoping some of the milk would spill in his direction.

"Because you are the kindest man I know," Dottie assured him. "But I can't keep living in your house forever, John. Surely you'll want to move home at some point."

"At some point," he acknowledged, setting down the pail. Brian immediately put both paws on the rim and began licking at the residue.

John turned, wiping his hands on his trousers. "Tomorrow's Sunday. May I escort you and Peter to church?"

Such a little request, yet it filled her heart. "Of course. And I hope we can join your family for dinner again."

"Of course." He shifted on his feet as if trying to prolong the moment. "Well, I suppose I should be going."

She wasn't sure what came over her, but she darted

to the stove. "You could stay for dinner. I'm frying the trout you brought earlier."

He grinned. "Sounds lovely." Immediately his grin faded. "That is, I'm sure it will be very good. Great even." He dropped his gaze to where Brian was now winding around his ankles.

Dottie dropped her hand. "What's wrong, John?"

"Nothing," he assured her. "I'll just go wash up. Anything you need while I'm waiting?"

She couldn't think of anything, but that didn't stop him from helping. After he'd washed his hands, he chopped the potatoes she'd planned to fry with the trout, set the table and brought in more wood for the box. By the time she'd laid out the food, he'd also filled the box in the parlor and swept the front porch and the back stoop.

Dottie regarded him as he waited for her to take her seat. "I truly appreciate everything you and Harry do, John. But have I given you the impression I'm utterly helpless?"

His brows shot up. "By no means."

"Good." She took her seat next to Peter, and John sank onto the chair opposite her. "Would you say the blessing, then?"

After last Sunday's meal, she knew his family didn't resort to memorized prayers but spoke from their hearts. She thought he would thank God for the food and the farm. As usual, he surprised her.

"Dear Lord," he prayed, head bowed and hands clasped. "Thank You for bringing Dottie and Peter to Wallin Landing. Their talents and characters bless everyone who comes near them. Give them strength and wisdom to see Your path. Open it wide before them. Thank You for the good food You've blessed us with as well. May it build our bodies as Your word builds our hearts. Amen."

"How are you so perfect?" Dottie asked.

Hand reaching for the trout, John paused. "I'm hardly perfect, Dottie."

"You are to me. I've never known anyone who consistently puts others' needs before his own."

"Isn't that what Christians are supposed to do?" He dug into the fish and heaped a serving onto his plate.

"I suppose so," she admitted. Funny how she'd never seen it lived so well before coming to Wallin Landing.

She wasn't sure afterward what they talked about, but conversation flowed, Peter beamed, Brian circled the table waiting for something to fall and dinner ended on a congenial tone. However, as she rose from the table, forcing John to his feet as well, Peter's face turned stormy, and he began to whimper.

"What's wrong, little man?" John asked, bending to lift Peter from the baby chair.

Peter rested his head against John's shoulder with a sigh.

The sight pierced Dottie's heart. That was what Peter deserved, a loving father who would guide and protect him. She knew Harry was trying to take that role, but he still paid Peter little attention when he was in their company. John always thought about Peter.

Even now. He walked the baby around the room, Brian following as if just as concerned, while Dottie put the dishes in the sink and pumped water on them to soak. She thought surely Peter would fall asleep with the movement, but each time they passed, her son's eyes were wide-open.

"I know what he needs," John murmured. "We'll be in the parlor when you're ready to take him."

She nodded, and he moved into the other room.

She scraped the last of the trout into a bowl and set it on the floor for Brian. The cat scampered over without even a glance in her direction and set about devouring the fish.

"So," she said, turning to put the pan in to soak as well, "it seems you like John more than Harry. I suppose I shouldn't be surprised. You are John's cat, after all."

Brian twitched his tail, but he kept his head down.

"And I suppose you think I'm being foolish not to pursue John," she told the cat. "He's everything I could want in a husband. But he doesn't seem to want to get married. Any ideas why?"

In answer, Brian shifted around the bowl to put his back to her.

"Ah, the silent type," Dottie said with a shake of her head. Then she laughed. "And perhaps I ought to be silent as well. Now not only do I talk to Peter, but I talk to you!"

The dishes dealt with for the moment, she started down the corridor. Immediately she heard John's voice. Was he talking to Peter, too? She hurried to the parlor.

John was sitting in one of the chairs near the hearth, Peter in one arm and a book open in the other hand. "'Chivalry!—why, maiden, she is the nurse of pure and high affection—the stay of the oppressed, the redresser of grievances, the curb of the power of the tyrant. Nobility were but an empty name without her, and liberty finds the best protection in her lance and her sword.'''

Peter's eyes were wide, his foot twitching, and he kept glancing between John's face and the book, as if understanding that the words were coming from the little black lines on the page.

Dottie went to sit on the other chair and picked up the mending she had from Nora. How peaceful to sit and listen to John's warm voice. She could imagine herself safe, loved, happy.

She could imagine John as her husband.

She poked herself with the needle and laid down the work to rub at her finger. John said he didn't want to marry. He was only being kind to treat her and Peter this way. She shouldn't build up hopes for something that might never be.

John walked back from his house through the dark April night, drizzle making his cheeks wet. He had never felt jealous in his life, until today. Oh, at times he envied his brothers their strengths, but, in general, he'd been satisfied to be the peacemaker, the helper. Harry's possessive attitude toward Dottie, however, was starting to get on his nerves.

Harry had a tendency to show off. When it came to Dottie, he acted as if he alone had the strength to be a husband. From what John had seen of his brothers and their wives, husbands needed a great deal more than physical strength. But then again, he'd never been a husband, so what did he know?

Given Harry's antics, John wasn't entirely surprised when the logger showed up Sunday morning as John was meeting Dottie and Peter. Harry insisted on walking with them to services. But his attentions didn't end there. He grabbed branches along the path and snapped them off with his bare hands, leaped over a log and did a handstand on the porch of the main house, making Peter crow. The fellow was insufferable!

John made sure to position Dottie at the end of the circle of chairs and took the seat next to hers. That didn't stop Harry from pulling one of the chairs out of the circle and shoving it into place on the other side of Dottie. Drew, who was going to be commenting on the reading this week, eyed his crewman and pointed wordlessly to where Harry had removed the chair. Harry merely grinned at him as if he had no idea what Drew meant.

"Harry, you've destroyed the symmetry," James scolded. "I doubt Simon will bring himself to worship unless everything is even."

Simon glared at him.

Dottie stood. "I'll move my chair."

Immediately Harry leaped up to move it for her. John was only glad that Beth and Nora were on either side of the space, so Harry couldn't plop himself beside Dottie.

But then again, neither could John.

As Simon stood to play, John drew in a breath. He needed to put this all from his mind. Now was the time for worship, for thanks, for supposition. Hadn't Jesus said that if you had anything on your mind before worship, deal with it before worshipping?

His family began singing the hymns, but John bowed his head instead.

Lord, forgive me. All I want is for Dottie and Peter to be happy. I can't convince myself that Harry will make them happy. Is it just jealousy? A competitive nature? I didn't think I had that. I've been Your peacemaker since I was a child, but I can't help thinking that Dottie needs more than that.

John didn't sense a response as the songs ended, or when James said the opening prayer. Then Drew stepped up to the hearth to read. John had heard today's story countless times over the years, how Jesus had healed a man who had been lame from birth.

Have I been lame from birth, Lord? You asked the man if he wanted to be healed. I didn't know I needed healing. Or am I just too complacent?

Greater love has no man than this, that he should lay down his life for a friend.

He remembered the verse. He believed it. That was the measure of a man, the measure of a hero. Would Harry be willing to lay down his life for Dottie and Peter?

Would John?

He thought about the matter as the service concluded and his family began moving around him. He was so deep in thought, in fact, that Harry beat him to Dottie's side.

So did Beth. His sister was already talking as she reached out to take Peter. "It's so nice to have a baby to hold again. All our nieces and nephews are growing up so fast." She jiggled Peter on her hip, and he beamed at her.

"He needs some little brothers and sisters, if you ask me," Harry said with a sidelong look to Dottie.

"What a lovely idea," Beth said. She held out Peter to him. "Let's see how you do with a baby, Mr. Yeager."

Harry blanched, but he opened his arms. Peter clung to Beth, face scrunching.

John stepped up. "I'll take him."

To his surprise, Beth turned Peter away from him. "No. It's my turn. You've had him entirely too often. Why don't you and Dottie take a walk along the lake? I promise you won't be needed for some time."

"I'd be happy to stroll along the lake with you, Dottie," Harry said, offering her his arm.

Beth looked pointedly at Nora, who practically leaped from her chair. "No, Harry, I need your help."

Harry frowned. "With what?"

"With…" She glanced at Beth as if for inspiration.

"With rearranging the furniture in my cabin," Beth said. "Nora has a far better eye for it than I do, and she once lived in that cabin, so she knows exactly how things could fit." She batted her eyes at the logger. "I'd be ever so grateful for the use of your muscles, Harry."

Harry preened, casting John a glance as if to rub in the fact that he had been chosen to do something more manly. "Anything for you, Miss Beth."

John took Dottie's arm and led her away before anyone else could chime in.

"I can see I'll have to speak to my sister again," John told her as they left the main house. "She's still trying to play matchmaker."

"I can see I'll have to speak to Harry," Dottie countered. "I truly appreciate his kindness, but I do not think we will suit."

John wanted to raise his head skyward and burst into song, but he kept step with Dottie instead as he turned them to the north around the building, where a path led down to the shore. "That's a shame."

Dottie swatted his arm. "Oh, you never wanted Harry to court me. I could see that."

He didn't like that his jealousy had been that obvious. "I just wasn't sure he was the man for you and Peter."

"I don't think he is," she confided. "I suppose he might become accustomed to dealing with Peter eventually, but why take that chance?" She picked up her skirts with her free hand to navigate the slope.

Take a chance, she'd said. That was what she'd be doing with any man she decided to marry.

That was what she'd be doing with him.

They reached the lake. The day was overcast, Mount Rainier hidden behind clouds. The waters looked dull and gray, as heavy as the sky. "It must be hard to think of marrying again after the death of your husband," John murmured.

She wrapped her arms about her, and he realized it was chillier here by the water. He drew off his coat and draped it around her shoulders.

"You're doing it again," she said. "Being noble."

John laughed. "Well, then allow me to shiver in my nobility." The wind whipped past him, moist with the coming rain, and he fought not to show her that shiver.

"My husband wasn't noble," she said, gaze out on the waters. "He didn't think like you do. He thought only of his needs, his happiness."

John suddenly wanted to meet her dead husband. "I don't think I'd like him."

She puffed a laugh. "Oh, everyone liked him. He

was friendly, charming, but there was no depth to it. I didn't realize that until it was too late."

"And then he died and left you alone with Peter," John said.

"Then he left," she agreed. "And I tell myself it's a good thing that Peter never knew him. I couldn't bear for him to hurt Peter, too."

"I would never do anything to hurt Peter," John promised her. "Or you."

"I know that." She reached up a hand to press it against her chest. "In here, I know that. But sometimes—" she reached up to touch her forehead "—I doubt in here."

He knew the feeling. "It's easy to focus on our fears rather than our hopes."

She cast him a glance. "You, too?"

Especially him. "Yes."

She frowned. "But, John, what could possibly frighten you?"

Taking a chance. Risking his heart. Hearing that he'd never be anything but second best. He bent, picked up a stone and hurled it into the lake.

"Being less than who I'm meant to be," he told her.

She put a hand on his arm as if to keep him from throwing another stone. "That's impossible. You're already the finest man of my acquaintance." As if to prove it, she stood on tiptoe and kissed him.

Chapter Fourteen

She'd just wanted to prove to John he was everything a gentleman should be. But one touch of her lips to his, and he made her feel like everything a lady should be—loved, admired, protected. His arms stole around her, and he held her close. Once more, she didn't want the moment to end.

He drew back to gaze down at her. "Why did you kiss me?"

Oh, such a difficult question to answer! Dottie took a step away, for all she longed to draw closer. "You seemed to need it."

He laughed. "I'd imagine you could say that about every bachelor in Seattle."

She blushed. "Well, I don't intend to kiss every one of them."

He slipped his hand over hers. "Nor would I want you to. I'm having a hard time just seeing you with Harry."

Something was changing. She could feel it, and she was fairly sure he felt it, too. "Harry will never be more than a friend, and I doubt he'll even want to be that when I explain the matter to him. You have consistently called yourself my friend. Do you want to be more, John?"

He drew in a breath. That appeared to be an equally hard question to answer by the way he examined her fingers laced with his. "What I want isn't important. What's important is you and Peter."

Such a kind thing to say, heroic even. But oh, so unsatisfactory. "And what if I should tell you that I think Peter and I could be very happy with you?"

He raised his head to regard her. "I'd say you need to be very, very sure about that."

A cold wind raced across the lake, making whitecaps on the water. Even in John's coat, Dottie shivered. It was a huge decision, one she very well knew could change her life forever. She'd been willing to marry a stranger. Why was she so hesitant to marry a man she was coming to admire?

Something wet struck her cheek, and for a moment she thought she was crying again. Then John looked up, blinking, and she realized it was raining. Hand on hers, he pulled her back toward the main house.

He stayed near her side for the rest of the afternoon as they visited with his family. While Catherine played with Peter, Dottie helped John and Beth cook dinner. Then they all ate together.

Still, she longed for a moment alone with him, a moment to talk about what was happening between them. She thought surely he would escort her and Peter home, but Harry shoved next to her as she was preparing to leave.

"I'll walk you home, Dottie," he said.

Dottie glanced to John, but he nodded as if encouraging her to take the logger's arm. What was he doing? By the frowns on Catherine's, Beth's and Nora's faces, they wondered the same thing.

"Very well," Dottie said.

Head high, he led her out the door.

"Mighty fine day," he said as they crossed the clearing for the trees.

The rain had stopped, but the skies were still leaden, and she was fairly sure there would be more showers before the night set in. "I suppose we need the rain," she said, glancing to the fields before the trees closed around them.

"I meant, any day is a fine day when a man has a lovely lady beside him," Harry said.

Dottie nodded, but she found herself wishing it was John walking beside her. They would have found something more interesting to discuss than the weather.

And perhaps that was why John had let Harry walk her home.

"You've been very kind to us, Harry," Dottie said as they passed James's cabin. "I want you to know how much I appreciate it."

Harry stopped, the shadows of the trees crossing his face. "You can show your appreciation anytime you like." He turned his head and pointed to his cheek.

Was he angling for a kiss? Dottie kept walking. "I thought I had. But if you'd rather I paid you, I have a few coins saved up from my sewing."

Harry lengthened his stride to catch up to her. "I didn't help you for money!"

"Good," she said as they came out onto the field in

front of John's house. "Because I was under the impression we were friends."

Harry caught her arm. "If I've given you the impression I want nothing more than a friendship, I've been doing it wrong." He bent his head toward hers.

Dottie pulled back, though there was only so far she could go with his hand holding her. "And if I've given you the impression I want anything more than a friendship, I've been doing it equally wrong."

His face reddened. "You really prefer that mealworm to a real man."

Heat flushed up her, and she shook him off. "I prefer a gentleman who appreciates me and my son."

He started laughing, and there was nothing kind in the tone. "You just want a man you can coddle like your son. Well, that's not me. Good day, Mrs. Tyrrell." He turned on his heel and strode back toward the trees.

Well! Dottie was trembling, and she clutched Peter closer to keep from dropping him.

"I'm quite glad I didn't decide to pursue him," Dottie said aloud.

Peter patted her on the shoulder in agreement.

She started for the house. "Though, I do wonder sometimes whether I can attract no one but scoundrels," she told her son.

Peter scowled at her.

"Present company excepted, of course," she assured him with a smile.

And certainly John's company was excepted as well. He would never have spoken to her like that, all but demanding a kiss. And she didn't coddle him or Peter.

Still, he was hesitant to further their friendship. She

couldn't believe Harry's statement that John was a coward. She couldn't be so terrifying as to prevent John from proposing if he truly thought they'd suit.

She let herself in to find Brian waiting at the foot of the stairs. He came over and twined himself around her skirts.

"A shame you can't talk," she told the cat. "I imagine you could tell me all kinds of stories about your master."

Brian glanced up at her with a grin that showed his teeth.

She thought John might come in after he'd done the afternoon milking, but he must have taken the pail to one of his brothers, for she caught no sign of him. Neither did she see him Monday morning, though she was up early and had bacon frying in hopes of sitting down to breakfast with him.

"Did I scare him away?" she asked Brian, who was sitting by the milk can, tail twitching, as if he, too, expected John.

Peter waved his wooden spoon, ready to defend her. Too bad it wasn't that easy.

She was just cleaning up after breakfast when she heard a knock at the door. Her hands flew to her hair, and she immediately scolded herself. It couldn't be John. He'd walk right in. And besides, he didn't care what she looked like. She didn't need to primp for him.

She gathered Peter in her arms and went to answer.

She found Nora, Catherine and Beth on the porch. They had dressed in their everyday cotton gowns, but that didn't stop them from looking positively determined.

"We came to help," Nora announced.

"Drastic measures are clearly needed," Catherine agreed.

"In other words, my brother is being bullheaded," Beth said, "and we're here to see what can be done about it."

Had he told them about his and Dottie's discussion yesterday? Her stomach dipped. "There's no need to intervene, ladies," she told them.

Beth marched past her into the house, with Catherine a step behind. Nora entered more slowly with a supportive smile to Dottie.

"He's being perfectly unreasonable," Beth said, throwing herself onto the chair nearest the hearth in the parlor. "What does he mean, giving Harry an opportunity like that?"

"Simon would never have done that," Nora agreed, going to perch on the bench.

"Drew might have," Catherine admitted, joining her. "Men can be obtuse sometimes."

"I think John may have been more canny than obtuse," Dottie explained, taking the seat across from Beth and adjusting Peter on her lap. Her son was gazing about at the ladies, foot twitching with his interest. "He may have been giving me time to let Harry know I could not favor his suit."

Beth giggled. "And you must have done that, for Harry was in a fiery mood this morning. He yelled at Tom for taking the last piece of bacon."

Dottie grimaced. "I'm sorry for Mr. Convers, but I had to explain to Harry. I didn't want him thinking there was a future in courting me."

Catherine leaned forward. "And what of John? Do you see a future in having him court you?"

Dottie sighed. "I wish I knew." Peter wiggled on her lap as if determined to get closer to their visitors, and she moved her leg up and down to distract him.

Brian wandered in just then and began strolling from lady to lady, rubbing against their skirts and uttering plaintive meows until they reached down and petted his back.

Beth shook her head. "If you wonder at my brother's character, you have only to look at Sir Brian de Bois-Guilbert here. He should be sleek from mousing, but a more pampered cat you will never find."

So much for the theory that Beth had done the pampering.

"Perhaps Brian is company in the evenings," Nora said, giving the feline a good stroke. "I feel that way about Fleet." Brian circled for another pass.

"Very likely John agrees," Catherine said, "but I'd like to see him with a wife as well."

Beth clapped her hands down on the chair arms. "He nearly had one. Oh, but I could give Caroline Crawford a piece of my mind! What was she thinking, refusing him like that?"

Dottie had been about to protest on John's behalf. Now she didn't dare speak. Caroline Crawford? Had John courted before?

"So he did propose," Catherine said, ignoring Brian's attempts to get her attention.

"And Miss Crawford refused," Nora said.

"And none too kindly, if I were to guess," Beth told

them. "He moped for weeks, and I don't think he's been the same since."

Dottie shifted Peter closer. "Then he was in love with her."

"Surely not," Nora said with a look to Dottie.

Beth sighed. "Surely so. I know my brother. He's devoured the books Pa left us. You read *The Last of the Mohicans* and *Ivanhoe* too many times, and you'll hold a very high ideal for love."

Was that why he didn't propose? Was he still mourning Miss Crawford's defection? Dottie could certainly understand the desire to protect his heart. She'd been doing that since the moment she'd learned about Frank's other life.

Or was there more to it than that? Maybe Dottie didn't meet his ideal for love. Maybe she really did only attract scoundrels. An ache grew inside her, like an abscessed tooth.

"I could see why he might be attracted to Miss Crawford," Catherine said. "She has had more than her share of suitors. We simply must convince John to look elsewhere."

Nora smiled at Dottie. "At our new friend."

"Perhaps," Dottie made herself say, "John isn't ready to look elsewhere."

Beth waved a hand, as if it was that easy to eliminate heartache. "He's ready. He just doesn't realize it yet."

"Which is why we're here," Catherine told Dottie.

Beth rose. "We think you should be bold," she said, hand slicing the air as if she held a sword of righteousness. "Since he won't come to you, you must go to him. That's what Nora did."

Dottie darted a look to the quiet seamstress. Nora nodded, broad cheeks pinkening. "I asked Simon to marry me."

Could Dottie be that bold? What would she do if John said no? Just the thought made her chest hurt.

And, oh, what would she do if he said yes?

"I don't know if I could," Dottie confessed. "I came here to marry John Wallin, but he's not as I pictured him. I don't want to hurt him."

Beth's face melted. "Oh, Dottie, you couldn't."

She could. If John had already lost one woman he thought he loved, she didn't want to add to that pain.

"I'm certain you're exactly what he needs," Catherine assured her. She turned to her sister-in-law. "Nora, how soon could you make a new dress for Dottie?"

Nora eyed Dottie as if calculating inches. "Four days, if I had the fabric."

"John's heading into town today," Beth told her. "I'll tell him to pick some up. There's the loveliest lavender wool at Kelloggs'. It will match your eyes, Dottie."

"Oh, I couldn't—" Dottie began.

"Nonsense," Catherine insisted. "You'll need a new hat, too."

"I can make it," Beth promised. "I have ribbon and a frame saved."

"Ladies, please," Dottie said. "I don't want to put you out."

"It is no trouble," Catherine assured her. "It is a privilege to help a friend."

Nora nodded. "You'll want to look your best for the May Day picnic on Friday."

"For John and for the other eligible bachelors in attendance," Catherine agreed.

"We're just gilding the lily," Beth told her. "All you have to do is be yourself, Dottie, and the gentlemen will come running to meet you, even John."

John clucked to the horses, more than glad to accept Beth's commission on his trip to Seattle that morning. Truth be told, he was avoiding Dottie, but for a reason. He wanted to give her time to think about their exchange by the lake yesterday, to be sure he was the right man for her. She deserved that.

And he hadn't been ready to face another rejection.

He sighed as he drove the team into town. He preferred to discuss differences, settle arguments peacefully. Did that make him less than a man? His brothers didn't seem to think so, but they were kin, after all. Should he have challenged the logger to a duel instead of letting Dottie decide whether she favored him or Harry?

Harry was definitely willing. He'd lobbed sarcastic comments at John through breakfast, had even gone so far as to try to trip him as John climbed off the bench. John had avoided Harry's foot, but the way the logger had raised his fists, John could tell he was spoiling for a fight.

John wasn't willing to give it to him, because he was feeling too good. Harry's increased antagonism could only mean one thing.

Dottie preferred John.

He caught himself whistling as he guided the horses onto Second Avenue. Dottie preferred him. He wanted to preen, do a handstand on the boardwalk, run through town shouting it to the sky. But not yet, not until she told him. He had to be sure. And so did she.

He tied the horses to the hitching rail outside Kelloggs' and went inside. He needed more paint for the church, and he wanted to see if the seeds Nora had ordered had come in. Besides, Beth had given him a special commission for fabric, and he knew how particular his sister could be in that area.

He went to the counter and placed his order with Weinclef, who'd been the clerk at the general store for more than ten years. Short and whip-thin, he tended to lean forward slightly, as if he was pointing his long nose at his customer.

"We are expecting the seeds from San Francisco any day," he informed John, hefting the pail of paint onto the counter. "But be advised we will not be open this Friday."

Checking the label on the can, John looked up with a frown. "Why? You're generally open every day now."

"We are building a railway," Weinclef informed him, as if anyone could have missed the posters all over town or the accounts in the last year of newspapers. "It is a civic duty." He shook his finger at John. "Seattle will not be left behind, sir."

"And rightly so." Another man stepped up to the counter. He was tall and slender, with a shock of curly black hair and a trim mustache. "I moved up from San Francisco in part because Seattle is expected to grow."

John shook his head. "We will grow, but I don't think this railway is going to have much to do with it."

Weinclef's lean face scrunched up, but the stranger laughed.

"Where's your sense of civic spirit? Any time this many people can agree on anything, I call it a good day." He tugged down on his striped waistcoat. He was too well dressed for the town, though John thought James and Nora would approve of the tailored coat and pressed trousers.

"That's true enough," John agreed. He stuck out his hand. "John Wallin. My family settled the northern end of Lake Union."

"Frank Reynolds," he said, giving John's hand a hearty shake. "I don't suppose you know of any jobs out your way. I was a salesman before I headed west."

Weinclef immediately busied himself looking for Beth's fabric among the crowded shelves.

"No sales jobs out at Wallin Landing, I'm afraid," John told him.

Reynolds's face fell. "There must be some way for an enterprising fellow to make a living here."

"Coal," Weinclef advised, returning. "Most of the single men head for the fields at Newcastle beyond Lake Washington." He thumped the bolt of fabric down on the counter.

John could see why Beth favored it. The wool looked warm and soft, and it was a delicate shade of bluish purple that reminded him of Dottie's eyes. But then, lots of things reminded him of Dottie these days.

"Too far from civilization for me," Reynolds told the clerk. "I like the ladies, if you know what I mean."

Weinclef wrinkled his nose, and John felt a similar distaste. The way Reynolds said the word *ladies* smacked of property. But maybe John was still frustrated about Harry's attitude. He had no reason to think Reynolds was less than the gentleman he appeared.

"Besides," Reynolds said, leaning on the counter, "I prefer not to dirty my hands in manual labor."

Perhaps too much the gentleman? "A shame," John said, pulling the money for his purchases from his pocket. "There's plenty of work to be done for a man willing to farm or log. I wish you good fortune, Mr. Reynolds." John picked up the pail and bundled the fabric under one arm.

"If you are intent on meeting the right people," Weinclef told Reynolds, "you should join us for the May Day picnic. Everyone will do his or her part to build our great city, even our city fathers." He raised a brow at John as if to dare him to disagree.

Reynolds smiled. "Well, then, gentlemen, count me in. Perhaps I'll see you and your family there, Mr. Wallin."

John nodded. "We're planning on going. Look for me, and I'll be sure to introduce you."

Chapter Fifteen

Over the next few days, Dottie helped the Wallin ladies prepare for the big May Day event, baking pies, cakes, bread and biscuits.

"I still say no one makes biscuits as good as my brother Levi," Beth had remarked with a sigh.

From conversations, Dottie had gathered that the youngest Wallin brother had ever been the most adventurous. Unwilling to farm, ranch or log, he had left home with his friend Scout Rankin to seek their fortunes. The last the Wallins had heard, the two men were at the Omineca gold rush in Canada, but the last letter had come months ago, and all were concerned.

Dottie couldn't help thinking about her aunt and uncle. Did they miss her? Wonder where she'd gone? They had wanted nothing to do with her when they'd learned she was with child and had no husband to support her.

"I knew there was something wrong with that man," her uncle had railed, for all he'd been the one to introduce Frank to Dottie.

"We told you not to marry him," her aunt had lamented, even though she'd nearly dragged Dottie to the altar.

Somehow she couldn't imagine them caring the way the Wallins cared about their lost brother.

Or the way she was coming to care for John.

He did not press her about whether she was willing to have him court her in earnest, but he resumed his usual pattern at the farm. He was waiting for her, smiling, when she went out to gather the eggs in the morning, and, more often than not, he joined her and Peter around the breakfast table. When he didn't, her son would look at the empty chair, face scrunching.

During the day, she could see John out the windows, working on the fields that ringed the house, tending to the animals and fixing things around the house and barn. One day, he came to the door midmorning, face red from his work but smiling.

"To what do I owe this visit?" Dottie teased him.

"I promised to show you that big cedar," he reminded her as he took Peter and offered her his arm.

Peter straightened in John's other arm as if eager to see, and Dottie felt her own spirits rising as John led them down the drive. Of course, it could have been the man beside her rather than the prospect of seeing the tree.

He veered off the drive onto a narrow path that wound deeper into the woods.

"Just a little ways," he told Dottie. A moment later, and he strode into a clearing, then paused as if to let Dottie take in the sight.

The tree was massive, the trunk like a wall in front

of her. Tilting back her head, she couldn't make out the top through the branches, but it had to be more than forty feet tall. The entire Wallin family holding hands would have had a difficult time encircling it.

Peter just stared, foot twitching.

"Drew figures it's hundreds of years old," John said. "We had a few like it on the other claims, and they fetched a pretty price in board feet. I've seen whole families live in one of these hollowed-out stumps."

He let go of Dottie's hand to reach out and pat the rough bark. "But I couldn't see this grandfather of the forest come down."

Dottie knew she was regarding John as fixedly as Peter regarded the tree. Friend to widows, children, lost cats and even trees. She could not help but admire him.

And there lay the problem. John had given her an opening to tell him how she felt, to encourage him to court her. But now that she knew he had loved and lost, she hesitated. He'd been through pain not unlike her own. Was he truly willing to try again? Especially if he knew about Frank?

Beth and his sisters-in-law seemed determined to have him notice Dottie at the May Day picnic. Beth had created a darling hat from deep blue velvet with a matching pleated satin ribbon that sat on Dottie's upswept curls and made the gold of her hair all the more apparent. She'd had two fittings with Nora for her new gown and knew it would complement the hat as well as her figure.

Yet all of her new finery would be in vain if John wasn't truly interested. If he was still grieving the loss of his sweetheart, she could understand his reluctance to try again so soon. Yet she felt every hour that passed like the toll of a bell. At some point, it would strike the final note, and she would have to leave Wallin Landing. She could not live on the Wallins' charity forever.

By arrangement, everyone was up earlier than usual on May Day. The sky was still dark, clouds so low they touched the tops of the firs and hid the stars. John came to collect her, holding the lantern while she carried Peter through the hush of the forest to the main house, where everyone was to gather.

Simon, who seemed to share John's opinion of the futility of the event, was staying behind with Nora and the children. Like Dottie, the women were swathed in cloaks or coats against the chilly damp air. The men in their thick coats looked as bundled as little Peter.

Beth stepped up on the back porch of the main house, her long, dark blue coat making her look a bit like a little general, and began issuing orders. "Drew, you take Catherine, Harry and the lads up with you along with the tools." Her brother and his crew began loading the axes and shovels into the bed of Drew's waiting wagon.

"James," she continued, "you take Rina and the food with you."

"'Here with a loaf of bread beneath the bough,'" James quipped, offering his arm to his wife, "'and thou beside me singing in the wilderness.'"

Beth frowned. "Wait, sending the food with just you and Rina will be entirely inconvenient. She won't want to keep looking backward to make sure it's securely stowed. I better ride in the bed with the food. Pickles have been known to explode when not properly tended."

Had they? Dottie didn't remember that from her days on her parents' farm. "Perhaps I could help," she offered.

Beth shook her head. "You need to focus on Peter." She waved a hand. "John, you take Dottie and Peter and the blankets for the picnic."

Dottie didn't know whether to thank Beth or scold her for arranging things so neatly. John's sister hopped down off the porch, picked up the blankets that had been piled there and carried them to where John stood by one of the farm wagons. Dottie followed.

He offered her a smile and held out his arms for Peter.

Before Dottie could hand him her son, Beth all but threw the blankets into the bed of the wagon and leaped between Dottie and John. "Let me hold him, Dottie. John, help Dottie onto the bench. We really must be going if we're to reach Seattle in time." She scooped Peter out of Dottie's arms.

John's arms fell, and he frowned at his sister as if he wasn't sure what she was on about.

Beth stamped her foot, startling Peter. "Well, go on! Must I do everything around here?"

With an apologetic grimace, John stepped forward and put his hands on Dottie's waist.

She was certain time stopped. His gaze met hers and held. Her breath lodged in her chest. She felt his muscles tighten, sending a jolt through her. His name whispered past her lips as he effortlessly lifted her onto the bench.

Then he drew back, and sound and movement returned.

"He's such a sweetheart," Beth said.

Dottie blinked, then she realized Beth was talking about Peter.

"Thank you," she said as John came around and hopped up beside her.

Beth beamed at the baby in her arms. "Could I keep him with me on the drive? We'll be just behind you, so we can stop if he needs you."

"I would think you wouldn't want Peter to ride with the exploding pickles," John drawled.

But Beth was already hurrying away with Dottie's son.

Dottie watched her, then glanced at John. "Do you think the pickles are truly dangerous?"

"Not in the slightest," John said, gathering up the reins. "But I'm not too sure about my sister."

They set off after Drew's wagon. Dottie glanced back in time to see James and Rina pull in behind them.

The way was slow. Lanterns at the front of each wagon gave enough light for the horses and oxen. The jingle of tack played the cavalcade along, the wagons swaying in time. She could imagine Peter closing his eyes, safe in Beth's arms, surrounded by pickles, pies, cakes, bread and biscuits.

"I must apologize—again—for my family," John said beside her. "I'm not sure what it would take to get through to them we don't need their assistance in courting. Shall I write it in the rain clouds? Outline it on the snows of Mount Rainier?"

Dottie smiled. "At least we know they have our best interests at heart."

John snorted. "Sometimes that's just a handy excuse for meddling."

"Or helping," Dottie insisted. "The way you helped me by bringing me out to Wallin Landing."

He glanced her way, gaze shadowed in the lantern light. "Did I help you, Dottie? Sometimes it seems you'd like to be somewhere else."

Dottie readjusted the cloak about her. "Not somewhere else. Just settled. It would be nice to know I could stay where I am, without having to look for something more."

He returned his gaze to the road ahead. Drew's wagon was no more than a lumbering dark shape beyond the golden light. She could feel the mist gathering on her cheeks.

"Is that why you suggested we consider courting?" John murmured. "So you'd know you're settled?"

Dottie stared at him. "Of course not! I suppose it may seem otherwise because I came out here as a mail-order bride, but I take marriage very seriously. The Bible says that God created Eve because it wasn't good for man to be alone."

"And look at all the trouble that caused," he said, but she could hear the teasing tone in his voice.

"Oh, come now," she protested. "What would your brothers do without their wives? What would Wallin Landing be without everyone's contribution? You'd have no school without Rina, no dispensary without Catherine."

"James would have to go to town to find someone to sew him a new waistcoat without Nora," John added.

He was in a rare mood. She found she liked it. But then, she liked a great deal about John Wallin. The only thing she didn't like was his refusal to wed. He seemed to think he wasn't good enough to be a husband.

"Caroline Crawford has a lot to answer for," she said.

He started, and the horses picked up their pace. Immediately he slowed them again. "What did you say?"

She'd known speaking her thoughts aloud to Peter and Brian would get her into trouble one day. "Forgive me, John. It's really none of my affair. Your sister mentioned that you had courted Miss Crawford, and you and she decided you would not suit."

"She decided." The words were said quietly, all humor gone. "I thought we were meant for each other. She did not share that opinion. It seems when it comes to being a husband, I lack a key characteristic."

Dottie decided she did not like Miss Crawford in the slightest. "Nonsense. I can't imagine what she thought was lacking, but she was clearly mistaken."

"No, she was right," he insisted. "Once the fault was pointed out to me, I saw it as well. And I'm not sure it's something I can change."

Dottie swiveled to face him. "John Wallin, surely a well-read gentleman like you knows that we are always capable of changing."

"When the fault is in our very nature?"

He sounded skeptical, yet under the tone she heard a yearning. The lantern light outlined his cheeks, made his green eyes dark pools. She had wondered whether this man was hiding a flaw. Now that he had seemed to confess as much, she found she couldn't believe it. Her faith had grown, in him and in her own judgment.

Even in God's provision. For all her trials, He had led her to a good place, surrounded her with people who cared. The least she could do was treat others the same way.

"What did Miss Crawford find so very objectionable?" she asked. "That you give too much of yourself to others? That you put the needs of friends and family before your own? I find those characteristics heroic, sir."

He stared at her. "Heroic? When I can't find time to fix a stuck window or fund the library?"

"Those things will come," she assured him. "But I insist that your nature is the very essence of a hero. If Caroline Crawford can't see that, she isn't worth your time."

A laugh bubbled out of him. "If only I could see the world through your eyes."

Dottie smiled. "And I'd like to see it through yours, full of opportunities to do good for those we love. You notice the wonders in everyday life, John. Look for them in yourself."

He reached out a hand and laid it over hers. "Perhaps we can both catch hold of a new vision together."

Together. They had started as strangers, become friends. Now she could see that they had a chance to end as something far more.

John kept his hand on Dottie's until they reached the outskirts of Seattle. Her words said she believed in him, wanted him at her side. She'd called him heroic. Him! For her, he wanted to be. He was only sorry the crowd made it prudent to put both hands on the reins.

Indeed, it seemed as if Seattle had heeded the call, and every man and woman above the age of sixteen had turned out. From the tracks, from the woods, others joined them on foot, on horseback and in wagons. They went ahead, beside, around, voices growing louder in excitement and anticipation.

The actual location for the work was three miles south of town near where the Duwamish River turned for the bay. As he guided the horses into the city, a boom echoed across the hill, and the church bells began ringing. Dottie glanced his way, brows up.

It had been so dark at Wallin Landing he hadn't gotten a good look at her this morning. Now with the sun setting the city to glowing, he saw the color high in her cheeks, the sparkle of her lavender eyes under the velvet blue of her hat.

The rosy warmth of her lips.

"What was that?" she asked.

It took him a moment to find coherent thought. "That had to be the cannon at the armory. They're certainly doing this up right."

So it seemed. Now he heard the sound of horns playing a rousing march. As they turned the corner onto Second Avenue, he spotted Seattle's brass band, horns flashing in the light as they moved south, a parade growing behind them.

"It's as if the circus came to town," Dottie marveled.

John could only agree. Townspeople shouted and cheered as the Wallin group moved past, then fell in behind. Men carried the tools of their trade, women bore baskets or casks of provisions. As they crossed the old skid road, John spotted other people heading toward the wharves, where the steamer *Comet* was waiting, stacks smoking, to tow the scow *CC Perkins* down to the work site by water.

The parade continued the three miles into the woods, with people singing, laughing. Loggers and sawmill workers leaned on John's wagon, peered up at Dottie and grinned.

"Quite a lady you got there, Mr. Wallin, sir," one asserted.

"I'll save a spot at the picnic for you, ma'am," another offered.

Dottie kept her face forward, her chin up, not so much as giving them a look of encouragement. John waved them back from the wagon.

"Go along now, lads," he told them. "The lady has better things to do than to dawdle with the likes of you."

"A shame, oh, a shame," one lamented. Then they noticed Beth in the wagon just behind and hurried off to petition her instead.

Dottie clasped the opening of her cloak. "And I thought Beth intended to introduce me to *suitable* bachelors!"

He knew there would be others at the work site, but suddenly he had no interest in sharing. He reached out and took one of Dottie's hands in his. "If you believe I'm suitable enough, Dottie, maybe you don't have to look so hard today."

Her head snapped around, her gaze searching his. Then she smiled, cheeks pinkening.

"Perhaps I don't," she said.

This time he didn't release her hand as they rolled into the work site.

If the parade through town had been wild, this place was in turmoil, with older people milling about while the youth dashed from one group to another. John had thought his sister's attitude this morning a bit dictatorial, but it was clear someone needed to take charge. He called to a redheaded fellow who seemed to be directing traffic.

"Pull your wagon in over there," the man said, pointing to a cleared field near the shell of a gristmill that was under construction. "We'll need your horses to help pull the stumps after the loggers take down the trees." He nodded to Dottie. "All the ladies are gathered at the mill, ma'am."

Dottie turned in her seat, but her gaze went back the way they had come. "Where's Beth with Peter?"

John glanced back, too. James had been right behind them, but the number of people had obviously forced his brother to slow. Now it took John a moment to locate his sister, his brother and Rina.

"They're heading for the gristmill," he reported. "They're probably dropping off the supplies before James finds a spot for the wagon. I'll take you to them."

She nodded, but she seemed taut as a bowstring as he maneuvered the wagon into an open space. He asked a lad he knew to watch the horses, then came around to help Dottie down. Her gaze skittered past his in apparent panic. She'd probably never been parted from her son for more than a few minutes.

"It's all right, Dottie," he murmured, running a hand up her arm. "Beth won't let anything happen to Peter."

She drew in a breath and nodded, but her feet skimmed the grass as she hurried with him over to the mill.

The outer walls and roof of the building had been erected, but the inside remained hollow, awaiting the machinery that would grind the grain. Open doors at either end brought in people, light and sound. Someone had laid long boards across logs and sawhorses, and the makeshift tables dipped under the weight of the foodstuffs.

At least the ladies were organized. Already the foods had been grouped by type, and James and Rina were ferrying supplies while Beth pointed out locations as she jostled Peter on her hip. Dottie dashed forward and took Peter from John's sister, cradling the baby close as if she'd thought she might never see him again. Beth hurried off toward the open door, where another wagon had just pulled in.

As John joined James and Rina, his brother clapped him on the shoulder. "The food has been delivered. Let's escape before they put us to work."

Beside John, Dottie stiffened. "Who's that dark-haired man talking with Beth?"

Chapter Sixteen

Dottie's heart was pounding in her throat, and she couldn't think. It couldn't be Frank, not here, not now. She started backing away, and John caught her arm.

"Dottie? That's Michael Haggerty. He's married to Maddie, who owns the bakery where we met. She's the redhead over there. The lads helping him unload his wagon are his son, Stephen, and his brother-in-law, Aiden O'Rourke."

As if he knew he was being discussed, the man turned and looked their way. The friendly, open face was sturdier, stronger than Frank's. She'd never met him before.

Still, she felt as if she was going to keel over. She must have swayed, for John's grip on her arm tightened.

"Dottie?" he asked, peering into her face. "Are you all right?"

She nodded, unable to say the words. What would she tell him, anyway? That she was terrified she'd meet her husband, whom John thought was dead? That she'd let John and his family think she was a widow when she was an abandoned woman?

That she was letting fear get in the way of good sense?

In her arms, Peter began fussing as if he knew her thoughts were in a knot. She was thankful Maddie Haggerty strolled up to them then with a grin. She tipped her chin at John's brother, even as she put her hands on her hips.

"I heard that, James Wallin," she declared, the lilt of the Irish in her voice. "And who was telling you the only work was outside, me lad?" The bakery owner pointed to the dozens of loaves of bread, cakes and cookies her family had begun unloading. "Go on now. Make yourself useful for once."

James clapped his hand to his chest as if wounded, but Rina pushed him toward the waiting wagon with a smile.

John was watching Dottie. "Are you sure you're all right?"

She stroked Peter's hair, felt her son begin to relax. "Yes, I'm fine. I'll go see what I can do to help."

He nodded and took a step back. Suddenly she realized he wasn't going to be at her side today. It was all she could do not to latch on to his hand and keep him there.

Which was silly. Beth was here. As were Catherine and Rina. Even Mrs. Haggerty would be willing to help her if needed, she felt certain. She should let John go.

So she smiled, reached down and took Peter's little hand, and gave it a wiggle. "Say bye-bye to John, Peter."

Peter gabbled something that didn't remotely sound

like goodbye, but John grinned as if her son had sung an aria, then sauntered out of the building whistling.

Dottie felt a similar pleasure rippling through her. It would be all right. She was with friends. She turned to see what she could do to help.

The ladies of Seattle had been generous. Tables were stacked with chicken, ham, jellies and biscuits. She spotted a dozen crocks of pickles, all of which appeared to have reached the work site without damaging themselves or anyone around them. Other tables were laden with pies, cakes and cookies. Several younger ladies had been employed with fans. They stood over the tables, waving the lace or feathered accessories over the food to keep flies and other insects away. Other women were organizing plates, cups and cutlery for the repast to come.

"What a crowd!" Beth materialized beside Dottie. "All of Seattle really did turn out. Isn't it wonderful?" She bent and tickled Peter under the chin, and the baby grinned at her.

It was amazing to see so many people so intent on helping each other. Beth and Dottie took up places with those waving the fans. It was something Dottie could do while holding Peter, and Beth seemed more eager just to watch everyone.

"See that woman with the black hair all piled behind her?" she asked Dottie, nodding toward a slender older woman whose directions the others seemed to be following. "That's Mary Ann Denny. She's one of the ladies John tried to convince to donate money toward the library. Her husband is the president of this railroad everyone's trying to build."

Dottie was more interested in the lady than the railroad. "Would you introduce me?" she asked Beth.

Beth was delighted. She made the introduction, then hurried back to her place behind the pies with an encouraging smile to Dottie. Mary Ann Denny was equally encouraging. She beamed at Peter, who waved his fists at her as if wanting to touch her amused smile.

"I remember when mine were that small," she said to Dottie. "Sometimes I can't believe we made the overland trek with two of them and one on the way."

Dottie raised her brows. "That must have been difficult. I came by train to San Francisco, then took a boat north to Seattle, and I know how hard it was to see to Peter through all that."

Mrs. Denny touched one of Peter's little hands. "We make the struggle because we want what's best for our children. We want to give them a bright future."

Dottie nodded, throat tightening. "That's it exactly. And for that reason I hope you will reconsider John Wallin's request for funds for a library at Wallin Landing. Books and education are one of the ways we give our children that bright future. Indeed, I don't know how they persevere without the benefit of knowledge acquired no other way."

Mrs. Denny turned to stroll along the tables, Dottie beside her. She nodded to the other women, tugged a pie into line here, shored up a slipping cake there. "If I recall, it wasn't the idea of a library that we opposed. It was the fact that Mr. Wallin has chosen to invest in education to the exclusion of all else."

Dottie frowned, straightening a pickle cask. "I cannot

see that to be the case. He has a good farm, he's helping build a new church and he assists at the school."

"Commendable," Mrs. Denny agreed. She stopped to eye Dottie. "But above all else, Washington Territory grows through its families, with children and without. Mr. Wallin seems singularly determined not to marry. Or has he changed his opinion in that area?"

"I cannot say for certain, ma'am," Dottie admitted, shifting Peter in her arms, "but I have hopes in that direction."

Mrs. Denny's smile blossomed once more. "Well, then, have him reapply, if you will. We are always ready to support a man willing to do his duty."

She inclined her head and sailed off to the next group of women. Dottie hurried back to Beth.

"What did she say?" Beth demanded.

"She says John is welcome to reapply for funding when he reconsiders being a bachelor," Dottie replied, taking up her fan again.

Beth raised her chin. "Well, I like that! But how dare she tell John that he must marry."

Dottie glanced at her friend. "But, Beth, isn't that what you and the others have been telling him all along?"

Beth dropped her gaze. "Well, yes, but that's different. We're family." Another woman came up to help, and Beth handed her the fan. Then she turned to Dottie. "Come on, let's go see what John and the others are doing."

Knowing there were so many women available to work, Dottie didn't see the harm in slipping out for a moment. She followed Beth to the wide door of the mill.

A light rain was falling outside, but that didn't seem to have deterred the men. Coats had been stripped off and arms bared as they set to work. She spotted Drew, Tom, Dickie and Harry hacking away at several massive cedars, their strong bodies twisting with each blow. In the cleared space behind them, other men hooked oxen and horses to stumps, yanking the thrones out of the damp ground in an explosion of dirt and pebbles. Still others, some of them businessmen by the looks of their damp waistcoats and muddy trousers, followed with spades and wheelbarrows to grub out the last bushes and level the land.

A gentleman rode past, his gaze roaming over the groups as if suspecting trouble among the busy workers. He tipped his black wide-brimmed hat at Beth. "Miss Wallin."

Beth's normally happy voice came out strained. "Deputy."

So that was Deputy McCormick. Dottie could see why the Wallin ladies had mentioned him as an eligible bachelor. Under the shade of that hat, his face was sharply planed, strong, and he sat on the horse as if he owned the world. She didn't think he was the man for her, but she could see some ladies sighing in his direction.

Beth's face remained rigid until he passed, then it sagged.

"Has he done something to lose your favor, Beth?" Dottie asked.

Beth gathered her composure like a cloak. "Don't be silly. He's the town deputy. He has better things to do than talk to me." She linked arms with Dottie. "And we promised you a chance to look over all the bachelors. At least half of the men working today fit that description. See one that interests you?"

Only one. Dottie gazed out at the group again. Peter wiggled in her arms, throwing out a hand to the right and muttering. Her gaze was drawn in that direction, and she caught her breath.

John was working with a team clearing stumps. He'd just straightened from hooking a chain around a thick stub as the sun peered out from the clouds. The light sent flames rippling through his hair. He shouted something, then began backing up, coaxing the horses with him as the chain grew taut. His arms were bared to the elbow, his collar open. She could feel his strength, his determination. With a rumble, the stump pulled free, throwing up debris in its wake.

John looked up and met Dottie's gaze as if knowing she was there. His grin was all for her. She grinned back.

"Well," Beth said beside her, laughter in her voice, "it seems you've found one you like very much, indeed, and he seems to feel the same way. I knew that hat would be just the thing."

Dottie's smile of appreciation warmed something deep inside John, and he turned to the next stump with a will. In fact, he must have been working just a little too hard, for one of the other men grinned at him.

"What's the hurry, Wallin? You got somewhere you'd rather be?"

John glanced at the gristmill again, but Dottie and

Beth must have gone back inside, for he caught no sight of them. "Just beside my gal," he told the man.

"Well, who wouldn't want to be beside his gal?" the fellow returned. He called to the others. "Come on, lads. Mr. Wallin has a lady waiting. We wouldn't want to disappoint her."

They all laughed as the rain began pattering down again.

They had finished two more stumps when John heard the horns from the Seattle band blaring. Around him, men stopped what they were doing and raised their heads. Mrs. Denny appeared at the door of the gristmill, with a lid from a metal pot in her hand. She banged on it with a spoon, turning all eyes her way. "Luncheon is served, gentlemen! Gather 'round!"

John didn't need any urging. He settled the horses and hurried for the mill.

The ladies had attempted to make the place more festive. They'd spread blankets along the walls so the men wouldn't have to eat in the rain, and a few had brought colorful cloths to drape the tables. Red, white and blue bunting swung along the platform that would one day hold the grinding machinery. For now, it was the perfect place for the dignitaries to sit.

Husbands and wives were seeking each other, sweethearts had their necks craned. It took him only a moment to locate Dottie and Beth near the pie table. Beth immediately grabbed his arm and pulled him around behind the table.

"Here, John, you help Dottie. I'll go claim a blanket for us."

Before he could argue, she was gone.

Dottie offered him a smile. "It looks like work was going well."

"Better than I expected," John agreed. The other workers had begun lining up near the closest table and were shuffling along, filling their plates. It was only a matter of time before they reached him and Dottie.

Peter was beaming at him. John smiled. "And how did my little man do today? Was he a big help?"

"Extremely helpful," Dottie assured him, giving her son a fond jiggle. "He laughs through the dreariest moments and smiles at everyone."

Apparently not everyone. Peter's face was clouding, and John realized their first customer had approached the table.

Harry.

The logger thrust out his plate. "A shame you stayed with the women, Wallin. The men were out working in the rain."

"John among them," Dottie said before John could answer. "I saw him pulling up stumps."

Harry nodded to the apple pie in front of John. John pretended to misunderstand.

"He pulled up stumps after I chopped down the trees," Harry said as Dottie cut him a slice of the pie. Even one-handed, she managed to lift it and drop it onto his plate.

"And everyone works together," Dottie said cheerfully. "Just look at the cake Beth baked. I'm sure you'll enjoy it."

Visage brightening, Harry moved along to the next table.

It was like that for the next little bit. People seemed

to notice John for the first time, commending him on his work and glancing at Dottie as if surprised to see her beside him. It seemed they approved of him because someone like Dottie did. Or perhaps being with Dottie brought out the best in him. He found himself standing taller, serving up pie with a grin on his face. All too soon, Beth came to take their places, directing them to a blanket near the far wall, where James was standing guard.

Drew and Catherine let them slip through the line first. John filled a plate for himself and one for Dottie, then led her to the blanket. James nodded a greeting before sitting nearby with Rina, their own food before them. John said the blessing and began eating. He knew he was wolfing the meal. He'd worked too hard and felt too good to do otherwise. Dottie was watching him with an amused smile, picking daintily at her food, and Peter regarded him wide-eyed as if quite impressed by John's ability to shovel in the meal.

He'd consumed nearly half of the food on his plate when someone paused at the edge of the blanket. John glanced up to find Caroline Crawford regarding him steadily, head cocked so that her dark curls fell along her perfect cheek.

"Why, John Wallin," she said, balancing her plate of food in front of her lilac-colored gown. "I never expected to see you here."

He waited for the sting of embarrassment, the pain of loss. Instead, he felt only a mild annoyance that she'd interrupted his time with Dottie.

Beside her, the ever-dapper Rupert Hollingsworth

managed a smile. "Sure is crowded. Mind if Miss Crawford and I sit with you?"

Against his better judgment, John started to shift, but Dottie put out a hand.

"I'm sorry," she said with a pleasant smile, "but with the baby it's best not to introduce strangers. He's already been fussy. As you said, it's very crowded."

As if to back up her story, Peter began whimpering, his little face clouding.

Caroline took a step back. "I'm sure there's room elsewhere. It's good you found someone to sit with, Mr. Wallin, but then, I suppose a widow with child can't afford to be picky."

Dottie didn't so much as stiffen as she smiled at John. "Yes, those of us of a certain maturity understand the temperament and character needed for a good husband."

With a huff, Caroline stalked off to find more congenial seating.

"That's twice you've stood up for me," John pointed out to Dottie. "Much more of that, and people will start to talk."

Dottie tossed her head. "Let them talk. You've done nothing but help me. It's about time I returned the favor."

A loud bang echoed through the building, and Peter started. Arthur Denny set down the lid his wife had given him. "Everybody working hard?" the railway president asked, glancing around the room as everyone settled down.

Cries of "Yes, sir" and "You bet" echoed around them.

"I want you to know how much I appreciate it," he

continued. "This railroad will prove to the territory, to the country and, dare I say it, to the world that the people of Seattle are to be reckoned with."

Cheers broke out all around. James waved his hat in the air. Peter started laughing, setting Dottie to smiling.

The gentleman wasn't finished. He went on for another quarter hour, extolling the virtues of Seattle, her people and her future. He was followed by an even longer speech from Orange Jacobs, Chief Justice of the territory's Supreme Court. Peter began dozing in Dottie's arms. John wouldn't have minded laying his head down, either.

Finally, Mayor Yesler came to the edge of the platform. He'd put his coat back on and stood for a moment, gazing out at the crowd, hands gripping his lapels. John resigned himself to yet another speech.

"It's time to quit fooling," Yesler drawled, "and get to work." He jumped down from the platform and led the way back outside.

John rose and offered his hand to Dottie to help her rise. Peter opened a sleepy eye and smiled at him.

"How much longer will this go on?" Dottie asked with a frown.

"Probably until sundown," John told her. "Will you be all right?"

She glanced down at Peter. "I will if he will."

Mrs. Denny strolled up to them. "Mr. Wallin, I was introduced to your friend Mrs. Tyrrell this morning. Such a sweet lady and a dear child. I hope I will hear something encouraging from you soon."

John glanced at Dottie in surprise, but Mrs. Denny was already turning her way. "We just learned that the

CC Perkins was stuck on the tide flats. The captain couldn't move her until the water rose. We expect more than one hundred hungry people any moment. Dare I ask you to stay and help, dear?"

"Of course," Dottie said.

John could see the latecomers now, trickling in at first, then pouring through the door. He recognized Weinclef, face red in obvious embarrassment that he had been so tardy, the owner of the livery stable and the newcomer, Frank Reynolds. He turned to Dottie to find her once more ashen.

What had happened to frighten her so?

Chapter Seventeen

Dottie barely heard John say her name. All she could do was stare past the wide-open door of the mill at the man standing just outside. That rain-slickened hair and the more common coat could not disguise her false husband. Just seeing him made her feel as if the walls of the mill had crashed down upon her.

She clutched John's arm. "I must leave. Please don't ask me to explain. I have to go back to Wallin Landing. Now."

John frowned at her, and she thought he would protest, but he nodded. "Very well. I'll fetch the wagon. Do you want to wait here or come with me?"

Better in the mill, where she could hide among the women, than out there with Frank.

"I'll wait here," she told him. "Only please hurry."

He squeezed her arm in support and strode out the door.

But Frank intercepted him. She thought John would brush him off, perhaps point him toward whatever

Frank was seeking. But they stood a moment talking. Talking! As if they were acquaintances.

She swayed on her feet. What had she done? Had she placed her faith in a man who was Frank's friend?

Disgust at her own naïveté and fear mingled, clutching at her stomach. She couldn't seem to tear her eyes away from the two men, as if by looking she could somehow keep them from seeing her and Peter.

Suddenly Frank glanced her way. Dottie whirled, set her back to him and darted in among the women serving those who had come from the ship. Shifting Peter closer, she took up a serving fork and began passing out slices of ham. The women on either side nodded approvingly.

The action made her breath come easier. Peter gazed at the people passing and cooed a greeting, raising smiles. She was safe; she was among friends. Glancing to the left, she spotted Beth serving up the last of the cake. Rina was helping people find places to sit and eat. Catherine offered blankets to those who had been soaked in the rain. What had John said? All she had to do was cry out, and someone would come running.

But would they still come if they knew the truth about Frank and Peter?

Would John even speak to her if he knew the secret she'd been hiding?

Her hand was trembling on the fork again. As if he sensed her concerns, Peter began fussing, twisting in her arms and tugging at his ear.

The woman next to her touched her hand, making Dottie jump. Her coworker's smile was kind. "Go see to him. I can serve the rest."

"Thank you," Dottie said, handing her the fork. She eased herself deeper into the building to the far wall, where she could keep an eye on the door.

Both Frank and John had gone from the opening, but she couldn't shake the memory of the two of them together. How could they know each other? Frank had traveled for work, but she never thought he'd journeyed as far as Seattle.

She forced herself to draw in a breath even as she rocked Peter. Her son hiccupped back a sob and sucked on his fist. If only she could calm herself so easily.

What if John wasn't the man she thought he was? What if she'd been mistaken yet again?

What if she'd entrusted her future to a monster?

No!

She nearly stamped her foot. She was tired of living in fear, always looking over her shoulder. Wasn't that what had driven her from Cincinnati in the first place? She refused to give in this time.

She had known Peter's father so little that it had taken a stranger in the form of Frank's wife to show her the truth of his character. She didn't need someone else to tell her about John's character. She'd seen it firsthand, in the way he treated her and Peter, the way he helped his family and neighbors. He was her noble knight. He would do nothing to hurt her or her son. She had to have faith in him.

As if just as pressed by the crowd, a pretty brunette with rosy lips moved closer with a smile, a plate of food in one hand.

"Thank you so much for being willing to feed us so late," she said, taking up a fork to pick at the ham.

"I'm sure you were ready to clean up." She must have caught sight of Peter, for she giggled. "You and your helper, I see."

Dottie managed a smile. "I'm sorry. I'm not much use, and I can't stay."

"That's all right," the woman said. "I don't know how long I'll stay, either. I'm really not sure why my husband insisted that we come. He isn't a laborer."

"Neither is mine, dear," another woman said, bustling past with dirty plates in her arms. "But every man and woman in Seattle must contribute today."

The brunette smiled in her wake. "That's probably true, but I think my husband and I can be excused. We've only been in Seattle a week." She turned to Dottie again. "We just moved here from San Francisco."

She paused as if waiting for Dottie to introduce herself, but Dottie didn't dare offer her name, not when Frank could wander into the building at any moment. "I haven't lived in Seattle long, either," she said instead.

"Mrs. Reynolds!"

Dottie gasped at the name, heart thundering in her chest. But the brunette turned toward the voice. An older woman with a feathered hat wilting from the rain came up to them.

"I'm very glad to see you here, my dear," she said to the brunette. "I was just telling your charming husband that he would do well to assist the mayor's work gang. Mr. Yesler appreciates a man with Mr. Reynolds's ambitions."

Dottie felt as if the ground was tilting up toward her. Another Mrs. Reynolds? It couldn't be!

The brunette simpered. "My Frank is going places.

That's one of the reasons I married him. I can't believe it was only a month ago. I feel as if I've known him forever."

Or not at all.

Dottie cuddled Peter closer. She had to think. It was possible Frank had finally divorced his first wife, but Dottie was number two and that made this poor woman number three. Like Dottie, she was building her future on mist. Yet how could Dottie warn her without revealing herself and risking Peter?

Frank had threatened her about what would happen if she ever told anyone else. She'd thought he'd been trying to protect his reputation, his business connections in Cincinnati. If he'd been angry she might jeopardize them, how much angrier would he be if she told his latest victim the truth?

Yet how could she live with herself if she didn't at least try to save the new Mrs. Reynolds from the same fate?

Out of the corner of her eye, she spotted John coming through the crowd. It was now or never. Making up her mind, she leaned forward and touched the woman's arm.

"There is something you must know about your husband, Mrs. Reynolds. Go to the Pastry Emporium tomorrow afternoon for a message. Go alone. It's very important."

She frowned at Dottie's hand. "My husband? What do you mean?" Her gaze, dark and troubled, met Dottie's. "Do you know my Frank?"

"To my sorrow," Dottie said, releasing her and backing away. "Please, go to the Emporium, ask for a message. It will explain all." She turned and ran to meet John.

* * *

John had never seen Dottie like this, eyes wide, face pale and steps jerky. They'd been having a perfectly fine day, despite his original misgivings about the event. She seemed to be making friends, enjoying serving with the other women. And then panic had set in. She was so fearful, he half expected to see a ravenous wolf on her heels. Jiggled in her arms, even Peter frowned. But before John could ask her the trouble, Dottie seized his arm and tugged him out of the mill.

The rain had stopped again, though the clouds hung low over the area. She kept herself on John's right, though she glanced beyond him. Once again, he tried to see what had so concerned her, but he didn't notice anything that seemed out of the ordinary, unless one counted the likes of Frank Reynolds grubbing plants out of the mud alongside Henry Yesler.

Dottie started resolutely toward a row of wagons, but John pulled her up short.

"This way," he said, nodding toward a cart at the side of the clearing, where two horses waited in the traces. "My wagon was needed. This cart belongs to Mr. Blaycock. He'll get a ride home with James and Rina. I told my brother to let Beth and the others know where we'd gone."

She bundled Peter close and accepted John's help to climb into the seat. But his touch only raised a shiver in her. He felt it along his hand. Trying not to feel defeated, he went around to climb up beside her.

Dottie sat with her face averted as he started back toward Seattle. She clung to Peter as if afraid he'd be taken from her. The last stragglers were just reaching the work site, calling out jokingly that John and Dottie were going the wrong way. Then the trees closed around the wagon, and they were alone.

"Thank you," she said in the quiet. "I realize it would probably have been advantageous for you to be seen working among Seattle's luminaries."

He shifted on the bench. "No advantage that I can see. I'm not trying to impress the mayor or his cronies. If Henry Yesler doesn't know he can count on the Wallins by now, he never will. Drew's been supplying him with timber for ten years." He glanced at Dottie. "I'm more concerned about you. What happened back there?"

She dropped her gaze to Peter, who was nestled in her arms and watching her as closely as John was. "With the crowd coming in from the boat, there were too many people for me to feel comfortable with Peter. I might have been jostled and dropped him, and I certainly couldn't see to his needs easily with so many around. I should have realized that might be the case and stayed back with Nora and Simon, but I never dreamed there'd be so many people."

That seemed logical. It had been a messy scene. Men unused to working with picks and axes could harm themselves and others as they flung the tools about. But Dottie had largely stayed with the other ladies in the mill, where she'd find nothing more risky than a badly canned jar of peaches, exploding pickles notwithstanding. So why insist on leaving? If someone had accosted her or belittled her, he was certain his sister would have brought them to task if Dottie didn't feel comfortable sticking up for herself.

"I never dreamed Seattle had so many people," John

assured her. "They must have come from the north and east as well, as far as the coal fields by Lake Washington."

She perked up. "Do you think there were people from outside Seattle, then?"

John shrugged. "I've never met half the people who were working, that's for sure, and I thought I knew most of the people in the area."

She took a deep breath, as if he'd somehow alleviated her concerns. "In any event, I'm sorry you had to leave." She cast him a quick glance. "I noticed you talking with your friend."

He frowned, trying to think who she meant. "Friend?"

Now she was watching him, as if judging what he would say. "The dark-haired fellow with the solid chin. He came with the crowd from the boat."

John relaxed. "Oh, Frank Reynolds. I met him in town the other day. He's new to the area."

She licked her lips. "Is he planning to live here?"

The comment sounded casual, but the stiff way she held herself told him it wasn't. "I think so. He just moved up from San Francisco. He was looking for work."

"And did he find any?"

Again, he felt the undercurrent in the question. "Not yet, or I don't think he'd be out working in the rain. Mr. Weinclef at Kelloggs' suggested the coal fields. Reynolds didn't seem too keen on that."

If possible, she sat even stiffer. "Then he's determined to stay in town."

Why did she care? "I suppose. Did he say something to you after I left, Dottie?"

"No, no." She took Peter's hand, held it in her own while her son studied their joined fingers. "I was just curious what the two of you found to discuss. Did he ask you any questions about people in the area, perhaps an old acquaintance?"

An ache was starting inside him. He was fairly sure Beth would have said that a woman only asked such questions when she was interested in a fellow. He'd thought he'd won Dottie's heart, but perhaps he'd been mistaken again. Likely Frank Reynolds would be considered handsome with his dark wavy hair and confident manner. And he certainly had the ambition to get ahead in this world.

"He never asked after friends in my hearing," John said, slapping the reins so that the horses picked up their pace. "I'm not sure he has any friends in Seattle."

He nearly winced at the tone that had crept into his voice. There he went again, feeling jealous, and why? Didn't Dottie deserve the best? Didn't he want the best for her and Peter?

Didn't he love her that much?

He drew in a breath. *Are You smiling, Lord? Here I thought I'd hidden my heart. You knew better. Beth may think she brought Dottie out to marry me, but I see Your hand in this. It seems I'm meant to protect her, provide for her, encourage her, regardless of whether she loves me in return. I'm here to be her hero, and that's what heroes do, put the needs of others before their own.*

Peace and surety flowed from the prayer. He slowed the horses, glanced Dottie's way again. Her head remained bowed, her shoulders slumped, as if she carried a burden too great for her. He could help.

"Frank Reynolds is going places, no doubt about that," he told her, careful to keep his tone light. "But, Dottie, if you're considering him for a suitor, I'd advise against it. He doesn't seem to hold a very high opinion of women. I don't think he'd make you a good husband."

Dottie's head came up, and she started laughing. The release shook her chest, brought tears to her eyes. The force of it startled Peter, who blinked and altered between a frown and a smile, as if he wasn't sure of her mood. Truth be told, neither was John.

"Oh, John," she said, eyes shining, "you needn't worry. I have absolutely no interest in marrying Frank Reynolds."

Relief washed over him, cleaner than a spring rain. "Well, good."

She chuckled. "In fact, I don't think much of Mr. Reynolds's future in Seattle if even the kind Mr. Wallin has taken him in dislike."

"He'll survive without my endorsement," John said, guiding the horses around a bend in the road, feeling as if the air tasted sweeter than it had a few minutes ago. "In fact, he appears to be busy ingratiating himself with all the right people. Very likely he'll be running for government office a year from now."

She sobered. "That's what concerns me."

She obviously didn't like the fellow. Why the questions, then? Simon would have blurted out his concerns. Drew would have demanded answers. James would have teased and cajoled until she told him the truth. But this time, John thought his way was better.

"I'm sorry he frightened you," he said.

She stiffened again. "Fr-fr-frightened?"

If she hadn't been before, she was now. Why? She'd said she hadn't even talked with the man.

"At the picnic," he clarified as gently as he could. "Something frightened you, made you want to flee. I'm guessing it was Frank Reynolds."

She pressed her lips together as if to keep from saying a word.

"I hope you know you can trust me, Dottie," he said as he sighted the town through the trees. "I won't let anything happen to you. If Frank Reynolds or anyone else has given you cause for concern, tell me, and I'll see the matter settled."

She shook her head, tipping the blue velvet hat on her curls. Once more, he could feel her distress, see it in the tears pooling in her lavender eyes. In her arms, Peter wiggled, face clouding, as if he felt his mother's pain, too.

"Forgive me, Dottie," John said. "Whatever happened at the mill, I didn't mean to compound the problem by pressing you over it. But I can't help you if I don't know what I'm fighting."

"It's not in you to fight," she said with a watery smile. "So let's just drop the matter. Would you like to stop at the Pastry Emporium for a cookie? My treat."

Was he a child she had to coddle? Frustration pushed up inside him. He refused to take it out on her.

"I believe Maddie closed up shop for the picnic. You'll probably find most of the town empty."

Once more, she slumped. He couldn't conceive she was that disappointed about missing out on a sweet. He almost relented, but it turned out he was right. Seattle looked abandoned as they drove through, the streets empty and silent, the businesses closed. Some of Sheriff Atkins's men were patrolling, and John nodded his thanks for their efforts to safeguard the community.

Dottie remained silent as they reached the far side of town and started toward Wallin Landing. John racked his mind for a way to break through the wall she had erected. Peter slumbered in her arms, head heavy. John's heart felt just as heavy.

"I love you, Dottie Tyrrell," he murmured. "I wish I could convince you of that."

She swiveled, eyes wide, mouth open in an O of surprise, and he waited for her to tell him he wasn't the man for her after all.

"I love you, too, John Wallin," she said, her voice hinting of more tears to come. "You are a fine and noble man. I never imagined there was anyone left in the world like you. That's why I have to tell you the truth about why I came to Seattle, and why I must leave."

Chapter Eighteen

Dottie felt as if her insides were on fire. She'd meant what she'd said to John—she loved him. How could she fail to fall in love with a man so gentle, so kind? Her heart seemed to heal a little more every time he was near.

And, loving him, she had to tell him everything, even if her explanation cost her his love. He deserved the truth. She was merely glad Peter had fallen asleep, so he wouldn't see her disgrace.

"I met Frank Reynolds in Cincinnati," she said. Oh, but her voice sounded so soft, so scared. No more. She raised her head and took a breath before plunging ahead with a firmer tone. "My family thought he was the right man for me, and I began to hope so, too. You must have seen how charming he can be."

He shifted on the bench, and she reached out a hand to touch his arm.

"Please believe me, John. Life had seemed empty since the day my parents died. Frank made me feel valued, loved. When he proposed, I happily agreed to marry him."

He sucked in a breath. "But I thought your husband was dead."

"Dead to me," she said, trying not to squirm under the worried look he shot her. "You see, though Frank is Peter's father, he was never truly my husband."

His brows tightened. "I don't understand."

"Neither did I, at first. Why would I doubt him? He took me out of town to a darling country inn for the wedding ceremony, just the two of us with a minister I'd never met and my aunt and uncle as witnesses. I thought it was so romantic at the time. Later, I realized it was the only way for him to convince me we were wed. If he'd tried to marry me in Cincinnati, someone might have realized he already had a wife."

John reined in the horses, brought the cart to a stop at the side of the road.

"Frank Reynolds married you when he already had a living wife?" His face was harder than she'd ever seen. Would she finally witness John Wallin angry? A shame she had more to confess.

"I didn't know he was already married, John. I honored my vows." She hung her head. "But he didn't."

She risked a glance in his direction. His jaw had tightened, and he gazed out toward the road ahead. She felt as if someone had shot her in the chest.

"What happened?" he asked.

The pain of remembering wasn't nearly as bad as the thought of hurting John.

"His true wife showed up at my door," Dottie explained. "I was stunned, hurt, humiliated. I vowed to have nothing more to do with him. But he wouldn't let me go so easily. He threatened retaliation if I ever told anyone about my situation."

His hand moved as if he meant to reach out to her, but his body remained stiff. "Did you go to the authorities?"

Dottie shook her head. "I was too embarrassed to tell them, even if I hadn't feared what Frank threatened. Then I learned I was carrying Peter. I was so sick, in heart, in body. I couldn't tell Beth the truth in my letters. I thought surely I'd lose the baby and, to my shame, at times I thought that might be a good thing."

He was so still he could have been carved from the wood his family logged. Then he turned to her, and she could see her pain shining in his eyes. "Frank Reynolds violated your trust," he told her, voice gentle. "He took advantage of a nature I suspect was far more trusting then. You are not to blame."

She gazed at him a moment, feeling she had been lost in the desert and offered a cool cup of water. "Don't you understand? I wasn't married when Peter was born. I let you believe a lie."

He winced as if she had struck him. "I was afraid I wasn't enough of a man that you could trust me, Dottie, but I'm beginning to understand why trusting anyone had to have been hard."

Dottie sighed. "I can't even trust myself sometimes. I see so many things about Frank and our so-called marriage I should have questioned."

His smile was soft. "Amazing what more we can see looking back. But God didn't give us eyes in the back of our heads. Our eyes, like our feet, face forward, toward the future. And that's what you did by answering Beth's advertisement."

She knew her trust was growing, for she only felt relief at his response. It was as if her noble knight had somehow taken the pain onto himself. Even her breath came easier.

"I wanted a better future. But as soon as I responded to the advertisement, I knew I shouldn't have. What did I have to offer a husband? My heart was shattered, my body ill. Yet Beth's letters were so encouraging, so normal, that I found myself daring to dream. And then Peter was born, and I knew I had to try, for him." She bent and pressed a kiss to her son's head.

John wrapped the reins around the brake and turned to her, opening his arms. She leaned into his embrace. The warmth, the strength of him, surrounded her. Her head against his chest, she closed her eyes a moment and allowed herself to be cherished.

"You don't have to be afraid anymore," he murmured against her hair. "You're not alone. I won't let Frank Reynolds hurt you. I can see why it was important to protect Peter. Was Reynolds angry when you told him he had a son?"

She swallowed, unable to look at him. "I never told him. He still doesn't know."

John leaned back to eye her. There was no censure in the look, only confusion. "Did he see you with Peter today?"

"I don't think so. But that's why I had to leave the picnic, John. Frank can never know about Peter. I don't want him anywhere near me or my son."

Now his face sagged, as if she'd wounded him anew.

"But, Dottie, surely even someone like Frank deserves to know he has a child."

Guilt tugged. She pushed it back. "That's not the issue. If Frank learns about Peter and decides he wants to raise my son as his own, he could take me to court. A father's preferences always prevail over a mother's."

"Even if the father is a bigamist?" he challenged.

She shuddered. "He may not be a bigamist. Perhaps he learned his lesson with me. Perhaps he divorced his first wife to marry the one he brought with him to Seattle."

John stared at her. "He brought a wife with him? *Another* wife?"

Dottie nodded, throat tight. "I met her today. She's so happy, John, so much in love. I couldn't stand by and see another life ruined. I told her to go to the Pastry Emporium tomorrow afternoon. I thought I could leave her a note, explain the situation so she can protect herself. That's why I wanted to stop there on the way back from the picnic."

He ran a hand up her arm. "Even though it might have endangered you, you thought of her needs first."

She could not see herself as brightly as he did, not yet. "Well, perhaps second," she acknowledged with a glance down to her sleeping son. Then she met John's gaze again. "But after I warn her, I must leave Seattle. I can't risk that Frank might learn about Peter and claim his fatherly rights."

"I still think the court will take a dim view of the situation," John insisted. "Bigamy is against the law. He could well go to jail."

"Not if he claims we never wed. He held the marriage certificate, for safekeeping, he told me. I have no idea whether my aunt and uncle would stand by me. He could easily say I was the one who seduced him. He threatened as much." She shuddered again. "Oh, John, sometimes I despair of the woman I was."

He took her hand. "And anyone who has met you here in Seattle can only praise the woman you've become. You're a good mother. You try to do what's right. Don't let Frank chase you away from where you belong."

She had once. Did she have the strength to fight him off this time? She stroked Peter's silky hair. "I don't know what's right anymore."

"Stand your ground," John told her. "My family and I will support you. We won't let Reynolds win."

He looked so determined, with his lips tight and his eyes snapping fire. He believed in her, would likely do anything to protect her. But was it right to put John between her and Frank? Who knew how Frank would react if he found her in Seattle. She'd feared for Peter, and now she feared for John. What would her gentle suitor do when faced with Frank's evil?

"You don't understand," she said. "He can appear friendly, kind even, while all the time he's playing his own game. When I told him we were through, he was violent. I can't inflict him on you, John."

He took her by the shoulders. "You're not putting a burden on me, Dottie. I'm taking it with my own hands. I will stand beside you no matter what happens. I hope you've come to see that I'm a man you can count on."

Tears were starting to fall. She wanted to trust him so badly. If only she could put her fears away, once and for all. "Oh, John, I hate pulling you into this mess."

His smile brushed her heart so softly she was certain

she could feel it mending some more. "But together, we'll sort out the mess. We can find a way to make a future for you and Peter."

Hope bubbled up inside her. "I want to stay in Seattle, but if anything should happen to Peter, I would never forgive myself."

He released her shoulders to take her hand in his once more. "Trust me, Dottie. I won't let anything happen to you or Peter. Let me take you home, where I know you two will be protected. Then I'll ride back and speak to the sheriff. Frank Reynolds may have finally married one wife too many."

John took up the reins and called to the horses, determination building inside him. Reynolds was a worm, the lowest of the low. Just the thought of how he'd used Dottie lit a fire inside John that he doubted would be quenched anytime soon. She'd been alone, friendless, and Reynolds had preyed on her dreams. John may have been called the peacemaker, but all he could think about was going to war.

Beside him, Dottie looked drained, her face pale under her jaunty blue hat. Yet the smile she gave him offered hope, hope that she could be free of Reynolds, hope that she and Peter could have a future here. When she leaned over and put her head on his shoulder, he wrapped an arm about her. He told himself it was to keep her and Peter safe on the bench, but he knew he had another reason. He wanted to hold her, protect her. He wanted to be her husband.

Her real husband. Whatever Reynolds had tried to be, it was never that. Husbands and wives shared all their lives. They didn't keep parts hidden. They didn't lie about their intentions. And they didn't abandon each other in their time of need.

For richer, for poorer, in sickness and in health.

He'd heard Drew, Simon and James take those vows. He saw them live out the words every day. That was the kind of husband Dottie deserved. That was the kind of husband he would be. Now he just had to convince her of that.

He kept her close the remainder of the drive, sorting through options in his mind. But when he passed the drive to his house and headed for the main cabin, Dottie protested.

"Please, John, I can't face Nora and Simon right now." Her look was nearly as scrunched as Peter's when he was about to start crying.

"You need to be around people," John told her. "I always wondered why you were so worried about staying alone at my house. You kept expecting Reynolds, didn't you?"

She sighed, rocking Peter, who was just starting to wake by the way his little face wiggled. "Yes. I heard my first week here from an old friend in Cincinnati that he had headed west. But I hoped he wouldn't come all the way to Seattle."

"Seattle has a way of drawing people," he said as they rolled into the clearing. "Good and bad. It promises a new future. And I mean to give it to you and Peter, Dottie."

Her smile strengthened his resolve. He set the brake, then came around to help her down.

The yard was quiet, but he could see faces lined up

at the window of the main house. His nieces and nephews must have heard the sound of the horses coming in. Now the little heads disappeared, and the door opened. The oldest children spilled out on the porch, Simon just behind them.

"Did you build the railroad?" James's oldest son, Seth, asked, fairly hopping on the planks.

"All the way over the mountains?" His cousin Lars, Simon's oldest, wanted to know.

"When may we ride on the train?" Victoria, James's daughter, asked, steps as regal as her mother's, but eyes bright.

"I'm not sure how far they cleared today," John told them as he led Dottie and Peter up to the porch. "But I don't think it was much beyond the edge of Seattle. And no tracks were laid, so no train for now."

They all looked disappointed.

"Where's Mama?" Drew's son Davy asked, gazing up at him with a trembling lip.

"Not far behind us, sweetheart," Dottie assured him with a smile.

John escorted Dottie and Peter into the house, meeting Simon's frown with one of his own before his brother went to see to the horses. The children's smiles, the curious questions and the games Nora initiated seemed to put Dottie at ease. Peter watched the children as they passed, reached out hands to touch. Most of John's nieces and nephews had had to deal with siblings or cousins younger than them, so they were careful in how they dealt with the baby.

"He has pretty eyes," Mary, Drew's daughter, told Dottie. She smiled. "You have pretty eyes, too."

"Thank you," Dottie said. "And you have your mother's eyes. I can see that."

They had been in the main house only about an hour, helping Simon and Nora with the children, when Drew and the others returned. John heard the wagons coming in. Dottie stiffened.

"It's all right," he assured her. "We'll face this together, remember?"

She nodded, and he went out onto the porch, even as the children lined up at the window.

Catherine's head was on Drew's shoulder, and Rina was yawning as James pulled up the team. Mr. Blaycock went to take charge of his cart and horses. Tom and Dickie climbed down and loped for the house. Harry sauntered past with a nod to John.

"See you couldn't make it through a day of work," he gibed. "Did Dottie have to drive you home to rest?"

John bit his cheek to keep from responding.

"Cleared a whole mile of track," Harry continued, as if he'd done all the work himself. "The mayor and his like were impressed."

Yesler probably hadn't even noticed Harry in the crowd, and if he had, John couldn't have cared less.

"They ate more than a mile of food as well," Beth countered as she climbed down from the wagon. "I don't want to see another piece of chicken as long as I live."

"And the fact that Beth ended after a mere two sentences should tell you how tired she is," James added with a grin. He pressed a hand to his back. "I worked hard enough for three days. I'm taking tomorrow off."

"You always take Saturdays off," Rina reminded him with a fond smile.

"I know you're all tired," John said, ignoring Harry's snort of an answer. "But Dottie and I would like to talk to you before you head for your beds. It's important."

Beth brightened. "Oh, John, did you finally propose?" Before he could answer, she threw her arms around him. "Thank you, thank you, for giving me another sister, a friend and a nephew."

John disengaged, conscious of Harry's scowl behind her. "Congratulations are premature. Something's happened, and I need your help."

"Of course," Harry grumbled.

Drew towered over his foreman. "When Wallin Landing's main helper asks for help, we oblige," he said.

Beth cast a longing glance toward the path to her cabin, but she nodded. "All right, then, ladies, gather in the crockery, gentlemen, see to the horses and wagons. We'll gather in the parlor in a quarter hour."

As usual, no one argued with his sister. The mothers headed for the house, where squeals and laughter greeted them, while the fathers and loggers did as she had bid. John took his sister aside.

"Dottie is going to need a friend," he said. "Would you be willing to move into my house to help her for a while?"

Beth frowned. "Of course. But, John, is it truly so bad she must have company?"

"I'm not sure," John told her. "But I'd like to be ready."

As it was, it took a few minutes to get everyone settled. Nora agreed to continue watching the older children, taking them into the kitchen for a snack while the youngest remained with their parents. Even Tom, Dickie and Harry joined the family as everyone else gathered on chairs and benches.

Dottie was soothing Peter in Ma's old bentwood rocker, face troubled, as John leaned closer.

"I'll explain, if you'd like," he offered, wanting only to shield her from the pain that seemed to be radiating from her body.

She drew in a breath, and for a moment he thought she'd agree. Then she raised her chin.

"No," she murmured. "This is something I must do for myself. Just stand beside me, John, for I don't know whether any of them can react as kindly as you did to the story."

Chapter Nineteen

Dottie handed Peter to John, afraid she might squeeze her son too tight in her concern. Around her, voices went silent, bodies stilled. They were all looking at her. Those who knew her only a little, like John's brothers, were frowning for the most part, as if wondering what she would say. Tom and Harry had their arms crossed over their chests, and Dickie was wringing his hands. Those who knew her better, like Beth, leaned forward, eyes bright with trust. Would she see that look dimmed?

She stood taller. Her path had led her to Wallin Landing. Now it was time to see whether she'd be welcome to stay.

"I must ask your forgiveness," she said, and her voice echoed against the beams overhead. "I allowed you all to believe something that wasn't true. I'm not a widow. I've never been married."

"But she has a child," Dickie protested to Tom, who elbowed him.

Shame swept over her. "I thought I was married at the time, but I also believed something that wasn't true. The man I thought I'd married was already married."

She heard an intake of breath, and she wasn't sure if it came from Beth, Catherine or Rina. The trio wore stormy faces now, and she nearly faltered.

John touched her arm, and she met his gaze. In the expanse of green, she saw faith and confidence. He nodded as if encouraging her to continue. Cradled in John's arm, Peter beamed at her as if proud of her no matter what she did.

Dottie faced his family once more. "I came west to make a new life for me and Peter. I intended to start fresh, bringing with us nothing of the darkness that had been our lives. Only today, I realized Peter's father has moved to Seattle. I saw him at the picnic."

Murmurs ran through the group, and Drew and Catherine exchanged glances.

"He's what chased you off?" James asked. "Why you wanted to leave early?"

Dottie nodded. "I wasn't sure it was wise for us both to be in the area."

Harry stepped forward, dusting his hands together. "That's easily settled. We'll run him out of town on a rail."

Dickie and Tom nodded their agreement, pushing forward as well. Even after she'd refused their suit, they were ready to rally to her side. As if he knew the emotions that bubbled up inside her, John gripped her hand and gave it a squeeze.

"Bit of a problem," James said. "We don't have any rails. We haven't finished building the railway yet."

Rina frowned him into silence.

"My first thought was to leave," Dottie admitted. "That's what I did in Cincinnati." She looked to John and Peter. "John convinced me a future here is worth fighting for."

"A shame Mr. Wallin isn't known for fighting," Harry drawled.

"On the contrary." Drew rose and leveled a look at his foreman. "John has ever fought for all of us to do what is right."

Simon stood as well. "It took courage to tell us this. Thank you, Dottie."

He was thanking her? He could not know how his words honored her. She could feel tears starting even as James, Rina and Catherine joined Simon and Drew on their feet, children bundled in their arms.

"You are a woman of character," Rina said. "Just as John is a man of character."

Catherine nodded. "There's only one question in my mind. How can we help?"

Dottie looked from one determined face to another. She'd feared their disdain, their censure, yet they offered support. She'd forgotten what it was like to have friends in times of trouble. She'd been nearly alone in Cincinnati. Here she had people who cared. She felt as if the sun had come out after weeks of rain.

"I don't know what to say," she murmured, wiping at the tears flowing down her cheeks.

John's family converged on her then, the ladies patting her shoulder and hugging her, children laughing at the movements, gentlemen vowing support. John kept his hand on hers, the gentle pressure making her aware that the only one who mattered other than Peter was the man beside her.

"I agree with Harry," Beth declared, earning her a

surprised look from the logger. "We have to stop him. Who is he, by the way?"

Dottie squared her shoulders. "His name is Frank Reynolds."

Beth's brows shot up. "Frank Reynolds? I met a Mrs. Frank Reynolds today at the picnic."

Rina nodded. "As did I. She seemed quite in love."

Dottie felt ill at the thought. "I believe her to be his next victim."

All the women blanched.

Beth smacked her fist into her palm. "That tears it. We have to do something."

"We will," John promised her. "I intend to ride to town tomorrow morning and talk to the sheriff about arresting him."

His brothers and the loggers were nodding, but Dottie felt her stomach tightening. "Arrest him?"

John frowned. "Does that trouble you? Frank Reynolds treated you and at least two other women abominably. Jail is the least he should face."

"I know," Dottie told him. "But do you really think he would be sentenced? None of his wives will want to parade their mistakes in public. I certainly don't."

Beth rubbed Dottie's arm as if in comfort.

"I know it will be hard, Dottie," John said, his voice once more gentle, "but you are a brave woman. If you weren't, you wouldn't have left Cincinnati to start a new life with a stranger."

"I promise you, it wasn't bravery but fear that drove me."

"Then let it drive you one more time," he urged, "to see justice done."

She felt his convictions, and she knew them to be right. Frank should be stopped from hurting anyone else. And she still had a note to leave at the bakery.

"Very well," she said. "I'll come with you and swear out a complaint. That should give your sheriff enough to make further inquiries at the least."

Beth stepped closer, eyes bright with determination. "Don't go to the sheriff, John. Talk to Hart—that is, Deputy McCormick. He'll take this seriously."

Dottie wasn't sure why the lawman would react differently than his superior, but Beth obviously had faith in him, for all her protests otherwise. The plan agreed on, the Wallins and Harry, Dickie and Tom chorused their approval, and people began moving toward their own beds.

Beth patted Dottie's shoulder. "John thought you might feel better with company tonight."

"Oh, I couldn't..." Dottie began.

"You most certainly can," Beth said. "And you should. Give me a moment to collect my nightgown, and I'll move into John's house tonight."

"You think of everything," Dottie told him as his sister bustled out.

He looked down at Peter, who was slumbering in his arms as if he knew he was safe there. "Just trying to be the man you can trust at your side, Dottie."

Even having accepted her story, he could not know how hard that trust was to extend. She leaned in and kissed his cheek, feeling the scratch of a day's growth of beard against her lips. "I don't deserve you."

Dottie wasn't sure why she slept so well that night. Perhaps she was exhausted from the exertions of the day followed by her confession to John and then the Wallins and writing the note to the latest Mrs. Reynolds. Perhaps it was Peter's rhythmic breathing in his cradle beside the bed. Perhaps it was Brian curled up in a warm bundle near the foot, or Beth resting beside her.

But she rather thought it was knowing that, in John, she might finally have found someone to protect and love her.

She would have preferred to leave Peter in Beth's care the next day, but she was concerned she might be gone too long for the baby. So she bundled him up and was ready to go when John brought the wagon around that morning. He kept up a pleasant conversation as he drove her into Seattle, telling her stories of what had happened outside the mill yesterday while she and the other women had been preparing the luncheon. Peter nodded along, as if drinking in every word.

John had explained that it might take a while to track down the deputy. The sheriff and his men had to cover all of King County, from the Cascade crest to the shores of Puget Sound. But it seemed the May Day picnic had brought enough people to town that the deputy had felt inclined to stay close. They located him in a rough area not far from Yesler's mill. He turned his horse alongside the wagon and followed them back toward the business district.

On a quiet side street, Dottie told her story once more. Funny how each time seemed less daunting. Of course, Deputy McCormick was an entirely different audience from John or the Wallins. For one thing, she didn't know him well. For another, he listened intently, leaning forward in the saddle, his gunmetal-gray eyes narrowed. He was so still Dottie wasn't sure what he was thinking. John had told her the deputy had dedicated himself to protecting the citizens of the area. He'd brought down bandits, horse thieves and vandals. Surely Dottie's story wouldn't shock him.

But it concerned him more than she had expected. She saw him stiffen, heard him suck in a breath as she explained how Frank had treated her. Still, he said nothing, though she felt as if she could see thoughts winging behind his eyes. She glanced at John for guidance.

"What do you advise, Deputy?" John asked.

"Telegram," McCormick spit out, making Peter jerk in her arms, most likely at the sudden unfamiliar voice. "To the police commissioner in Cincinnati. These sorts of cases are usually tried in the area where they were committed."

Dottie's heart sank. Frank had so many friends in Cincinnati, and she had so few. He could easily sway a judge to see things his way.

"Usually," John pressed him. "But not always? What would it take to arrest and convict him here?"

McCormick rubbed the back of his hand against his chin. "It would help if Miss Tyrrell and the first wife swore out a complaint for bigamy and desertion. I can write Miss Tyrrell's for her to sign."

"Then let's send the first Mrs. Reynolds a telegram, too," John said.

Dottie shivered. Her whole future could well rest in the hands of a woman who could bear her no love. But she went with John and the deputy to the sheriff's office, gave the information to the deputy so he could send the telegrams and signed the form he offered her.

The deputy put a hand on her shoulder, then hastily withdrew it as if feeling he'd overstepped.

"You're doing the right thing, Miss Tyrrell," he told her. "Men like Reynolds must be stopped."

He was so intent, gaze drilling into hers, that she asked, "Have you had other cases like mine, Deputy?"

He took a step back. "No, ma'am, but I don't much like men who make women their victims."

It seemed John wasn't the only hero in town.

And now it was Dottie's turn. The note felt heavy in the pocket of her cape, and she knew she'd rest easier once it had been delivered. McCormick looked ready to talk further with John, so Dottie touched John's arm. "I'm going to the bakery to leave the note. Meet me there?"

He put his hand over hers. "Right behind you, I promise."

She carried Peter out of the sheriff's office.

Dottie had hoped to leave the note with Beth's friend Ciara, but another young lady with blond hair was standing behind the Pastry Emporium counter, looking decidedly bored, when Dottie entered. She brightened as Dottie approached and smiled at Peter, who waved a fist before sticking it in his mouth. The girl giggled.

"Is Ciara O'Rourke working today?" Dottie asked.

The girl nodded. "She works most days. She's earning her tuition for the Territorial University."

Dottie could hear the envy in the girl's voice. She would have liked to ask the girl about her own dreams, but it was nearly one o'clock. Mrs. Reynolds might come through the door any moment, and Dottie didn't want to be around when she read that note.

"Could I trouble you to fetch her?" Dottie asked. "I have something for her."

The girl nodded, openly curious, and disappeared through a curtained doorway behind the counter.

Alone in the bakery, Dottie pulled the note from her pocket and gazed down at her son. Peter was eyeing the scrumptious goods on display, as if unsure of their purpose.

"You wait and see," she murmured to him, free hand stroking his curls as the bell signaled the arrival of another customer and footsteps clumped closer. "One day you're going to like these all too well."

"So, that's what you're hiding," Frank said.

Dottie's head jerked up. He was standing beside her, gaze fixed on the baby in her arms.

"By the looks of it, I'd say it's old enough to be mine." He said it quietly, but there was no mistaking the anger underlying the words. "When did you plan on telling me about my child, *Mrs. Tyrrell*?"

Dottie scrambled back, bumping the counter, but he seized her arm and pulled her close, his gaze hard. "We're going out the door together, somewhere we can talk in private."

Peter began crying. Dottie rubbed his back, praying Frank didn't notice her trembling. "I'm not going anywhere with you."

His mouth tightened into a sneer. "Oh, I think you will. You'll come with me, or I'll tell the fine John Wallin just what kind of woman you are. He's the fellow you've taken up with here, I understand."

Her stomach roiled, but she couldn't give in. Who knew what he'd do to her or Peter when they were alone?

"You won't tell anyone about us," she said, "because the story reflects worse on you than it does on me. And you wouldn't want your new wife to hear about it."

He blanched, and she knew she'd scored. She took no joy in it.

"Stay away from me, Frank," she said. She yanked out of his grip, and the note she'd intended to leave his so-called wife fluttered to the floor.

Frank pounced on it.

The curtain was whisked open, and Ciara came out into the bakery. Dottie nearly ran to her side. One look at her face, and the girl's smile disappeared. She glanced back at Frank. "Is something wrong?"

Behind Dottie, Frank's voice was chipper. "Not at all. Just making acquaintances. Young lady, would you happen to know the whereabouts of the owner of this fine establishment? I'd like to make him a business proposal."

"My sister owns the bakery," Ciara told him. "She's out this morning. Perhaps I could take your card."

"No need," he said. "I'll come back another time. Seattle will be my home now. I intend to establish deep roots. Good day, Mrs. Tyrrell."

Dottie refused to look at him as he exited. Even the sound of the bell made her twitch.

"You wanted to speak to me, Mrs. Tyrrell?" Ciara asked.

Dottie drew in a breath. "Yes. The man who just left is a liar. Tell your sister never to do business with him."

Ciara's eyes widened. "I certainly will. Thank you for warning me."

The bell tinkled again, and Dottie hunched in on

herself, sheltering Peter. If Frank had come back, he would find her ready to fight to protect her son and the man she loved.

Something was wrong. John could see it in the way Dottie stood, shoulders bunched and arms tight. Even Ciara was frowning in concern. He came to their sides and placed a hand on Dottie's arm. She flinched back.

"Dottie?" he asked, concern rising. "Are you all right?"

At the sound of his voice, she raised her head and took a shaky breath. "Oh, John. I'm so glad it's you. Take me home, please."

He would have liked to know what had happened, but the most important thing was to put Dottie at ease. He asked Ciara to give his regards to Maddie and Michael, and led Dottie and Peter from the shop.

Out on the boardwalk, her steps were so quick that her skirts swirled around her like a river at flood stage. Peter was bouncing in her arms as if ready to run beside her. John couldn't feel so pleased.

"It's all right, Dottie," he murmured. "No one's chasing us."

She was going so fast she nearly plunged off the boards where the walk ended. John caught her arm, felt the tremor go through her.

"What happened?" he murmured.

She hesitated a moment before answering, as if struggling with her thoughts. "Frank came in the shop. His new wife must have told him about my conversation with her. He took the note. I don't know how to help her now. She still thinks she's married. She doesn't know about his first wife, or me." Suddenly she swiveled, eyes wide with panic.

"John! What if he divorced his first wife? Would that mean Frank and I are legally wed?" She looked as if she might cast up her accounts on the boardwalk.

Conscious of a dozen people moving about the street, John pulled Dottie back against the mercantile they had been passing. "I'm no lawyer, but since you said your vows while he was still married, those vows should be null and void, regardless of what he did later." He squeezed her hand. "You're free of him, Dottie. He can't claim you for his wife."

The thought did not seem to calm her. "I'm just as worried for you. He knows you're courting me, John." She looked up at him, face troubled. "You must be careful. He may think you're a threat now."

"I hope he does," John said. His voice came out hard enough that even Peter frowned. "I'd like to show him how big a threat I can be."

Dottie's eyes widened. "Why, John, I've never heard you speak so forcefully."

"Perhaps I've never felt so strongly before," he told her. "You make me want to be a hero, Dottie, something I'd never thought I'd be. I'd fight off the combined Seattle militia single-handedly if it meant keeping you and Peter safe."

She lifted a hand to his cheek, the touch soft, sweet. Sweeter still was the look in her eyes. "You weren't meant to be a fighter, John. And I'm very thankful for that."

Was she? One moment with Frank seemed to have driven any thought of protection from her mind. It seemed she still didn't trust John with her future. Perhaps it was time she realized the depths of his devotion.

To curious stares and whispered words from those passing, he took Dottie's hand and went down on one knee on the boardwalk.

"John?" she asked, obviously confused.

"Dottie Tyrrell," he said, gaze turned up to hers, "I love you. I want to spend the rest of my life with you. I want to wake in the morning at your side, spend the day helping you make your dreams come true and fall asleep with you in my arms. I want to be your friend, your husband and Peter's father. I will honor and cherish you all the days of my life. Will you marry me?"

He thought she might hesitate again, perhaps even protest. Instead, the response seemed to fly from the deepest recesses of her heart.

"Yes." She started as if surprised by the vehemence of the word, then plunged on while Peter gazed up at her raptly. "Yes, John, I will marry you. I love you, too. You make me believe a happy future is possible. You are everything I could have asked for in a husband."

He heard applause and realized the people nearest to them were congratulating them. Men were grinning, ladies were teary-eyed. One fellow clasped both hands over his head in a sign of victory.

Now they just had to claim victory over Dottie's past for Peter's future.

Chapter Twenty

The next few days would have been the best of John's life, if it hadn't been for the lingering threat of Frank Reynolds. Beth remained at John's house, sleeping with Dottie to satisfy propriety so John could bed down in the loft and be on hand if Dottie needed him. He and Dottie spent every moment together, except when he had to tend the animals or she had to feed Peter. They talked about their wedding, the library they both wanted to build and the normal schedule for sowing and harvest. If there were moments she gazed out the window with a troubled frown, he understood. There were moments he still feared he would never be worthy of her love.

Still, he could picture other, more tender moments together—reading by the fire, walking by the lake, taking the pins from her hair and letting the gold spill through his fingers.

He could hardly wait.

It was Thursday before he spotted the deputy coming up the road. Dottie and Beth had been playing with

Peter on the porch. Now his sister scooped up the baby and headed inside, as if determined to avoid speaking with McCormick. John and Dottie went to meet the lawman.

McCormick handed John a telegram, then swung down from the saddle.

Dottie craned her neck to see over John's arm as he opened the note. He didn't know whether to sag with relief or shout for joy at the words.

"The first Mrs. Reynolds has agreed to swear out a complaint for abandonment and bigamy against Frank Reynolds," he told the deputy. "Does that give you what you need to arrest him?"

McCormick's smile was grim. "It sure does. But the town's still swollen with newcomers and rail workers. We could use another deputy." He eyed John.

A deputy? Now, that was a hero, someone Dottie could look up to. John took a step forward. "I'm your man. Nothing would make me happier than to know Reynolds was behind bars."

Beside him, Dottie stiffened. She put a hand on his arm as if to keep him at her side. "No, John, you've done enough. I wouldn't want anything to happen to you."

John covered her hand with his, smiled down into those lavender eyes. "I need to see this through, Dottie. For you and for Peter." And for himself.

She searched his face, as if struggling with her own concerns, then nodded. "Very well. I trust you to do the job and come home safe."

She trusted him? It was such an easy thing to say for his family, but how he'd longed to hear the words from her. Dottie trusted him. The thought kept going through his mind as he saddled his horse and headed for Seattle with McCormick. Dottie trusted him at last. He had won her heart.

Still, the ride back to Seattle seemed longer than John remembered. Perhaps it was his eagerness to have things over and done so he and Dottie could get on with their lives. Perhaps it was the silence from his riding partner. McCormick's gaze kept moving, as if suspecting threats from every quarter, but his mouth remained mostly shut. John tried several gambits to start conversation only to be answered with monosyllables.

Finally, John asked a question that had been bothering him for some time. "By the way, Deputy, did you and my sister have a falling-out?"

McCormick's face went still. "She tell you that?"

"No," John admitted. "But I got the impression she was upset about something."

The deputy shook his head. "Nothing of any lasting import. The best thing your sister could do is choose one of the fellows chasing after her and settle down."

John chuckled. "That won't happen for a while. Sometimes I think Beth's goal is to see all her brothers married before she is." He grinned at the lawman. "And she's succeeded with me."

"I wish you and Miss Tyrrell every happiness," McCormick said, raspy voice deepening.

Was he getting emotional? No, that couldn't be. Not hard-as-nails Hart McCormick. Still, as if deep in thought, he didn't speak again until they reached the outskirts of the city.

"I checked around town," he told John as they rode onto Second Avenue. "The Reynoldses are staying at the Occidental Hotel. We'll see the sheriff first and get you deputized."

The sheriff was more than glad to deputize John. As John raised his hand and made his pledge to uphold the law, a thrill shot through him. He was doing this for Dottie and for all Frank Reynolds's victims, women who had had little voice or recourse. There was something right and good about that. He thought Pa would be pleased.

A short while later, he and Deputy McCormick reined in in front of the hotel. The whitewashed exterior was neat, and the number of wagons and horses waiting testified to the popularity of the establishment. Inside, the crowded lobby boasted polished wood floors and tufted red velvet upholstery on the furnishings.

The clerk sent a porter up to ask Frank down to the lobby.

"We need to do this quietly," John told the deputy, glancing around at the number of people coming and going. "There's no need to bring up Dottie's name."

McCormick nodded, then frowned, and John turned to see a lady returning with the porter. She had brown hair piled up behind her and wide-spaced gray eyes that now were rimmed with red. Her hands twisted a handkerchief in front of her fine gray silk gown.

"I'm Mrs. Reynolds," she told the deputy with a glance to John. "If you know something about my husband, I need to hear it."

The shadow John had felt all week hovered closer.

"We were hoping to speak to Mr. Reynolds," McCormick told her, widening his stance and hooking a thumb in his gun belt, as if ready to fight off anyone who told him otherwise. "I'm Deputy McCormick, and this is Deputy Wallin."

She glanced between them again. "Deputies? Is Frank in some kind of trouble?"

John wasn't about to explain everything where anyone might overhear. Already, several of the other guests were looking in their direction.

"We just need to ask your husband some questions, ma'am," he told her.

Her lower lip trembled. "I wish I could help you, but Frank left the hotel yesterday morning, and I haven't seen him since. I've been so worried. My friend Mrs. Maynard came to stay with me today." She blew her nose in the handkerchief.

McCormick met John's gaze, and John saw the same concern written there.

"I'll stay in Seattle, start the search," the lawman said. "You make sure Miss Tyrrell and her son are safe."

"Miss Tyrrell?" Frank's latest victim said, head coming up. "Who's Miss Tyrrell? What does she have to do with my husband?"

Her voice was rising. John could see the panic on her face. McCormick stepped back as if unsure of his response. He was a good man, but he was used to dealing with facts, logic. John had long ago learned to deal with emotions and feelings. Much as he longed to return to Dottie, he knew he couldn't leave the other Mrs. Reynolds in such fear.

He put his hand on her arm. "Would you allow me to come up to your room to explain things to you? Mrs. Maynard will vouch for me."

She drew in a breath as if gathering her strength.

"Yes, that should be appropriate." As McCormick strode for the door, John followed the woman up the stairs.

The hotel room Reynolds had arranged was far nicer than the one Beth had been able to afford for Dottie. The iron bedstead had a crimson bedspread edged with gold fringe, and two chairs and a small table sat next to a window looking out over Puget Sound.

Mrs. Maynard rose from one of the chairs as John and the other woman entered. Her easy welcome, kind smile and indefatigable energy had warmed many a heart in Seattle over the years. Like Drew's wife, she was a nurse. She had partnered her flamboyant husband, Doc Maynard, until his death last year. Her dark hair was slicked back into a bun, and her black gown had all the lace and furbelows one might expect of a wealthy widow.

"Mr. Wallin," she said with a nod. "I didn't expect to see you here."

John inclined his head. "Mrs. Maynard. I understand you're a friend of this lady's. She will need one now."

Mrs. Reynolds sank onto the opposite chair. "Why, Mr. Wallin? What do you know about Frank?"

John went to sit on the edge of the bed so he didn't tower over the pair. "I believe Mr. Reynolds said you were from San Francisco. Have you family there?"

She shook her head, fingers pleating the handkerchief. "I was a foundling. I grew up at Mt. St. Joseph Orphan Asylum and was placed into service when I grew older. When I met Frank, I was the companion of his employer's mother. He quite swept me off my feet."

The anger was burning inside him again, a coal lodged in his heart. Like Dottie, this Mrs. Reynolds had nowhere to turn, no one to protect her. Frank Reynolds chose his victims well.

"There's no easy way to say this," John told her, keeping his voice gentle. "You aren't the first woman your husband has married. You aren't even the second. And the first Mrs. Reynolds is very much alive and well, and prepared to swear out a complaint of bigamy."

She refused to believe it at first, then sobbed and railed at Frank for his betrayal. John nodded, listened, offered encouragement, but all the while he saw another woman with golden blond hair and lavender eyes in pain. Had Dottie reacted this way? She must have cried. Her heart had been torn out, spat upon. And she'd had no friends around to support her. Small wonder trust was so hard for her.

But no longer. Now she had his family for support. Now he stood beside her. She didn't have to fear any longer.

Leaving Mrs. Reynolds to Mrs. Maynard's tender care, he went for his horse and urged it out of town.

Please, Lord, protect her. Let her know that You never left her side, and I won't leave it now.

If the way out had seemed long, this ride seemed unending. It didn't matter how fast he urged the horse. The miles crawled past. Finally, he made the last climb up to the house and burst out of the trees.

Dottie, Beth and Nora were huddled on the porch. At the sight of him, Dottie broke away and ran to meet him. He reined in, leaped from the saddle and gathered her close. Thanksgiving rose in his heart.

She pulled back to search his face. "What is it, John?

You rode in so fast. Did Frank say something to concern you?"

John shook his head. "I never saw Frank. I failed you, Dottie. He left Seattle, and we don't know where he's gone."

Dottie listened to John's words, saw the anxiety on his face. Once, she would have crumpled with the fear of knowing Frank could be coming for her. No more. Now, thanks to this dear man, she knew she wasn't alone. His embrace was gentle, but she appreciated the strength in those arms—strength to lift a loaded trunk, strength to cradle a crying baby, strength to carry her burdens when her strength faltered. For the first time in a long time, she could open her heart.

"You could never fail me, John," she told him. "If Frank left Seattle, it was because he wanted to, not because of anything we did."

He released her from his embrace and took her hand to walk her back to the porch, where Nora and Beth were waiting, Peter in Beth's arms. The baby babbled a greeting.

"Reynolds left yesterday morning, according to his current wife," he explained to them all, fingers cradling Dottie's. "Deputy McCormick is searching the town."

"The poor woman," Nora said, broad face sagging in sympathy.

Dottie felt for this Mrs. Reynolds, but her concern had to be for Peter. "Then we don't know if Frank's left the area."

John shook his head, grip tightening. "He may have

caught wind of what we were planning, though I don't know how."

"If I were him," Beth said, hand protectively on Peter's head, "I'd jump aboard the first ship sailing north. Tell Deputy McCormick to check at the port, John. The shipping companies will have noted any passengers taken aboard. I imagine the same could be said for the livery stable, if Frank Reynolds bought a horse."

If only he had sailed away. If only she knew he was gone.

"Good idea," John said to his sister. "Unfortunately, there are too many places a man like Frank could hide out here."

Dottie glanced at the trees, which seemed to be closer to the house. She'd once feared Frank could be hiding nearby. It seemed he could be now. She turned to John. "Searching Seattle won't be enough."

He nodded. "Agreed, but Sheriff Atkins is low on men. The best thing we could do is find him some more."

Nora gathered her skirts and stepped forward. "I'll fetch Simon and the others. I'm sure they'll want to help."

"We'll need even more than that to search the entire area," John advised. "Tell Drew and Simon to go north, and James and I will head south. We'll meet back here in an hour with however many men we can gather."

Nora nodded and hurried off.

John turned to Dottie. "I don't like leaving you, but we both need to know Frank is somewhere he can't hurt you and Peter. Besides—" he grinned at his sister "—Beth's nearly as good a shot as I am."

"Nearly!" Beth sputtered. "You watch me, John Wallin."

He chuckled, then returned his gaze to Dottie. "Will you be all right?"

His presence drove out fear. Wasn't that what love did? Now she had to be brave even if he wasn't standing at her side.

"We'll be fine," she assured him. "But isn't there anything we can do to help?"

"Round up the ammunition," he told her, releasing her at last. "Make sure the lanterns have plenty of oil. I hope this doesn't last until sundown, but you can never tell." With a quick kiss, he made for his horse.

"Will they come, do you think?" Dottie asked, watching him head down the road.

Beth moved in beside her. "They'll have plenty of reasons to refuse. It is planting time. The weather's finally nice enough to start building. But don't worry, Dottie. They'll come when they hear John Wallin is asking."

Dottie smiled.

Beth was right. Over the next hour, men arrived on horseback, by wagon and on foot, most carrying guns. Dottie and Beth welcomed them, offered them coffee or tea while they waited. More than one congratulated Dottie on her upcoming marriage, and she couldn't help wondering if they, too, were threaded onto Beth's spool of information.

"Fine man, that John Wallin," an older farmer said, cradling his cup of coffee in his worn hands. "Fixed our roof when I was down with the influenza last year.

Wouldn't have made it through the spring rains without that."

Another man with a grizzled beard nodded. "Remember the year old man Rankin tried to raise cattle? Foolish beasts got into my corn. Would have wiped me out if John hadn't come by to help me move them into pasture."

A younger man wiped his hand over his mouth. "I won't forget when he rode to Seattle for the medicine Annie needed. I might have lost her but for him."

Dottie's heart swelled with pride just listening.

John returned shortly after with the last of his friends, head high like a knight riding into battle. Even his brothers behind him paled before the determination that rode his broad shoulders like a cape. Dottie was sure Ivanhoe had never stood as tall as John did when he stepped up onto the porch, fingers laced with hers, to address his army.

"Thank you all for coming. As you've heard, we have a criminal on the loose, a threat to this dear lady and her son, Peter. Mrs. Tyrrell and I are engaged to be married. That makes me the closest thing Peter Tyrrell has to a father. And I'm not willing to stand by while my son's in jeopardy."

Dottie felt tears gathering even as murmurs of approval ran through the crowd. Drew and Simon were nodding, and James was grinning.

"The sheriff and his men are searching town," John continued. "We're taking the outlying areas. I don't know how long the search will last."

"With us at your side, it won't be long," one of the men predicted, and the others shouted their agreement.

John smiled his thanks. "Make any last preparations you need. We leave at the quarter hour."

As the men began checking gear and mounts, John turned to Dottie. She'd been afraid for herself, afraid for Peter, concerned for the Wallin family when they'd taken her in. Now all her worries seemed to be centered on John.

Father, please protect him. I never thought I'd find love again. I can't lose him.

"You will be careful," she murmured. "Catching Frank means nothing if you're hurt in the process."

Beth must have overheard, for she tossed her head. "Frank Reynolds is no match for my brothers. I just wish I could come with you. I'd like to give him a piece of my mind."

Dottie shook her head. "I'm glad you're staying here. I don't want to worry about you, too. Who knows what Frank may do?"

"A predator cornered is at its most dangerous," John said. "Pa taught us that. But this time, Dottie, Frank Reynolds isn't the predator. He's the prey. And I won't rest until he's caught and brought to justice."

He kissed her, hard and fast, a promise of devotion. Then he was striding for his horse.

Dottie and Beth stood on the porch, watching John and his army ride down the hill. Pride warred with concern inside her.

"They'll be back soon," Beth told her. "Then we can finish planning your wedding." She linked her arm with Dottie's and led her into the house.

Dottie went to check on Peter in the cradle, where she'd put him to sleep earlier. The soft sound of his breath and the tilt of his little head spoke of peace, of security.

Please, Lord, soon!

She returned to the parlor to find that Beth had taken out her brother's rifle. John's sister did indeed try to interest Dottie in wedding planning, but the gun resting in easy reach was a constant reminder of the danger outside these walls. Dottie had a feeling she was agreeing to all kinds of things she'd likely regret, but she couldn't seem to focus her mind. She was glad Brian stayed close, for petting the cat was the only thing keeping her calm.

Suddenly Brian leaped from the sofa and stalked into the corridor. He stood staring into the bedchamber, tail twitching.

"He must hear Peter stirring," Dottie told Beth, rising. "It's about time to nurse him. If you'll excuse me."

Beth leaned back. "Of course. But when you return, we must talk about music. I think we should convince my brothers to install a piano at the church. Do you know anyone who can play?"

Dottie shook her head, then headed for the bedchamber. Piano music? She didn't need anything so grand. She just wanted to be John's wife.

She thought surely the cat would skip ahead of her to see Peter, but Brian refused to follow her inside. Frowning, she stepped through the door.

Frank stood beside the cradle, holding Peter in his arms. It seemed Brian had finally decided to embrace mousing, because he'd found a rat.

Chapter Twenty-One

"You're in trouble now," James teased as he rode with John and the others back along the road toward Seattle. "You left your bride with Beth. They'll have planned your whole wedding by the time you get back, and you may just find they've convinced Nora to sew you a pink suit to match the roses."

John shook his head as the men around him chuckled. They had agreed that Frank was too green to have navigated the wilderness on foot alone the last two days. He had to be on horseback, which likely meant he was traveling by road. Drew had taken a group north toward the top of the lake; the road ended there, but Frank might not have known that. Simon was with a group on his way east along the bottom of the lake. John, James and their neighbors were covering the route south.

It had seemed like a good plan at the time, but, in truth, each mile that separated him from Dottie made it harder to press forward. He knew she was safe with Beth; between the two of them they could likely handle any trouble. But she'd been struggling alone for so long. He didn't want her to feel alone again.

A shame they didn't know the direction Reynolds had taken. Only so many roads led in and out of Seattle. If Reynolds was on horseback or had hitched a ride with someone, most likely he was heading south, toward the more populous cities of Tacoma and Olympia. The only other way out of Seattle was by boat, as Beth had noted, and they wouldn't have much chance of catching him if he was sailing for Canada or the Orient. And if he'd ridden north, along Lake Union, he'd have had to travel this way. John could see the tracks in the mud; only three horses had headed that way recently, and he knew one of them was Deputy McCormick's and another was his.

Could the third be Frank's?

He felt as if cold water ran down his spine as he reined in. James slowed his horse, glancing back.

"I've got to go home," John told him. "Keep the others riding forward. I need to know Dottie is safe."

Harry, riding past in a wagon, sat up straighter. "Want company?"

John waited for the gibe, the complaint that he wasn't strong enough to make it all the way to Seattle. But Harry seemed sincere.

"I can handle this," John told him.

As the wagon moved on, Harry nodded. "It seems you can at that. Keep her safe, John."

John turned the horse and put his heels to her flanks.

Once more, he galloped toward home, praying that nothing had happened to Dottie, Peter and Beth. Fear sat like a second rider in the saddle with him. He couldn't lose his family. They were his to protect, his to love.

He reached the foot of the drive and forced the horse to slow, then dismounted. If Reynolds was at the house, John didn't want him to know that help was coming. Letting the animal out into the field, he crept up the road, staying among the trees. The house sat quietly. Too quiet? He could hear his heart thundering in his ears.

He let himself in the back, listened. It seemed he heard the murmur of voices, but it could have been Beth and Dottie. He opened the door from the kitchen, peered into the parlor. Beth was sitting on one of the chairs by the hearth, rifle in her lap, her tapping foot making her skirts swing.

"Beth."

Her name, even said so softly, brought his sister's head up. She rose, beaming.

"You're back! Did you catch him so soon?"

John shook his head, feeling foolish as he moved into the room. "I needed to make sure Dottie and Peter were safe."

"Oh, that's so romantic." Beth tipped her head. "They're fine. Dottie is in the bedroom feeding him."

John glanced that way. "I thought I heard voices."

Beth dimpled. "Me, too. But you know what? Dottie likes to talk to Peter when she thinks no one else is around. It's so sweet."

John nodded. It was rather endearing, but it was also another sign Dottie had been alone for too long. He didn't like to interrupt Peter's feeding, but he just wanted to see her before he returned to the other men.

Harry and the others were sure to give him a ribbing as it was; what were a few more moments? Resigned to his fate, he started across the hall for the bedchamber.

Brian darted in front of him with a hiss, but his gaze wasn't on John for once. He appeared to be staring into the bedchamber, tail lashing. John felt as if the air had chilled. He eased into the doorway.

The tableau that met his eyes brought him up short. Dottie was pressed against the wall nearest the door, hands outstretched, as if begging Frank Reynolds to return her child. Reynolds had Peter and was gazing into his face.

"Those are my eyes," he told Dottie. "You can't deny that."

"I can," John said. "I don't think Peter looks anything like you, and if I have any say in the matter, he'll never act like you, either."

Reynolds stiffened, even as Dottie ran to John's side.

"Oh, John. We have to stop him. He'll take Peter."

As if in answer, Reynolds hefted the baby closer. "He's my son. I have every right to him."

John put Dottie behind him. Perhaps because he was no longer able to see his mother, Peter started to cry. Reynolds frowned as if he'd had no idea babies could make that kind of noise.

"Everything all right?" Beth called from the parlor.

If John didn't answer her, his sister would come to investigate. With the rifle. John couldn't see that Reynolds was armed, but he couldn't take any chances with Peter.

"Give the baby back to his mother, Reynolds," he said. "She knows how to take care of him."

"And you don't think I do?" Reynolds shifted Peter

closer, and the baby's sobs ratcheted higher. "If she can learn how to take care of him, so can I. That's why I came out to Wallin Landing. To see my son." He jiggled Peter up and down, and the baby's arms flailed out.

John edged closer. "He's a good, strong lad. A son a man can be proud of. That's why I know you're not going to hurt him."

Reynolds frowned. "Hurt him? Of course I wouldn't hurt him. He's my son, for all she tried to hide him from me. Make no mistake, Wallin. I'm the victim here."

That he could believe it made John ill. Still, he had to focus on Peter. "You want the best for your boy. I can understand that. But you can't give him the best, Frank. There's a warrant out for your arrest. I was leading a posse to find you. If you take Peter, you'll be on the run for the rest of your life. That's no way to raise a child."

He frowned, then held the baby out to peer into his face. "You hear that, son? Your father's a wanted man."

"Not wanted by anyone around here," Beth said from the doorway, raising the rifle.

Frank turned his back on her, shielding Peter. That told John all he needed to know.

"Put down the gun, Beth," he ordered, keeping his eyes on Peter's father. "I promise to protect your son, Frank. But you have to give him back to Dottie."

Slowly Reynolds turned, eyes narrowed. "I'll give him back so long as you let me go free."

John shook his head. "I can't do that. I was sworn in as a deputy today. But I can promise that you'll get a fair trial."

"Fair," Frank scoffed. "She'll testify. I won't have her turning my son against me."

John took another step closer. He was nearly in reach of Peter. He could see the baby watching him, lower lip quivering as if he wasn't sure whether to cry or smile.

"You want Peter to remember you as a hero," John said. "That's what every father wants. But if you don't give yourself up, he's sure to remember you as the villain."

Frank shifted on his feet, as if some part of him struggled with the decision. Then he thrust Peter at John. "Here, take him. I wouldn't want to mind him all day anyway."

John snatched the baby out of Frank's hands and whirled to offer him to Dottie. She clasped Peter close and backed away from Reynolds. Then her eyes widened. "John, watch out!"

John turned in time to see Reynolds rushing toward him. Crouching low, John caught Reynolds under the ribs and turned with the momentum. Reynolds slammed onto the floor, with John on top.

Beth darted forward, gun trained. "You stay down," she ordered Reynolds.

John had never seen his sister look so fierce. As if just as determined, Brian pounced into the room and glared at Reynolds, eyes like fire. Reynolds opened his arms in surrender.

John climbed to his feet. "Fetch the rope from the barn," he told Dottie, who hurried to do as he bid. Only when Reynolds was safely trussed did John feel comfortable leading Dottie, Peter and Beth onto the porch. Brian swept out with them and jumped up on one of the chairs, where he daintily licked one paw as if well satisfied by his role in the whole affair.

Dottie was less calm. With Peter in Beth's arms, she

clung to John's neck, trembling, before pressing a kiss against his cheek. "You did it, John. You saved Peter."

Her gratitude and relief bathed him. Still, he couldn't quite believe he'd done it. Drew would probably have picked up Reynolds and thrown him through the window. James would have made some quip before darting in to save the day. Simon would have tried to reason things out. John had appealed to the man's character, a chancy thing. But, as it turned out, Reynolds had some fatherly affection.

John wrapped an arm around Dottie, rested his head against hers. For so long, he had wondered whether he could be the sort of man to partner a wife, to raise a family. Dottie believed in him, cared for him. With her, he was a hero. For her, he always would be.

"Who's that?" Beth asked.

John frowned, raising his head even as Dottie stiffened in his arms. A lone rider was coming up the hill. His broad-brimmed hat hid his face. His black horse plodded as if he'd traveled far. John didn't recognize man or beast.

Beth handed Peter to Dottie, picked up the rifle and held it at the ready. That didn't stop the stranger from reining in in front of the porch, face shadowed.

"I heard there was trouble here," he said. "I thought I could help. I'm a minister."

The voice was familiar, but it sounded deeper, more mature than John remembered, as if sorrow had softened the youthful tenor.

Beth lowered the gun, brows up and eyes wide. "Levi?"

Chapter Twenty-Two

The man tipped back his hat. His face was lean, cheekbones evident, as if he hadn't eaten well in quite some time. In the caped duster, it was hard to tell if his shoulders were as broad as John's, but his legs were long. What drew Dottie most, however, was the deep blue of his eyes. They were nearly as dark as Beth's.

Peter reached out a hand and babbled a greeting. The stranger smiled, the gentleness of it reminding Dottie of John.

"It is you!" Beth put down the rifle and leaped off the porch. Their youngest brother threw his leg over the horse and slid down to catch her.

John shook his head, smile growing. "Dottie, may I present my brother Levi."

"The prodigal son," Beth said, leaning back after giving him a squeeze. "Why didn't you write? We were so worried about you. And what do you mean you're a minister? You can't be a minister, not you."

Levi shrugged. "I found my calling thanks to a missionary on the gold fields, trained at a seminary in San

Francisco and was ordained there a month ago. I haven't
been assigned a church or circuit yet. I wanted to come
home first." His smile faded. "I stopped at the house.
Catherine told me John and the others were out with a
posse. How can I help?"

"No help needed," Beth promised him. "John van-
quished the villain. It was just like in *Ivanhoe*. You
should have seen him!"

Levi glanced between his sister and John, and Dottie
felt John stand straighter. In her arms, Peter reached out
and patted John's chest as if as proud of him as Beth.
Brian, watching from the chair, appeared just as sure.

"It seems I'm not the only one who's changed in the
last few years, brother," Levi murmured.

The faintest of pinks tinged John's cheeks. "That
doesn't mean I don't appreciate help. We need to send
word to the posse and Deputy McCormick in town so
they know the search is over. And I suspect there's a
horse tied in the woods nearby. But your horse looks
spent, Levi. Can you stay with the ladies while I escort
Frank Reynolds to the sheriff?"

He was leaving? Disappointment shot through her.
But before Levi could answer, Beth turned and stamped
her foot. "John, no! You should stay here with Dottie
and Peter. They need you."

John gazed at Dottie, and she felt warm all the way
through. Peter wiggled happily against her.

"I won't be long," John murmured. "I promise." He
turned to his brother. "Levi, this is Dottie Tyrrell. Peter
is her son. Dottie and I are engaged to be married."

Why was it her heart beat faster every time he
said that?

Levi's midnight blue eyes widened. "Congratulations. Welcome to the family, Dottie, and, of course, Peter."

Peter crowed an answer.

Levi turned his look on his brother. "And you're right about my horse. I don't think she'll make it much farther. If I could borrow a mount, I'd be happy to deliver Reynolds to Seattle and let the posse know it can disband. I take it there's a warrant for his arrest."

John nodded. "Dottie may have to testify."

She waited for the fear to come but felt nothing but determination. "I'll do it," she told John. "Frank will never silence me again."

Levi gathered up the reins of his horse. "I'll take Belle around to the barn. John, I'm glad to see you finally have what you deserve, a wife and child who love you."

John gazed at Dottie, the green of his eyes as bright and pure as the forest around them. Peter reached for him, and he took the little hand in his.

"What about it, Dottie?" he asked. "The danger's past. You don't need a hero anymore. Do you still want to marry me?"

He said it in a teasing tone, but she wanted to make sure he had no doubts. Perhaps he wondered whether she'd accepted his offer from desperation, as she had in Cincinnati, and, gentleman that he was, he was giving her the opportunity to bow out gracefully.

This time, she refused to give up. She was done running, done worrying. With John, she was home.

"Are you going back on our arrangement, John Wallin?" she challenged. "You said you didn't think you measured up to a hero, but you are the only man I've ever known who makes everyday life heroic by his attitude and his actions. I came to Seattle to marry you, and that's what I'm going to do."

"Far be it from me to argue," John said, and he took her in his arms and kissed her. She sighed against the sweet pressure of his lips. Why would she ever want to be anywhere else but at his side?

She heard a cry of joy, and it was a minute before she realized she hadn't made it. John raised his head, and Dottie saw that Beth was fairly bouncing with excitement.

"Oh, I love weddings!" his sister cried. "Dottie and I have it all arranged. Nora will make the dress. She has it half-finished already."

Dottie raised a brow. "Were you so sure of me?"

"Of course," Beth said, as if there had never been a doubt in anyone's mind. "And we'll have flowers soon. This may be just what we need to get everyone to pitch in and finish the church so we can hold the ceremony here. I wondered about the minister, but Levi can preside."

Peter clapped his hands as if he quite approved.

John didn't look so sure. "Is that legal?" he asked with a frown.

"It better be," Dottie said. "Because this time, I intend to marry and live happily ever after."

And they did.

* * * * *

Dear Reader,

Thank you for choosing John and Dottie's story. I love getting a chance to peer in on the Wallin family from time to time. I hope you do, too. If you missed the earlier stories, try *Would-Be Wilderness Wife* (Drew and Catherine), *Frontier Engagement* (James and Rina) and *A Convenient Christmas Wedding* (Simon and Nora). Their friend Maddie married in *Instant Frontier Family*. Catherine, Rina, Maddie and Nora came to Seattle in *The Bride Ship*.

In case you wondered about the library John hoped to build, Mrs. Maynard convinced the other ladies of Seattle to help fund the endeavor. A real-life pioneer lady, she opened her own reading room in her home in Seattle in 1875.

To learn more about life in pioneer Seattle, visit my website at www.reginascott.com, where you can also sign up for a free email alert to hear when my next book is out.

Blessings!
Regina Scott

Get 2 Free Books,
Plus 2 Free Gifts—
just for trying the Reader Service!

Love Inspired HISTORICAL

LIH17R2

"Mr. Arness—I'm sorry, Preacher Arness—I'm here to apply for this position."

"How old are you, Miss Marshall?"

"I'm nineteen, but I've been looking after my brothers, my father, my grandfather and, until recently, my niece since I was fourteen. I think I can manage to look after one four-year-old boy."

That might be so, and he would have agreed in any other case but this four-year-old was his son, Evan, and Annie Marshall simply did not suit. She was too young. Too idealistic. Too fond of fun.

She flipped the paper back and forth, her eyes narrowed as if she meant to call him to task.

"Are you going back on your word?" she insisted, edging closer.

"I've not given my word to anything."

"'Widower with four-year-old son seeking a marriage of convenience. Prefer someone older with no expectations of romance. I'm kind and trustworthy. My son needs lots of patience and affection. Interested parties please see Preacher Arness at the church.' I'm applying," Annie said with conviction and challenge.

"You're too young and…" He couldn't think how to voice his objections without sounding unkind, and having just stated the opposite in his little ad, he chose to say nothing.

"Are you saying I'm unsuitable?" She spoke with all the authority one might expect from a Marshall…but not from a woman trying to convince him to let her take care of his son.

He met her challenging look with calm indifference. Unless she meant to call on her three brothers and her father and grandfather to support her cause, he had nothing to fear from her. He needed someone less likely to chase after excitement and adventure. She'd certainly find none here as the preacher's wife.

"I would never say such a thing, but like the ad says, Evan needs a mature woman." And he'd settle for a plain one, and especially a docile one.

"From what I hear, he needs someone who understands his fears." She leaned back as if that settled it.

Don't miss
MONTANA BRIDE BY CHRISTMAS by Linda Ford,
available October 2017 wherever
Love Inspired® Historical books and ebooks are sold.

www.LoveInspired.com

Inspirational Romance to
Warm Your Heart and Soul

Join our social communities to connect
with other readers who share your love!

Sign up for the Love Inspired newsletter
at **www.LoveInspired.com** to be the
first to find out about upcoming titles,
special promotions and exclusive content.

CONNECT WITH US AT:

Harlequin.com/Community

 Facebook.com/LoveInspiredBooks

 Twitter.com/LoveInspiredBks

LISOCIAL2017

SPECIAL EXCERPT FROM

Love Inspired®

*When an accident strands pregnant widow Willa Chase
and her twins at the home of John Miller, she doesn't
know if she'll make it back to her Amish community for
Christmas. But the reclusive widower soon finds himself
hoping for a second chance at family.*

*Read on for a sneak peek of
AMISH CHRISTMAS TWINS by USA TODAY
bestselling author Patricia Davids,
the first in the three-book CHRISTMAS TWINS series.*

John waited beside Samuel's sleigh and tried
unsuccessfully to curb his excitement. He was almost as
giddy as Megan and Lucy. A sleigh ride with Willa at his
side was his idea of the perfect winter evening, especially
since he didn't have to drive. Lucy was the first one out of
the house. She quickly claimed her spot in the front seat
beside Samuel. Megan came out next and scrambled up
beside her sister. He'd never seen the twins so delighted.

Willa took John's hand as he helped her in. He gave
her gloved fingers a quick squeeze and saw her smile
before she looked down.

Samuel slapped the lines and the big horse took off
down the snow-covered lane. Sleigh bells jingled merrily
in time with the horse's footfalls, and Megan and Lucy
tried to catch snowflakes on their tongues between
giggles.

John leaned down to see Willa's face. "Are you warm

enough?" She nodded, but her cheeks looked rosy and cold. John took off his woolen scarf and wrapped it around her head to cover her mouth and nose.

"Danki," she murmured.

"Don't mention it. In spite of the cold, it's a lovely evening to go caroling, isn't it?" The thick snow obscured the horizon and made it feel as if they were riding inside a glass snow globe. The fields lay hidden under a thick blanket of white. A hushed stillness filled the air, broken only by the jingle of the harness bells and the muffled thudding of the horse's feet.

Their first destination was only a mile from John's house. As Lucy and Megan scrambled down from the sleigh, John offered Willa his hand to help her out.

"Was this what you imagined Christmas would be like when you decided to return to your Amish family?"

She shook her head. "I never imagined anything like this. Do you do it every year?"

"We do."

"You aren't going to actually sing, are you, John?"

He threw back his head and laughed. "*Nee*, but I will hum along."

"Softly, dear, softly," she suggested.

He wondered if she realized that she had called him "dear." It was turning out to be an even more wonderful night than he had hoped for.

Don't miss
AMISH CHRISTMAS TWINS
by Patricia Davids, available October 2017 wherever
Love Inspired® books and ebooks are sold.

www.LoveInspired.com